The Levels:
Gateway Township
Book 1

Samuel Toller

Flowers of Purgatory—Conway, Arkansas
Paperback ISBN: 979-8-9902538-2-7
eBook ISBN: 979-8-9902538-3-4
Library of Congress Control Number: 2024913834
Title: *The Levels: Gateway Township: Book 1*
Author: Samuel Toller
Digital distribution | 2024
Paperback | 2024

This is a work of fiction. The characters, names, incidents, places, and dialogue are products of the author's imagination, and are not to be construed as real.

Published in the United States by New Book Authors Publishing

Dedication

iii

I dedicate this book to my family. You are the adventure in life with which I've been blessed. I will always fight my way back to you, no matter the circumstance.

Acknowledgements

I wanted to give my gratitude first to my wife and children. You have been at my side through all of this and have encouraged me every step of the way. Thank you, I love you, Naomi, Zeke, Emma, Desmond, and Ronan.

I'd like to also give my gratitude to my friends and beta readers who have also encouraged me, keeping the fire lit under me, so I didn't stop, when I was overwhelmed. Thank you, I may forget some of you, and for that I'm sorry. Thank you, Laura W., Milly and Justin J., Bill and Laura F. Matt and Beth H. and Cassie, Angelina and Blake H., Olivia G and Caylin, and of course my siblings and their spouses, Chris and Sarah, Shaun and Sarah, Stephanie and Kirk, Christine and Nate, Nathan and Laura, and James.

You have all been an inspiration and have given me gentle shoves within the foundry that is my mind. I love you all.

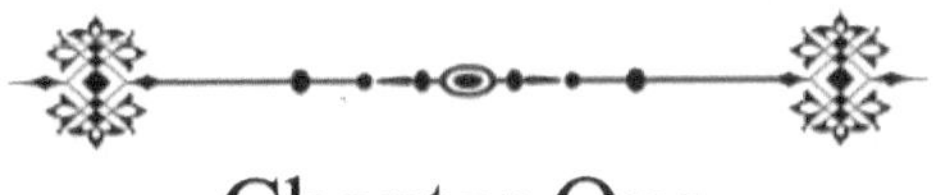

Chapter One

Dust billowed and blew over the crumbling cities of Earth. The sun had to fight with much of the atmospheric debris just to shine enough light to feed the plants.

What's odd is that it didn't get cooler, with the sun being shaded in places, on the contrary, it got much, much hotter. In some places, there wasn't an overshadowing presence of dust and other detriment in the atmosphere, which allowed the blistering sun to elevate the temperatures even more. It goes to show that the ozone protecting our planet from the harmful rays of ultraviolet radiation were, indeed, incredibly important.

The year was 2087, it was late April in a small southern dystopian town in Arkansas called Sparkstown. A tall thin, almost emaciated young man, with a solid proportional build, and stringy muscular arms from tossing hay bales and tilling the ground, is standing in a freshly planted field. He has sandy brown hair, and tan, almost leathery skin, from countless hours spent in the sun. Wiping his brow of sweat that had gathered there, twenty-year-old Sesh was just about finished with a grueling day working in the garden of one his neighbors.

Mr. Fallow was a cranky old man, and a cattle farmer. He had been hardened by the loss of his entire family, and only tolerated Sesh because he reminded him of his late son. His farm used to be massive, full of cows, goats, and horses with sprawling acres of harvestable plants. Unfortunately, with the change of the world, many of them had been stolen, or died to the elements.

Now, there wasn't much left of his gardens or of his cattle, it was mostly some very thin and slow-moving goats, with the occasional scrawny cow in the herd. Sesh would work around the cattle farm, doing whatever Mr. Fallow needed. Today, he needed Sesh to run the tiller in the garden, and plant some of the very scarce potato eyes. Only time would tell if they would even sprout.

Even with spending countless hours of work nurturing a garden, oftentimes it was only the heartiest of vegetables that could be grown. Most of the plants able to be grown were grown from seeds that scientific groups like Monsanto had spent decades developing drought resistant genetic modifications on. The governments around the world came together and worked with these scientific-minded groups, to provide these seeds for free to the rapidly dwindling groups of farmers, so they were able to grow crops in even the harshest of climates. In this particular part of the world, it was rhubarb, Swiss chard, potatoes, and corn that was being grown.

Working hard for Mr. Fallow would be rewarded with a little bit of money, or sometimes a morsel of meat from one of the butchered animals, or vegetables when it was time to harvest. Sesh preferred the meat and vegetables, because food was so hard to come by, and a lot of times money would not get you food at the market.

Fortunately for Sesh, with Mr. Fallow, being a solitary elderly man, Sesh would help him can some of the foods from his garden, and sometimes the meat. This would help put a meal in his stomach a couple times a week, and sometimes even enable him to bring home a meal to his mom and dad. Unfortunately, in today's generation, it wasn't uncommon for people to starve to death, because there just wasn't enough.

The Long Years is what this generation was called. This was due to the long hard days that people had to put in just to survive. An average man could work 16 hours at a factory, then come home and easily work 4-6 more on his garden, for he must have a garden to survive. It was a normal thing for a guy or gal to go to work every day after only 2 or 3 hours of sleep.

It made people angry, unhealthy, and terrifying to be around.

Folks would walk around gaunt in the face from lack of sleep and food. The Russians called not getting enough sleep and food, *Proklyatiye khodyachikh mertvetsov*, or the disease of the waking dead. The worst was that it wasn't unheard of and was becoming far too common for people to lose their minds to the point of devouring everything around them, including their families, complete strangers, and themselves.

When this happened, their minds would without fail, be completely obliterated of any reason, while their bodies gained a look of a decrepit, lipless humanoid, bones showing on their arms and legs where they tasted their own flesh. Oftentimes, the fingers would be nothing but fleshless bone shards with scrapes and gnaw marks running the length of them, like a ghost-given tattoo. While recovery from such a state was almost unheard of, it did happen occasionally.

Though without fail, every single survivor was missing fingers and toes, and stared around at the remaining world, with a thousand-yard stare. The state of civilizations and sociological platforms was failing. The world was falling into death, destruction, and decay.

The work that needed to be done was incredibly arduous work, it was the kind of work that would debilitate even the heartiest of people. Working in one of the many types of factories was probably one of the easiest jobs. Population was down because people were starving to death. Children weren't being born into this world full of anger and disease because no one wanted to reproduce, or even had time to.

The lack of sleep made the majority of women barren. At least that's what the doctors were saying. The lucky families were the ones who had children and had the children survive the first 10 years. They were lucky because at around 10 years old a man or a woman could put their child to work on the garden or their rapidly deteriorating farm. This would toughen him up or harden her to do what must be done in order to keep their bellies full, and their families alive. Some children would end up working for the factories or large corporations, because the lack of reproduction from the population had caused a severe lack of workforce to fill the core jobs needed to keep a civilization running smoothly.

Most of the factories that remained, were electricity producing factories, or water purifying factories. Very few of them had to deal with food, and only the luckiest people got to work for those that did. There just wasn't enough to go around. Unfortunately, the few vegetables and morsels of meat that were available weren't enough to give the proper nutrients to the remaining populations. This caused the faces of the masses to appear pinched and aged prematurely. Many had their teeth fall out and had festering wounds left uncovered and rotting in the open air. This encouraged the diseases to spread rampantly. Many of the dead had died from scurvy, from not getting any vitamin C, because most of the fruit trees in the world had withered and died. Others had died from marasmus, which is the severe lack of caloric intake, to keep the body functioning.

There are many theories as to how all of this began. Government scientists blame global warming. They blamed it on a lack of any sort of attempt to fight the greenhouse gases the world's population was emitting. Other theories pointed towards the great war, the final war. World War 3 happened in 2025, after a major controversial election. Angry countries who had promises made to them that were broken invaded America, and America retaliated with nuclear weapons. There are some theories that think the second coming of Christ had happened, and all that was left were the lost.

In truth, The Long Years was caused by a combination of the two primary theories. It was caused by out-of-control population growth and a severe lack of care about the intense increases in atmospheric temperatures. The Great War was merely the feather that broke the camel's back. Our planet couldn't take the strain from so much abuse. The parasitic species known as humans had finally done enough to destroy their host.

In the beginning people who had a little bit of money moved towards the northern and southern poles, trying to get away from the famine and dust that plagued the parts of the earth near the equator. Over time, the cacophony of disease, famine, and turmoil reached even the poles. The planet was dying. There were hundred-mile-wide hurricane-like dust storms plaguing the driest parts, and random extreme lightning storms that blasted and pummeled the earth into pebbles.

Humanity still persevered but it was clear that they were fighting a losing battle. Each day, the population dwindled, without some sort of divine intervention or miracle, planet Earth would become another barren wasteland floating aimlessly through the cosmos.

Chapter Two
The Life Stone

Sesh had just finished working in Mr. Fallows' fields on this singular fateful day, when he happened upon a small, strange green stone that seemed to swirl and pulse with a radiant green energy. Upon touching the beautiful green stone, he got a feeling of cool peace and new life. It was like stepping out of the house after a cool spring rain and smelling the wonderful smells of fresh grass and sprouting flowers. Sesh had never smelt or felt this feeling before, so it was entirely new for him, and brought him pure joy into his heart.

He placed it in his pocket to consider later, as he enjoyed collecting unique and bizarre objects that he would find here and there. Strange objects were things he liked to bring home and collect, as it was how he was able to disassociate from the world around him. He would sometimes share his oftentimes unique findings with his mom and dad. With so few people remaining, it was rather unusual that he had both of his parents still, because most people didn't have much or any family left. Of Sesh's once large and vibrant family, there were only three of them that remained, his mom, his dad, and him. He had lost his brothers to the government when they were participating in the early picket lines.

Way back when populations were still high, and people were begging for help from the government to no avail. They were shot down in cold blood by the very people they were requesting aid from. They were brave and he missed them completely, but he tried to make them proud, because they were willing to stand tall for what they believed in. Sesh lost his sisters too, one of them was murdered in a tragic sexual assault incident by a disgusting pig of a man who will never have his name taint the very air again, if he could help it. After hunting the man down for weeks, his father caught and killed that man with his bare hands.

The last of his family to perish was his baby sister. She died to a starving family; they had the disease of the waking dead. His mother was lucky to get out of that situation alive, but it still almost killed her. They beat her unconscious, and then ripped the small child to pieces, eating her still wailing body, alive. His mother hasn't been the same since, if it weren't for the bystanders, she would have been eaten too. That entire family was shot and killed in the street, left there for the carrion feeders to clean.

At the end of the workday, only fifteen hours today, Sesh turned around and noticed something spectacular. His row of potatoes he had just been planting had already started to push through the dry mounds of soil. The tiny green sprouts that broke free of the dirt and clay were bright and eerie in the domineering brown and oranges of the world. This was startlingly fast, because he shouldn't be expecting anything to sprout for weeks, and usually it would be only one out of every fifty that would even survive being a seedling to sprout into greenery. What he could see now was an entire row of an eye-catching greenish yellow of new growth.

"This is impossible…" Sesh thought out loud, as he quickly trekked back through the 30-acre field of potatoes he had been working that day.

"Of the eight rows I've done today, why is this one the only one growing? Unless…." He felt a small vibration in his pocket, which would not be unusual, if he were carrying his cellular phone, but he was not.

He never carried his phone when he was working in the fields, he could not get a replacement. Reaching into his pocket, he pulled out the slightly pulsing strange little green swirling pebble and gazed at it. Experimenting, he bent down and stroked a potato plant, and watched in amazement as it grew two inches, based solely on him touching it with the stone. Excitement, fear, and wonder blazed through him, and he couldn't wait to share what he had found. He was excited because this could be the answer to every person on the planet's prayers, a new chance at life. He was scared, because he knew that people would do the most viciously cruel things for this. Glancing around, he was grateful that Mr. Fallow had only hired him to work in the fields today.

He knew just how much this would mean, and he wondered how long it would take for life to get just a little bit easier.

After work, Sesh was heading to see his longtime girlfriend, Suzanne. He couldn't wait to tell her what he had found in the fields, and the magnificent powers that it seemed to contain. He pulled into her driveway and saw her sitting on a porch swing talking to her father. John was a big, gray, burly man, who worked down at the power plant like most of the folks from Sparkstown. They were a little more well off than most of the other people in their little town, because John was the president of the union for the power plant. People would oftentimes give them gifts of extra canned foods from their harvests, just to stay in their good graces. Sesh climbed out of his rusty old faded once black pickup truck and sauntered over to the front porch, with a huge grin plastered on his face.

"Hey John, Suzy, how are y'all doing today?"

"Sesh." Was all John managed to say, his voice deep and masculine.

To Sesh's surprise and concern Suzy said nervously, "Hey Sesh…uh…Daddy will you give us a minute?"

John got up slowly and grunted acknowledgement then walked into the house. Sesh could tell he was still near the door. He looked at Suzanne, seeing how beautiful she was. She was short, around five foot tall, with long straight dark brown hair. Her eyes were a dark blue, the color of the Caribbean Sea, before a hurricane crashed ashore. She had slightly crooked white teeth, but not unattractively so. He noted that if people having braces were still a thing, she would have been a perfect candidate for them. Her lips were always a ruby red, from being out in the sun all the time. They clashed with her darkly tanned skin, and voluptuous body, in a way that only cartoons seemed to create, when they drew the perfect woman. He noticed her eyes were downcast a little, almost teary, but disregarded it to the dust in the air.

"Suz! You will never believe what I discovered today!" Pausing, after noticing the look on her face, a look of sadness and distress, "Wait, what's wrong baby?"

"Well," She started, with tears forming in her eyes, "I don't really know how to say this Sesh, it's just that you've been so good to me. I just don't know, I really don't…I… I met someone else, and I would really like to start seeing him more often."

Sesh was immediately struck with heartache. Immobilized by the thought of seeing her with another man, all thoughts of his findings vanished. He didn't quite know how to process what he was hearing; she was all he'd known for the last three years. His only friend, she was the only thing he looked forward to every single long-drawn-out day. Is it betrayal if she's being honest and open with him?

"Why? Things are going great for us Suzanne; we were going to have a great life together." Sesh managed to ask while looking devastated.

"We would have had a great life together, you're right. But it just isn't what I want right now, I want to be able to look at myself in the mirror ten to fifteen years down the road and know that I have no regrets. I like this guy, so far, we have only spoken a few times, but you never know. He asked me out the other day, his dad is on the board with my dad… well, you know, I always promised that no matter what, I would tell you if I was interested in someone else. Well now I'm telling you, and I'm telling you that we are over. I'm so sorry…" She trailed off, bursting into tears and rushing into the house. Sesh stood there dumbfounded, watching as the door slowly closed behind her, the statue-like figure of her father standing next to the door. John stood there, a sad look on his face. He nodded at Sesh, then reached out and finished closing the door, shutting off a chapter of Sesh's life forever.

Devastated, Sesh turned to leave, without saying another word he climbed into his truck. Glancing through his windshield at the home of his three-year friend and companion, Sesh pressed the gas pedal as he slammed his truck into reverse and backed quickly out of the driveway. With all thoughts of his findings gone, Sesh could only think about getting home, and trying to get some sleep. He had a lot of work to do the next day.

Chapter Three
The Crash

All Sesh could think about as he flew down the highway, was how everything in his broken little world was beginning to crumble. All of his plans for the future revolved around his relationship with Suzy. When it was all said and done, Sesh really did not know who or what he wanted to be in this life, or what he wanted to become. None of that mattered right now, as all he felt was the hurt of betrayal and loss.

The first thing Sesh heard upon pulling into his driveway was angry shouting from his home. It was an old run-down dust covered single wide trailer house with window unit air conditioners that did not work. The walls were very thin, which is why he could hear that his mom and dad were fighting again. They always seemed to fight now, ever since the death of his baby sister Eloise. Every day it was some other little insignificant thing that set them off, always at each other's throats, trying to tear each other down emotionally, as they were already torn down physically from all the demanding work they had to do each day. Sesh felt his familiar feeling of wishing he could just get away, and find somewhere else to live, where he could get a little peace and quiet. He just wanted to be able to come home for once, and not be drug into another tug-o-war between his mom and dad. He wanted to come home and go to sleep, wake up and do his day all over again. Sesh knew that it was a normal thing for most families nowadays, all the fighting. There was just too much stress and weariness. Including the fact that being hungry and over-worked didn't help matters either.

"I swear to God Tam, I'm doing the best I can! I can't possibly do anymore around here. I can't possibly survive on three beans!"

"It's all we have! Sesh won't have anything to eat when he gets home either! We give the bulk of our food to you! You're the one that's working two jobs and is supposed to be bringing home 'the bacon.' Where the hell is the bacon, Frank?!"

"The jobs I work at are just paying me in cash, not food! You know damn well there's no food to be found at the market. I go there every single day between jobs! NO ONE has any food! We got thousands of dollars Tam! THOUSANDS! I can't buy one damn meal with any of it!"

"Then quit your damn jobs and work in the garden, go hunting. Do SOMETHING, ANYTHING! PROVIDE FOR THIS FAMILY!"

"There are no animals left to kill, they hang people who poach other people's cattle. I don't know what else there is to do."

"Figure it out then. You're a man, you're always saying that you'll figure it out, so figure. It. Out!"

Sesh's mom was just as fierce as his father- both of them he loved very much, they were just tired and worn out from having such a hard life. Most of the world was like this today... lots of poverty, people barely surviving. His dad, Frank, worked two jobs, one at the power plant, and the other at the water-filtration factory. He managed to get the twelve-hour shifts alternating, one day at each one. His mom, Tammy, also worked at the power plant. She worked extremely hard, and when she wasn't at work, she was at home working in their own personal gardens, trying to turn the dry dust and rocks into pliable growth and foods. They had the money from their jobs, which would pay for some of the non-necessities, if they lived in a major city, which they didn't. So, they had money sitting in the bank, without any way to spend it. The amount of death in the world left a hole in everything, including land ownership. They could literally take whatever land they could farm; no one would stop them. Unfortunately, there just wasn't a need, water was scarce, so they used their own urine to water their plants. Every little bit helped the growth. Without their garden, they would most assuredly starve.

The world had fallen into complete disrepair. Working jobs like electrical maintenance and mechanical engineering were nearly obsolete. Considering the poverty level and the demand for food, biologists and horticulturists are in huge demand. They worked night and day trying to find a solution to the drought and disease that plagued the country. Nothing was ever found or had accomplished anything.

Sesh stormed through the door and yelled at the top of his lungs at his mom and dad. "THAT'S ENOUGH! I'M TIRED OF HEARING PEOPLE FIGHT ALL THE TIME. JUST GIVE IT A REST. WE KNOW THERE ISN'T ENOUGH FOOD! WE KNOW THAT PEOPLE NEED TO WORK HARD! JUST DO WHAT YOU GOT TO DO TO SURVIVE AND STOP FIGHTING!" He started reducing his voice to a small tenor, on the verge of tears he pleaded, "Please, I can't…I just can't take any more of this. If I could save us, I would."

A look of shock passed over his mom and dad's face as he yelled at them, but it quickly turned into sour anger.

"Don't you dare raise your voice to me like that in MY HOUSE, YOU DISRESPECTFUL INGRATE! Just who do you think you are!"

Without a response Sesh turned on his heel and left, getting into his truck, churning gravel as he launched himself out of the driveway. He was flying down the highway, his foot pressing the gas pedal as far as it would go. The sound of the old engine roaring in his ears. He only knew his phone was going off because he felt the vibration of it between his legs.

BUZZ BUZZ, BUZZ BUZZ

Sesh glanced down at his phone, it was his mom. She always had a soft spot for her kids. She was sweet and gentle, though when angry she was hard as ice. Sesh picked up his phone and hit the ignore button, though after unlocking his phone, he decided to text his mom and tell her he was sorry. While he was still angry with his foot heavy on the gas pedal, he didn't want her to think he hated them. He still loved them with all his heart, they were his family, and family means everything. Sesh glanced down at his phone and typed five and a half words:

I Love you Mom, I'm Sor…

Bright lights are suddenly in his front windshield. He had time to glance up to see he was in the wrong lane. The horn of the oncoming vehicle screaming in his ears caused his ear drums to ring with a horrible chime that sounded like the wheels of the train of death screeching to a halt. He had time to think, 'I haven't seen another car on this road in forever.' Then as his truck slammed into the small SUV in front of him, time seemed to slow down. He wasn't wearing his seatbelt, and he felt his body rip out of his seat and his head shatter the windshield as he flew through it. Time dragged on. Time was moving so slowly that Sesh was able to turn his head as he passed the void over his crumpled truck hood and the crumpled SUV hood in front of him. Glass was flying all around, a headlight bounced painfully off of his right shoulder, he could see droplets of blood flying through the air, glistening in the evening sunlight. Looking towards the driver of the other vehicle, he saw a young blonde woman looking at him. She saw him too and she smiled as if forgiveness was all she had to offer him. Time dragged on. Sesh slammed into the top of her SUV sliding over the roof and off the back onto the scalding hot asphalt. Lying face down in the middle of highway W, Sesh could taste and feel blood and glass in his mouth. All of the sudden, time sped back up, and blackness hit him like an unmanned aircraft smashing into the side of a mountain, then he knew nothing, he saw nothing, he felt…nothing.

Chapter Four
The Gateway Township

Ugh.... The air conditioner must be out again, it's so hot. Come to think of it, am I laying on the road... oh yea, car accident. What happened...? I remember I was texting mom then... ugh that poor girl, I hope she's OK.

Sesh cracked his eyes open, seeing bits of orange and brown from the surrounding view. It was nothing but desert in every direction, as far as he could see. Spikey, green, and brown Joshua trees scattered the landscape, with sprawling green cacti and thorn bushes huddling around the bases of each tree.

Sesh was lying in the middle of an abandoned highway. A light breeze blew rounded spikey bushes across the road at intermittent intervals. There were some light gray mountains in the far distance, and what looked like the beginning of a distant storm stirring up. The combination of the desert landscape and the distant mountains led Sesh to believe that he was in one of the western states of America.

"Which way should I walk?" Sesh grumpily asked himself, aloud.

Looking down at himself, he noticed he was covered in blood. His normally dirty, once white, t-shirt was ripped and dyed nearly entirely pink with sweat and blood. His pants had some small tears from the glass and crumpled metals of the accident, and they likewise had some blood splatters. Even his shoes were missing, what happened to them, he wasn't sure. That car accident really did a number to him. His shoulder ached a little from where that light smashed into him. Every bone in his body seemed like it was creaking, as if it decided that waking up and going back to work, was an involuntary choice. While his bones reluctantly began to work, he stood and looked around, thinking to himself about the possibilities.

Sesh thought, *the mountains in the distance will probably mean a city in that direction, not to mention potential water runoff. I won't be able to last very long out here without finding some water. Mountains it is. God, I hate this heat.*

After walking three miles, though it felt to Sesh like it was thirty, and being completely drenched in sweat, he noticed a slight change in his horizon. A reflective green sign a few hundred yards ahead of him stood out because there was nothing else around but red-orange dirt and clay, a couple of Joshua trees, sporadic tumbleweeds, and very seldom cacti. As he approached the green sign, he noticed the letters had not been written in the normal white bold font that most road signs are written in. This one was written in a bright gold lettering that emitted a gentle aura of power.

The sign read:

GATEWAY TOWNSHIP
THREE STEPS AHEAD

Looking around, Sesh didn't see anything out of the ordinary other than the sign. He looked as far ahead as he could see and didn't see any signs of human life. There were no settlements or cities. There was absolutely no reason this sign would say that, unless someone was messing around, and meant "miles" instead of "steps." Even then, he should be able to notice a distant town or city, even at three miles.

Weird, there's nothing ahead of me... Same old mountains same old road. Heck, it doesn't even look like I've gotten any closer to these mountains, so they must be further away than I originally anticipated.

Continuing on his way, Sesh began walking in the same direction, towards the mountains, and as he laid down his foot on that third step, a town appeared around him, out of nowhere. It was like standing in the middle of a western. Most of the dusty wooden buildings were run down and ragged. They were hugging the sides of the huge road with huge wooden-covered decks out front. Most of them had shingles that were missing and hung loosely from the eaves. The paved road he was on seemingly disappeared beneath his bare feet, turning into an exceptionally wide pathway, wide enough for seven or eight wagons to comfortably ride, side by side. It was riddled with pits and ragged holes. There were people too, hustling about, some were riding horses, or on rugged wagons, but most were walking. No one looked at him, they very pointedly looked away, as if they refused to acknowledge that a visitor to their little township would dare enter by the road. Looking around, it appeared to Sesh that the town was entirely made up of wood and glass, and a thick layer of dust that seemed to cling to everything.

Sesh tried to figure out exactly where he was, in order to call home and set up some way to get back there. It would help too, if he were able to get a drink of water because he was thoroughly parched. Every time he tried to get someone's attention, they would turn away from him, or blatantly ignore him. No one would answer him when he asked them anything until a tall thin elderly man with abnormally sharp elbows rode up to him. He had a small thin pencil mustache on his narrow slightly wrinkled face, pitch-black curly hair, and the appearance of what looked like, a middle eastern decent. His appearance wasn't the strangest thing about him, even though he was wearing flowing white robes that repelled the dust and a creepy, knowing smile. The strangest thing about him was the enormous dog he was riding. This dog was almost completely black, the ridgeline on its back looked to be on fire, and it had small red burning parts of its fur. The dog possessed huge flaming red eyes and stood as tall as any horse. He could see the drool-covered fangs the horse-dog had and knew instantly that this dog would not hesitate to tear him to shreds.

"Greetings young Sesh, I have come to escort you to the Gatekeeper."

"What…Who is the gatekeeper? And how did you know my name? Where am I? What is going on here?"

"Many of your questions shall be answered by the Gatekeeper, now come-hither good sir."

"I guess I don't really have a choice, do I?"

"You do not."

The horse-dog-riding man grunted regally and started slowly trotting away leading Sesh towards the only building in the town made of stone. Not only was it the only non-wooden building, but it was the only building that didn't have the same old wood brown color, this building was pure white. It was as if it was just like the dog-rider's robes, it repelled the dirt and detritus. The latches on the doors were finely polished gold, and the windows were made up of light fluffy white clouds. Sesh was suddenly aware of what happened just a few hours before in his small southern Arkansas town. He remembered the car accident, and that it was his fault.

I have got to be dead, and this is the gateway to heaven and hell…. That's the only thing that makes sense. I hope I am the only one who died in that accident. Maybe this mysterious dog rider guy will tell me if my thoughts on this are right or wrong.

"Am I dead?" Sesh boldly asked the horse-dog rider.

Without answering, the stranger stopped in front of the white stone and cloud building and pointed gravely at the front door. Turning his head slowly, Sesh looks at the front door, extreme fear washing over his entire body, as he knew that he must enter this door to learn his fate.

"You want me to go in there?" Sesh asked stupidly.

Without answering, the man just continued to point at the door. Sesh took the last remaining steps to get there, and carefully put his hand on the golden handle. Sesh noticed that the handle felt ridiculously hot in his hand, uncomfortably hot. There was a knocker in the center of the door that looked like a mighty angel holding a sword much too large for its body in one hand, and a set of golden scales in the other. The angel had flowing golden robes and beautiful white wings that spread almost the width of the door. The wings stretched out of the door, as a three-dimensional design, so that the knocker had to step within the encirclement of the wings. As soon as Sesh noticed the door would not open by the hot handle, the Angel moved.

"Are you…. Are you alive?" Sesh hesitated. "Of course not, I'm just talking to a door knocker. Hi, how are you? I bet you hear a lot of knock-knock jokes."

As Sesh reached up to knock with the hanging scales that the Angel was holding, the angel burst to life, and quicker than he could blink, the angel was holding his golden sword at Sesh's throat, the scales automatically righting themselves. The Angel's wings burst out further than before, seeming to envelope the entire world in shadow, all that remained for Sesh to see, was the Angel, and the white feathers that lined the winged walls around him.

In a voice much too large for the Angel, much too deep for something so small, the Angel said, "Halt! Who dares try to touch the holy scales? Who would dare attempt to enter the Gateway without being judged? Who, but the living God has the right?" The Angel's eyes met those of Sesh's and then gave a knowing smile. The Angel's face was perfect in every way, a perfectly proportional nose, and mouth, and his eyebrows were perfectly spaced and evenly grown. Not one hair seemed out of place.

"Ah yes, Sesh, the most recent addition to the Gateway Township. You have a peculiar soul, though many peculiar souls pass through this way. I take it you are wondering who I am?" Without waiting for Sesh to respond, he continued, "Very well, I shall tell you. I am Gabriel, the Archangel, the Gatekeeper, though I am not the *key-keeper*. I am the Vanquisher of the souls that are unfit to reside in the great house with the one true God, among other things."

"Gabriel…. Vanquisher of souls…what…I thought Gabriel the Archangel was supposed to be a massive angelic figure guarding the gates of heaven? And why is the gateway to Heaven a white door on a building held together by clouds, in the middle of a scorching hot desert western town surrounded by a bunch of people who don't speak to anyone?" Sesh questioned.

"So full of questions aren't you child? Alas, as it is with the newly deceased or nearly deceased… I suppose I will answer a few questions for you." Gabriel acknowledged. "You are correct I am a massive angelic figure, God's chief angel, primary messenger, and guardian. This figure I currently occupy is merely that, a figure that I take, when I do the important duties, God has asked me to do. Holding the scales is especially important, where I will weigh your life, good or bad. This door that I guard IS the gateway to Heaven AND the gateway to Hell. How the scales weigh decide how you will be judged by God, if you are more bad than good, for instance, you will be judged guilty, and sentenced to eternal life in the fiery pits of Hell, and vice versa. For you though, a different situation has presented itself, being that you are not dead but nearly dead. Your body is currently in, what you humans call, a coma. As is the young lady whom you may or may not have killed with your recklessness."

Sesh was shocked, he wasn't dead! Somehow, they may still save his life, he may still come back from this! He didn't know how, or who would save his life, but he knew there was a chance that all of this was just a dream. Gabriel was eyeballing Sesh as if understanding his thoughts on this and spoke clearly once more.

"I know you think there is a chance that you may yet survive, but I promise you, unless you take your next task seriously, there is no chance. Right now, I have been given the right to offer you a chance to save yourself. That is the only way you may survive and thus by surviving, save the planet you call Earth. You can survive by overcoming the Seven Levels and coming forth from them victorious. Only then will your eyes open and you may go on back to your planet with to complete another difficult journey. You have many trials ahead of you. As for the Levels, you will need a holy weapon. It could possibly be a sword, not unlike mine, to carry with you when you enter the seven levels of Purgatory. It could be something else entirely, no one but The Eternal knows what exactly your holy weapon is, until you find it. Each individual will require a different relic or complete a special task in order to survive their own type of purgatory. You personally may meet up with people, as they go about their quest and declare formally in the name of Christ that they are your allies on your quest. Beware, Sesh, any whom you meet on your quest in purgatory, may essentially be trying to take advantage of you, or kill you. Not everyone can be trusted, though some can be. Also be aware of allies, for an alliance is a shared union, if you ally with someone, you must complete their trial as well as your own before either of you can move on. For instance, if you were to ally with someone who needed to defeat a sphynx, you would have to assist them, if you did not, and they should fail, you would also fail. This works both ways. Remember, even the dead have to go through purgatory sometimes, trying to find a solution to satisfy their souls. If you fail at your purgatory quest, you will be judged based on your deeds. Your body will only survive if you survive the Levels. Trust must be given easily and earned through arduous work. Before you can face purgatory, you must complete your initial task, which again, is finding your holy weapon. Therefore, I beseech you now Sesh, do you accept the trials that I have laid out before you? If you accept, you have as long as you need to complete the levels, but you only have eight hours to enter the levels with your holy weapon. Do you accept?"

"Can I ask a few questions first, before I accept?"

"You may."

"What do you mean I have eight hours to enter the levels with my holy weapon?"

"You must find your holy weapon, and then enter the first level of purgatory."

"What happens if I don't?"

"You will be judged."

"Why would people try to kill me?"

"Not everyone who dies, was a good person. You need to understand that The Gateway Township, and The Levels of Purgatory, are not on linear time. You will run into people who have not even been born yet in your time but have already died in theirs. You will encounter people who have died just yesterday in their time, but five hundred years ago, in your time."

"That's… I sort of get it, what if I ally with someone, and I'm just about done with my journey, and continue onto the next floor? Level? Anyway, I move on, and they fail. What does that mean?"

"You will be judged."

"Okay, where can I find a holy weapon?"

"Somewhere in the Doomed Maze."

"Last question, you said I was going to have a tough journey, but I was going to save the world? What do you mean by that?"

"The small life-stone you found on your last day in the fields, is the key to saving your world. If you put that stone in the small spring your village gathers what little water they can from, the water will expand, your planet will reverse its course of a dry death. Consider that all springs on your planet are connected, so all water comes from the same place."

"That's all I have to do?"

"Yes."

"That makes my choice easy then."

Sesh valiantly accepted, he now knew the only way to return home to keep his mom and dad from falling into turmoil and starving to death was to accept. The only way he could return home and save everyone, including Suzanne, was to accept. Sesh listened intently as Gabriel gave him a couple of clues as to where he could start his search for his mighty holy weapon.

"You will need to use cunning and endurance if you hope to survive this, speak with St. Peter about outfitting you in some appropriate attire, as you are not currently wearing any adventure clothing. As for the weapon, remember the only direction you need to go is forward, try to go no other direction and you will make it out within the allotted time slot, also not all dead ends, are dead ends, and not everything is as it seems in the Doomed Maze."

Sesh stared at Gabriel blankly, "that's the advice you're giving me? What does it mean? Is this even possible? And who is Saint Peter?"

Chapter Five
Outfitters

Without answering, the Angel smirked then returned to his static motionless state. The wings retracted from his surroundings, allowing the bright sunlight to overtake and warm him once more. Sesh was about to ask again when he heard a voice speak up behind him.

"I am, of course." Said the old man standing behind Sesh wearing flowing white robes and sitting regally on the front haunches of a dog the size of a horse. "And this is my sweet, sweet, good boy, Theodore. If you hadn't guessed, he is a hell hound. I will say though, he is a little more domesticated than most hell hounds."

Now that Sesh could get a better look at the hell hound, he noticed that Theodore's fur was a thick coarse texture, which looked like charcoal or burnt wood. There was a small glow in the dog's eyes that gave one the feeling of staring deeply into the fire on a bone chillingly wintry night. One thing Sesh knew for certain, he would never, ever want to fight a hell hound.

"So, Mr. Saint Peter sir, what exactly are we supposed to do about getting me a holy weapon? Where do I go to begin this quest? I know that I need to start as soon as possible to take advantage of all the time I have been allotted." Sesh dauntlessly asked.

"The entrance to the doomed maze is just outside of town, through the rose garden, and at the bottom of the eastern valley. You have plenty of time, because your journey's time requirement will not start until you step foot inside. Before we head that direction though, I must get you outfitted for your task, obsolete or not, you will need some comfortable shoes and breathable breeches. How does a pair of moccasins and overalls sound to you?" Saint Peter stared questioningly after speaking softly to Sesh.

Sesh stared right back at Saint Peter before saying tactfully, "If you think 'overalls' and 'moccasins' are what I need to succeed, then by all means outfit me looking like an early European colonizer who just learned to trade with the Natives."

"I do not think any of the clothing that I give you, will either aid or hinder you from succeeding, that will rely entirely on you. If you are to make it through the seven levels of purgatory, you will need cunning, adaptation, and the ability to make an ally with the most stubborn of individuals from all levels of society, from all timelines your planet has experienced. Try to consider that time here is fluid. We are all just tiny specks of matter inside a floating cosmos of swirling liquid. Almost everyone who passes the boundary of life and death, comes here to the Gateway Township. Occasionally, someone slips by and goes directly past, which is usually a case where their death occurred unnaturally, or not at any fault of their own. Of the people that come to the Gateway Township, each person is either judged immediately, and sent on their way, or they go through the levels. We do offer it as a choice, as the Eternal instilled choice into his favorite creation, more than any other feeling or thought. With choice some, who would normally pass the gates immediately, stay and attempt the Levels because they have, what humans have called in the past, unfinished business. Others have a more sinister desire, to end the journey of the recently perished, they may not know that's their desire initially, but the truest version of ourselves is what is here, this is each of our souls after all. There is little law or rules here in the Levels. You will face creatures you have never dreamed of, that are from the deepest, most terrifying of nightmares. You will meet the gentlest of souls who you may appear on the surface to be horrifying monsters. Everything ever imagined is here. The fact remains that no one but God knows entirely what exactly you will face when you enter the levels, or the Doomed Maze for that matter, as each level and room in the maze is different. I have personally never been, but the looks of those who have returned, are always distant." He paused for a moment, looking off into the distant, then with a nod said, "Now, let's get you outfitted."

Sesh stared at Saint Peter for a few moments not knowing what to say, before shrugging and following closely behind. They walked up to a building that had a dancing ballet dancer on the windows, with bright pink tutus on full display. Sesh raised his eyebrows at the serious looking old man but said nothing.

Suddenly, a beautiful sound burst forth in the air. It was high pitched and full of love and joy. As if a couple of cherubs were playing in a gentle stream. It turned out to be St. Peter laughing, his eyes a perfect half-moon as he looked at Sesh's reaction, "I jest, I jest, young Sesh, one must keep the mood light, in light of death."

He began walking again down the dusty dirty street. "How about we outfit you in a combat uniform, soft poly-propylene liner inside a cotton-Kevlar hybrid and leather on outside that should allow you to move properly as well as offer protection from sharp objects. Also, it will take the brunt of some extremely hard blunt blows. Have no fear, you likely will not face any bullets from your modern-day guns, but will probably face mostly arrows, spears, maces, barbed hooks, or other facets of torture. There are a great many things that you'll find inside the levels."

"Now that's more of the type of gear I was thinking about, will you be able to give me any sort of weapon? How about a bow and some arrows, or a spear and shield or something to protect myself? How about food supplies, water, fire starting materials, a tent, or some kind of shelter?" Sesh couldn't help rushing out a bunch of questions all at once.

St. Peter eyed Sesh carefully before remarking subtly, "Do you know how to use a sword, or shield? How about a bow and arrow?"

"Well…. No."

"Then why would I give you something that would ultimately just hurt you?"

"I guess you wouldn't…"

Looking at Sesh for a couple of breaths, Saint Peter continued, "As for the other supplies you requested, they will be given to you inside your pack after you are dressed for success. You will receive your pack after you return here with your tasks required item… if you return."

"Outstanding, I guess."

Not noticing the sarcasm, Saint Peter just nodded as if he was doing the biggest favor ever for Sesh. "Indeed, let's get started, shall we?"

Sesh followed St. Peter and his mount, Theodore, down the dirt street passing several old wooden buildings. Many of the windows had dirty dust-orange faces pressed firmly up against the windows staring at them as they passed. It must have been a novel thing to have someone new, beginning the journey through the Seven Levels of Purgatory. All the faces looked the same, they were all covered thickly in the orange dust from the streets. The dust seemed to permeate and cling to everything, though none had seemed to cling to Sesh yet.

As their casual pace slowed, they came to a grand building with swinging half doors that reminded Sesh of the saloon doors he'd see on T.V. when his dad would watch *GUNSMOKE* on the weekends, back when they had time to watch shows, and had a television. The walls were the same weathered wood, speckled with the burnt orange dust that was common here. There was a large wrap around covered deck, which gave a beckoning feeling. With no furniture on the deck, it seemed almost too empty. Glancing back down the street, Sesh couldn't see past two of the buildings they had passed. It was almost as if reality was being created one hundred feet ahead of him and deleted a hundred feet behind.

St. Peter stopped at the double doors and solemnly said, "this is where we will get your new things."

Taking a deep breath, Sesh said, "Let's do this."

Entering the facility, one would expect a musty dirty interior to match the outside, but Sesh was shocked to see it was not as it seemed. Through the doors, which showed a dark interior, was a very bright white light, which seemed to emit from everything. There were no shadows from the various pieces of furniture, there were also no visible light fixtures on the ceiling. The interior of the building was impeccably clean, as if everything inside it had small porous holes that vacuumed constantly. There were a couple of very white one person couches, separated by a small coffee table. A desk sat off to the side, with a person, who wasn't quite visible from the doorway, sitting there.

Sesh followed Saint Peter as they walked up to the front desk, behind which sat an incredibly old, very wrinkly woman or man, Sesh could not tell which, whose name was Pat, as it said on their name placard in front of their desk. Peter and Pat spoke in hushed voices for a few minutes, occasionally glancing at Sesh. Eventually, Pat nodded gravely, then turned and exited out a door behind the desk.

"Please be seated." St. Peter was pointing at one of the white couches. Sitting down, Sesh found that the couch was so comfortable that Sesh had trouble staying awake. It wasn't until St. Peter was shaking him awake that he realized he had been asleep. For how long, who knew?

"Do not fret Sesh, you were supposed to fall asleep, for that is one of the restful couches. They are designed to enable any being to get a full night's rest after only ten minutes of sleep. Though, the downside is, if you do not have someone to awaken you, you will sleep forever. How do you feel?"

"I feel great! Thank you for letting me get some rest… and for waking me, how… uh, do you mean they sleep until they die?"

"No Sesh, I mean that if you fell asleep, and no one were to wake you, you would not awaken. If you slept for forty-five years, you would not die, or be judged immediately, you would simply stay asleep, as time swirled around you. When you awoke, you would not have aged, merely the world around you aged."

"That's a bit terrifying, at least it wouldn't result in one's death."

"Terrifying indeed, when these were on your planet, someone had slept for one hundred and thirty-two years. He was awoken by a random person who stumbled upon his cave where the couch was. They were merely passing through when seeking a better life in a different part of the continent. He was so bewildered when he awoke, to find out that his entire family had perished in his absence.

You see, no one knew he was in there, he was exploring a potential new home for his family, found a hidden chamber that had those two couches in them, along with some ancient celestial texts. Naturally, at that time of your planet's existence, no one could read them, but they felt comfortable to the touch, so he decided to take a seat. He then fell asleep, and after he was awoken by the random passerby exploring a cave, chaos ensued. It ensued because while one hundred and thirty years was not a terribly long time, it was long enough for the prehistoric human species to have been evolved away from, into a more nomadic species. They were all humans, but different attributes of their body structures changed, based on the ease of their lives. Shortly after, the powers that be decided that all couches with this particular benefit or curse were not a good addition for your planet, so they put them here, and now we utilize them to help purgatory participants."

Sesh was curious as to who the man was and what became of him after he became a living legend, but decided his nervousness towards the upcoming trial he was about to face, superseded his curiosity. He followed Saint Peter to the counter and retrieved a small bag and a bundle of clothing.

"Here, put these on." Saint Peter tossed the bundle of clothing to Sesh, and jerked his chin towards a closed door that he swore, was not there before. The door was labeled: **CHANGING ROOM**

After Sesh got dressed, he noticed that he now wore a completed outfit. He thought the outfit made him feel even more like he was in the middle of a western movie. He wore a pair of fitted blue jeans, with a leather belt. His torso was covered in a white undershirt, a mahogany brown wool collared vest, and topped with a wonderfully comfortable leather jacket. Every bit of the clothes he wore felt like there were made for him and sized exactly to his preference. On his feet, he had put on a pair of poly-propylene socks and wool socks, before he shoved them into a very worn, comfortable pair of leather hiking boots. Sesh had never had an outfit that was this well fitted, or nice, in his entire life. He left the changing room, and looked at a waiting Saint Peter and Pat, as they both nodded in appreciation.

Saint Peter handed a mall leather satchel to Sesh and said, "In this bag, you will find a bottle of water, before you enter the first Level, you will not have need for finding a water source, as this water bottle will automatically refill, this will cease when you enter the first level. As long as you are in the Gateway Township, you will feel no need for food, water, or to use the restroom. The second you enter the doomed maze; you will function as normal. You will also find a small bundle of unleavened bread, a notebook, and a pencil. The pouch itself, you can use to pick up anything extra, there are some remarkable things inside the maze, but they are difficult to find. Come with me now, and I will take you there."

Chapter Six
The Rose Garden

After leaving the populated portions of the township, Sesh noticed the buildings became less, and less, sturdy. Many of them were merely piles of broken planks and orange dirt. Beyond the seventh building, was a change of the scenery. Color seemed to overtake the horizon, which dominated his perspective. He never felt like he was capable of feeling starved for vibrant colors, until this moment, when he could see a beautiful rose garden in front of him.

Walking towards a huge archway, the color slowly became more apparent with tangible shapes, through the dust and haze of the Gateway Township. The archway itself was woven with vines, and on the vines were roses of every color imaginable. There were even roses that glowed with an inner light. Some were a mixed swirl of colors, that almost seemed to twirl and dance in the light of the day, as well as the light of their neighboring roses. Under the archway was like being inside a rainbow tornado, without the wind.

Inside the garden, Sesh could see a well-worn path, which snaked back and forth through the myriad of bushes and vines. It was quiet and peaceful here; the only sounds were the soft humming of bumblebees and gentle chirping of small birds. Occasionally a distant bench could be seen, beckoning, and encouraging one to sit and read a book, or just enjoy the serenity of the garden.

Sesh reflected to no one in particular, "this garden is just absolutely stunning. I could stay here for a great many hours or days and be at complete peace."

Chuckling, Peter said, "this rose garden was once a small part of the garden of Eden. When Eden was taken from humanity, it was broken down and split into many distinct parts and spread out over several places. Some of which are in the holy city. This particular piece remains here, as a gift for the efforts that the staff. They manage and maintain the Gateway Township after all. I've been to a part of the garden of Eden that had the tree of forbidden knowledge, and you would never guess what the shape of the fruit was. It's funny, because everyone on your planet always thought that it was an apple, or apple-shaped fruit, but it wasn't. It was the shape of a banana. Not the genetically modified banana that you may have read about, before they became extinct, but the small, bitter, green, banana that used to dominate the coastal regions. It really is a shame that they have all disappeared from your planet. Perhaps one day, they will return."

Staring blankly at Saint Peter for a moment, Sesh could only utter one word without bursting into laughter, "Remarkable."

After a couple more moments of silence, they shared an unrestrained laugh together. "A banana? Didn't the bible say it was in the shape of an apple or something like that?"

"No actually, in the Torah it was considered to be a grape, but in your English translated bible from Hebrew, it was not mentioned as to what type of fruit it was. Regardless, there was only ever one tree, and it is no longer accessible by any living person."

When they came upon a small bench in the garden. Peter decided he was going to take a small break and sat down on the bench. Theodore took this opportunity to quickly bound off through the garden, towards a large tree that was completely enveloped with rose vines. Sesh watched as the hound twisted and turned, rolling around on the ground near the tree, scratching his back. The thorns on the bushes and vines must be able to scratch his skin through the thick course fur on his back.

"This may be one of the greatest places I've ever experienced in my entire life."

"It is one of my favorite places, as well, young man. In fact, Theodore here is particularly fond of that tree over there, he loves to lie under it and take his naps... as well as use the bushes and vines to scratch himself."

They continued to watch the dog in silence for around twenty minutes, just enjoying the level of solitude and peace the garden had to offer. Sesh's mind was completely blank, without a single thought screaming through his head, or any sign of discomfort or stress. Sesh was at a never felt before level of peace, while he sat in silence with the old man.

Sighing, Peter stood and said, "I believe it is time young man. It is always hard for me escorting someone through the garden towards the Eastern Valley."

"Why?"

Peter didn't respond, just gave a small whistle to Theodore, and began walking the trail again. The walk seemed to fly by even though it was the longest part of their walk so far. They slowed down to enjoy the tranquility the garden had to offer once more but didn't settle in for another break. Before long they stepped off into a small valley entrance. The valley entrance was obvious, as approached from the end of the garden. It was marked with evergreen trees, more particularly spruce trees of every variety.

The slope down into the valley was not entirely steep, but it did have a gradual grade to it, slightly increasing over time. The deeper they walked into the valley, the more strenuous the hike began. The rocks got bigger and bigger, until Sesh had to leap over deep cracks in the large stones they passed over. The trees began to thin the larger the rocks got. The sounds of the valley were a far cry different than those of the garden. Here the sounds were hushed whispers, as if the souls of the dead were warning them of the dangers that lay at the bottom of the valley. An occasional wisp of light could be seen through the distant trees growing up on the other side of the valley. Sesh could occasionally see the twinkling lights from a slightly elevated vantage point, at different spots on their hike into the heart of the valley.

"Are those… spirits?"

"Those are the lost souls who refused to enter the maze. They are unable to return through the garden without completing their task. If you chose not to enter the maze, eventually your outer shell will crumble away, leaving behind something akin to the wisps and spirits you occasionally see there. They are harmless and can no longer communicate with anyone. Fortunately, this does not happen often, unfortunately, over the course of eternity, it has happened enough that those shells are noticeable."

At the bottom of the Eastern valley, they came upon a large opening that seemed to fall straight into the earth, directly down. The opening was a darker stone than the rocks and pebbles that made up the rest of the valley floor. There was a small trickle of water that steadily poured off into the hole from a tiny creek. If Sesh looked closely, he could see the creek zig and zag through the trees on the valley floor. He thought that it would no doubt lead to a waterfall at the distant end of the valley. In front of him was a void in the earth. There was a swirling haze with a dim orange light that emanated from the hole. Sesh could not see anything past the orange portal's haze. He was stricken with fear, because he knew that he would have to take a leap of faith far sooner than he had hoped.

"This is the Doomed Maze. The place where many have to go for their holy weapon. It is the single place in the Gateway Township where souls have a chance to never return, but their journeys end and they are judged and weighed immediately." St. Peter stared ominously at Sesh. "In fact, only one has ever entered this maze, and returned from it, that is why it is called the Doomed Maze. It is truly the greatest trial of the Township. There will be many obstacles you must face and overcome. Your ultimate test will obviously come at the end, if that wasn't predictable enough, there you must be willing to face your inner-most demons, to exit the Maze.

If you return, and I emphasize the "if," come find me, and we will go speak to Gabriel together, from there you will be taken to the first level, good luck, and may The Eternal watch over you." Saint Peter and Theodore turned to leave, heading back up the valley incline.

"Wait! What do you mean only ONE person has ever entered the maze and returned!? And there are other trials that exist here? How come I was given this one?"

Turning partially towards Sesh, but still staring off up the valley, Saint Peter responded with, "Yes, only one. He was also in a coma, just like you. Do not forget... every trial you will ever face in your existence, you are fully capable of handling. The Eternal will not give you anything you are incapable of overcoming, sometimes... sometimes you just have to apply yourself a little more, and sometimes failure or success brings you to the actual trial."

The older man and the oversized dog continued their slow march back towards the town. Sesh watched them leave for a little while, then turned and looked towards the next step of his journey. With a deep sigh, and a look of determination, Sesh ran forward, folded his legs beneath him, grabbed his shins and pulled his knees to his chest, then tucked his head between his legs, performing a perfect cannonball into the swirling mist that was the entrance of the Doomed Maze.

Chapter Seven
Spider!

"Oof!"

Sesh landed in a sprawling mass of limbs and dust. Groaning in pain, he stood, then dusted his clothing off and looked around. He was standing at what appeared to be the entrance of a very long hallway. The walls were so tall, they appeared to come together over head, at such a high point, Sesh wondered for a moment if he was within a cave. Each surface was a beautiful grainy wood, inlaid with palm branches. The palm branches were all imprinted with a burnishing tool. Staring at all the palm branches, he wondered if there was a correlation between the palm branches in the Bible and the ones on the walls. It gave him a creepy feeling, to consider exactly how long it took someone to individually burnish each and every palm leaf here. He doubted he would ever have the patience to do such a thing. Looking around to see if there was any way he would be able to climb the walls, he found that there was absolutely no way he could find a handhold to climb the walls. Not that he would want to anyway, or even would have the stamina to be able to climb that high without eventually losing his grip and falling into a horrible pile of blood and guts. No, the best way for Sesh to go, was forward, into the heart of the Doomed Maze.

Taking a few steps into the Doomed Maze, Sesh became acutely aware that he had less than 8 hours to find this holy weapon of some sort and begin the seven levels of purgatory. He must not fail, his family needs him, the world needs him, Suzanne needs him. The world would die without the stone that was sitting in his pants pocket, likely next to his comatose body in the hospital. Without that stone, his parents would never find peace amongst themselves. What would they do without him there to temper the moods, and to help provide for their small family. They cannot work as hard as they used to. Their age is catching up with them, as it is with everyone. The famine took a severe toll on his mom and dad, causing them to be malnourished, dehydrated, and cranky. Their fights are getting increasingly aggressive, alcohol consumption is getting heavier and heavier, and it would eventually run out, no one could make alcohol anymore, there just wasn't enough grain or fruit. He needed to make it through this maze, and conquer the levels, or his parents would fall apart and likely die. Maybe Suzanne would want him again if she found out that he was a hero. Just maybe…

Sesh shook his head vigorously, "I can't think about any of that right now, I need to focus."

He noticed a sign a hundred yards ahead, and quickly rushed towards it, it read:

**HERE LIES THE SOULS OF MANY
THIS IS THE DOOMED MAZE.
ONE HUNDRED THOUSAND SQUARE MILES
SEPARATES THE OUTER WALLS.
YOU HAVE 7 HOURS AND 57 MINUTES.
BE WARY OF THE DARK CORNERS OF THIS ABYSS.
GOOD LUCK SESH
MAY THE ETERNAL BE WITH YOU.**

This sign instilled unadulterated fear in Sesh. Reading it, it was almost like he was being watched, and witnessed as the final moments of his life were upon him. What scared him the most was not the warning of caution that needed to be taken in the darker parts of the maze. No, it was the sheer number of miles this maze is said to cover. One hundred thousand square miles?

He had no idea how he was going to find what he needed to find in a single square mile, let alone a hundred thousand square miles. No man can walk that many miles in eight hours, let alone navigate a maze that's one hundred thousand square miles. There has to be a way. Taking a deep breath, Sesh began the first leg of his journey.

No sooner had Sesh started down the long tunnel-like hallway that the wall behind him seamed together, forming a singular wall, with no exits. Experimenting, Sesh jogged forward a bit, then turned quickly. He saw the walls behind him slowly sealing together. It was as if the entrance of the maze was staying at his heel. He turned and began jogging forward at a steady pace. He knew deep down that if he stopped to rest, or slowed to a walk, he would not make it in time. Sesh decided he would heed the advice Gabriel gave him, 'go forward.'

After running for what seemed like an hour, Sesh hadn't come upon any forks in the road, or turns to be made. It was as if he was running straight down a long narrow road. He slowed for a moment, turned, and noticed the back edge of the wall was still there, his constant companion. Pressing on, he noticed a minor change in his environment, the tunnel seemed to bend a little and slope downwards.

After rounding the first turn, which happened to be a left and down, Sesh notices another sign near the wall:

GOOD CHOICE.
YOU HAVE 7 HOURS AND 56 MINUTES REMAINING.
DO NOT READ EVERY SIGN.
GOOD LUCK SESH
MAY THE ETERNAL BE WITH YOU.

"Do not read every sign? What was that supposed to mean, if they didn't want me to read the signs, why would they put the sign there in the first place, unless…. UNLESS IT WAS MEANT TO SLOW ME DOWN!" Sesh screamed at himself.

"7 hours and 56 minutes? I guess time here flows more slowly than I'm accustomed to, being that I have been running for at least an hour. That's a good thing at least, I'm glad I got that going for me."

Continuing his relentless pace, Sesh rounds a corner to the right and just about ran right smack into a bright blazing line of light. The light stretched from one side of the maze to the other. Sesh squinted and looked closer at this light before realizing it was a very bright, very white, almost burning, web. The web was so grand and so beautiful to behold. He loved the intricate designs and all the work that a grand spider, for it must have been a very large spider, had put into this web. That was when Sesh heard it…

SCUTTLE SCUTTLE SCUTTLE SCRATCH SCRATCH

Coming from the other side of the web Sesh could hear the sounds of the giant spider. There was nowhere else for him to go, he knew he had to go through this gargantuan web. As he took an exceedingly small, very slow deliberate steps towards the web, he got more and more nervous. Eventually, his foot flattened on the floor in front of the web, the scuttling and scratching stopped. Sesh stopped and exhaled a terribly slow breath. Focusing on the web, he took another slow deliberate step, then another. He walked along the edge of the web's barrier trying to judge where the spider was by sound, but no noise emanated from the other side of the web.

Off to the right, Sesh noticed a small, narrow pathway that looked abnormal… it was rectangular, like a doorway. When he focused his eyes on the abnormally rectangular door, in an otherwise flowing environment, it disappeared. He would look away and see it again out of the corner of his eye, but just for a moment then look quickly, and it would disappear again. Someone had been intentionally attempting to hide this door, this pathway beyond the web. But who? Maybe this was just part of the innate design of this maze.

It figures, just what I would expect from a magical maze full of terrorizing creatures and death traps. A giant spider web with a hidden secret door. Frankly, I just don't know how I am going to get through this, but I have got to try. You got this, Sesh!

He gave himself a small pep-talk, trying to crank up his courage. It barely helped, as he became more and more nervous, the longer he stood next to the web. Deciding on trying the door, he headed that direction.

Sesh walked towards the door very gingerly, trying to make as little noise as possible. Just as he is about to enter the door, he heard a faint, scuttle, one time, no scratching just a soft, shifting scuttle. The noise sent shivers down his back, causing the hair all over his body to stand on end. Something told him he was in immediate danger. Pressing himself as flat as he could, and crouching to a stooping level, Sesh creeped through the web where he thought he saw the door. Just as he was crossing the threshold of the door, he could not see anything, and he had the distinct feeling he was going to walk right smack into the wall. His body passed through the space smoothly and eased off into a brightly lit web hallway.

This hallway appeared out of nowhere, surrounding his entire point of view. It seemed to be approximately one hundred yards long and fifteen to twenty feet wide. Much wider and much longer than the maze pathway he was in previously, which was confusing none the less.

Sesh cautiously edged down the webby pathway, being extra careful not to touch the free hanging strands of white lightning looking web. After creeping a couple dozen yards, a soft grunting can be heard just ahead. Sesh could not see where the grunting was coming from, but it seemed to be coming from around a bend in the path.

Rounding the bend, Sesh caught sight of a small glowing peanut with wings. The fairy, for it was a fairy not a peanut, had soft supple white angelic wings. Its arms and legs were thin and its body somewhat bulbous. Overall, it looked like an overweight miniature child, with a tiny little human head. The entire fairy gave off a small glow, not equivalent to the bright light that permeated the web, but a different type of glow that seemed more golden. Next to the bright web, it was very dim, as if a shadow had tried to block out a bright light.

The small creature was struggling to free itself from the tangling strands of the web. As Sesh looked closer, he noticed the little guy had dark hair and pointy ears. His very masculine face, and chubby little body, very clearly showed him to be a male. He had a pained look on his face, as if the web were causing him physical harm. His eyes widened a little when he noticed Sesh standing there looking at him in pure curiosity.

"Eh hem, Excuse me, Sesh... Will... ooomphgrrr, will you, ahh, help me get out of this blasted lightning web?"

Taken aback slightly in shock, Sesh jumped, lightly touching a free hanging strand of lightning web across his left shoulder. ZAPP. POP. Sesh hit the ground hard as the strand of web disintegrated into bright blinding pain. The strand emitted a powerful electrical shock that temporarily stunned him.

"Feel better? This isn't time for a nap, quit playing around, come help me, this isn't pleasant." the fairy peanut asked.

"Ughh, what was that? And HOW exactly am I supposed to help you out of the exploding lightning web?"

"Well, first of all, that is the electric web from a giant cloud spider. They are a rather rambunctious race of electric spiders, but most of them are completely blind and deaf. If you don't touch their web, they won't have any idea that you are around. Secondly, I am NOT a peanut fairy, I heard you thinking that... I am your guardian angel. And my name is Sir Trilion Pippenstein the Third, everyone just calls me Pip. I have been appointed to you since the day you were born. I would have not had to reveal myself to you, except I decided to advance a little further ahead to see if this spider would be a nuisance to you or not, and unfortunately, I miscalculated my advancement and stumbled, into this web."

"You...are my guardian Angel? Then how did I end up almost dead? How did I end up having to go through a series of purgatory levels just to get back to my body? And why are you so small? Huh Pip?"

"Well, I am your guardian angel, yes. You ended up, nearly dead, because you were not following the laws of the land. Had you been following the laws of the land; I may have been able to gently nudge you in the other direction to prevent you from having an accident. But fueled by your anger, and your misguided practices of playing with that unfortunate technologically primitive version of a cellular telephone, you were, so to say, 'un-*nudgeable*.' Also, I am not small, I am normal sized for a guardian angel who is in my circumstance. I am perhaps even slightly above average in stature, thank you very much. Though I may add that following you around has given me plenty of time to catch up on some well needed rest, boy, do you have a boring life. Work, sleep, work, sleep, work, sleep. My last charge was the strongest man in the world, until he unwillingly had his hair cut. He shouldn't have told that "Jezabel" if you asked me, but he did. He had a short life after that, pushing those blasted walls down on himself and his enemies. It was in Gods will I reckon, though God isn't too keen on suicide, but things didn't go according to plan, so he got a pass."

"Your last charge was Samson?"

"Oh, you know of him?"

"Who doesn't? I learned of him in church, like most everyone else."

"Right, well, yes, Samson was his name. Now, as for getting me out of this spider's web, could you assist me please? It will hurt, but you will survive. Afterwards, I will remain visible to you and help you throughout your ordeal here."

"Yea, OK, let me do this, I'm just going to reach in, and grab hold of you, then pull you out on my way to the ground."

"Right, one last thing before you…" ZAPP POP Sesh reached up grabbed the little angel and pulled, being stunned immediately, he didn't hear what else the angel had to say until he was coming to and heard, "Pulling me, uhm, out will alert the spider we are on his web and he or she will come looking for their meal, you should be prepared to run."

Great, save a talking peanut sized angel named Pip, and get attacked by a blind deaf spider. I hate spiders.

"Hey, why didn't me getting zapped earlier, alert the spider? How come you didn't alert it by being in its web trapped?"

"RUN SESH!!"

Sesh sat up and looked at the scarred, gashed up spider roughly the size of a two-story house, dangling directly over him. The spider was dripping green acidic goo from his mouth, which seemed to be filled with so many razor blades. His bulbous body was covered in bristly hairs the length of his arms and as big around as his calves. Sesh could notice a wild assortment of scars and ancient battle wounds. Most noticeable was the gray clouds that floated in the many eyeballs that hovered above the gaping green mouth, and the occasional crackle of lightning that skirted up and down its legs. He had never seen a spider that looked anything like this in his life. It didn't quite have eight legs, but only five. It had hundreds of tentacles and spikes coming off of its body. Each leg ended in a huge double spike, likely meant for fighting, and for climbing.

Sesh froze. He felt if he moved at all the massive spider would be on him in milliseconds. Standing there, staring at the big spider, he decided to try to distract the spider with a well-timed tossing of a small stone. Moving back and forth sniffing and scratching softly at the ground with his long feelers that came directly out of its large gaping mouth, the cloud spider was ready to pounce. The second Sesh tossed the small stone, making it bounce off the side of the spider's back leg, it turned in a flurry of speed, and launched itself at the motion vibration of the stone impacting the ground and its leg. It sniffed and smelled around at the spot, finding nothing.

Throwing another stone, further across the pathway, it clanked and pounded loudly off the floor and wall. In a flash, the spider hurled his entire body to the other side of the pathway, attempting to catch its prey in a deadly grasp. Hoping it was finally able to satisfy the hunger that has eaten away at its insides. The spider was sorely disappointed though, because as soon as it jumped across the hallway, Sesh grabbed Pip and ran like he had never run before, bounding around the corner of the maze before he decided to turn and look back. The great cloud spider was still searching the area with his feelers, sniffing, and feeling, sniffing, and feeling. Sesh's heart nearly jumped out of his chest when the spider momentarily turned in his direction, pausing and sniffing at the air, as if knowing his prey had rushed away. Sesh began slowly and gently working his way down the hallway towards the end of the webbed section.

"Be careful, that cloud beast is ancient. And currently you are not prepared to face it in battle. The exit to the webbed trap is over there, directly in the middle of the path, do you see it?"

Pip was whispering directions to Sesh for a few minutes before he could finally see the exit. It would be a little more complicated to get through, but it was definitely feasible to accomplish without alerting the creator of the web. The exit hole was roughly the width of a narrow closet door, and about half as tall. Sesh would have to crouch and shuffle slowly in order to make it without being zapped by the walls. The tunnel inside the doorway curved and turned, rising, and falling in gentle hills.

"How long is this tunnel pip? Not trying to complain or anything but my legs and back are killing me from holding this position for so long." Sesh complained.

"Honestly, I don't know how long it is. I was stuck in the main hallway, remember? Just hang in there, we can do this." Pip encouraged.

"If you say so buddy, I'll keep going. Mostly because I don't want to be on someone's dinner plate today. Do you know how much time I have left until I must return to Gabriel with the holy thing?"

"Well, think about this Sesh, you had already figured it out. The rules of the maze, the time needed to get through it. If you just take a moment to contemplate the time situation here, I believe you will understand. I cannot answer the question for you, it is one of the ancient rules of my trade. But I believe in you, I know you can figure it out!"

"Uh… OK well, when I entered the maze, time moved more slowly, adjusting to the pace I was setting by how fast I was going through the maze. Does that mean that I was given the exact amount of time I need to get through this maze, whether I move slowly or quickly through it?" Sesh asks rhetorically, while Pip very quickly was nodding his head with a giant smile on his tiny little peanut face. The realization hits Sesh that he could rest. The time required would adjust to him slowing down. He saw a small spot ahead of him where there wasn't a risk of him accidentally touching a hanging strand of web. Occasionally, the large spider would click overhead, on the outside of the web tunnel. Sesh sat ungracefully down on the bare floor, stretching his legs and back.

"What are you doing? You can't rest." Pip urges Sesh onward after he notices him flopping down roughly on the tunnel floor. "What I can tell you is that your time will not STOP running, if you stop moving, in order for it to adjust to your pace, you have to be setting a pace. I'm sorry Seshy, but you can't rest, or you will not make it through this maze."

Looking at the small angel for a quick moment, in shock. No one had called him Seshy since before his little sister passed away. It was her nickname for him. Instead of acknowledging the pain, Sesh just pushed it down, and got back to his task.

Shakily, he rose to his feet, and pressed on. "Ok, let us do this Pip. If I can't rest, then I want to hear your best cheerleading to encourage me onwards."

He began shuffling forward at a smoother pace. Before long, the duo noticed a change in the brightness of the tunnel. Almost falling,

Sesh entered a section of the tunnel that was much larger than the other parts he had been in. This one was a giant domed section. Clearly, centered in the middle of the dome was a nest with a huge pearly white sack resting in the middle of it.

"Oh no!" Pip screeched quietly, "This is the cloud spider's nest. The ground is laced with webs, everywhere we walk there are microscopic webs lying on the ground. Only one kind of cloud spider that I know of, can do this. It has to be a queen, the mother, who births all spiders of her species. There is only one way past her, oh my let me think, I know this…"

"Calm down Pip. Just relax, we won't move for a minute and just relax until you can think of what you need to so we can get past this without becoming a meal."

Looking around, Sesh noticed the size of the arena they stood in, it was huge. Like a giant Roman colosseum, it had sloped edges and a large oval shaped central floor where the huge twenty-foot-tall egg-sac sat, surrounded by lightning infused webbing. Pip began to sing quietly,

"My gentle harp, once more I waken.
The sweetness of thy slumb'ring strain
In tears our last farewell was taken
And nos in tears we meet again.
Yet even then, while peace was singing,
Her halcyon song o'er land and sea,
Though joy and hope to others bringing,
She only brought new tears to thee."

Midway through the song, the spider queen began to swing low from the highest point in the ceiling above her egg sac. Swaying back and forth from a single strand, she watched with all of her many eyes as Pip began the second verse. She dropped lower and lower until she lay, unmoving over her giant egg sac, which glowed white, and showed through her carapace like an x-ray machine. Sesh and Pip could see the fluids inside her body pulsing with her mighty heartbeat. Steady and smooth, she was asleep.

"Then who can ask for notes of pleasure,
My drooping harp, from chords like thine?
Alas, the lark's gay morning measure.
As ill would suit the swan's decline.
Or how shall I, who love, who bless thee,

Invoke thy breath for freedom's strains,
When e'en the wreaths in which I dress thee,
Are sadly mixed, half flours, half chains."

Sesh and Pip eased their way past the giant spider's nest and moved into the narrow tunnel beyond. It was a straight shot, directly to the end of the spidery tunnel, Sesh could see the exit long before they reached it.

"What song was that?"

"It is actually a poem by Thomas Moore, called *My Gentle Harp*. I just sang it instead of recited the poem because of the weird quirk about putting the queen to sleep."

"It was beautiful."

"Well, that was much easier than I expected. I'm so glad to be getting out of this nasty sticky web!" Pip exclaimed.

"First of all, I thought those giant spiders were all blind and deaf. Second of all, that spider was definitely watching us with those eyes."

"Well, I said 'MOST' of those spiders were blind and deaf, the queen-mother is not. She is the only one, when she births another queen, as soon as that queen reaches maturity, she will die. It is their cycle."

"That makes sense." Sesh looked at Pip in a quiet contemplation for a few moments, before adding, "Your singing reminded me that my dad used to sing to me. He would sing to me only when he was at his drunkest. He was incredibly sad. I think he was sad that he couldn't provide properly for his family, or sad that the demands of life, and the confines of the world now were so difficult that he has become a slave to his work, and thus could never be the father he wanted to be… The chains of starvation holding him to his job. The chains of his family suffering holding him even more. It really wears a man down. My father is a proud man." Sesh explained sadly.

They continued on in silence until they neared the exit of the spider tunnel. Where Pip thought they should be wary before charging out of the hole in case they ran headlong into another situation that was just as dire. Sesh agreed, so they eased up to the exit hole, very slowly.

"Now remember, just because there's an exit here that we can see the other side of, doesn't mean we are going to be exiting out this door there. Each of these doors is a portal that transports us to another part of the maze. Most of the doors we enter, and exit will be very obvious that they are portals… because they will look like a portal. When we exit, we will see what happens, the new location should appear around us, quite similar to how it did when we first entered the Doomed Maze. Just be careful and keep your head on a swivel."

Stepping out of the tunnel, the area dimmed immediately without the bright lightning web around. Sesh turned and noticed that the back wall was back. Taking a few steps forward, he noticed another sign.

"Interesting," Sesh said with a small smile on his face. "There's another sign over there, and I think… I THINK ITS SOMETHING AWESOME!"

"What does it say Sesh?" Pip asked, sharing his excitement, they read it together.

You are doing well Sesh.
Sir Trillion is a dependable friend.
This next area is designed for your rest. TIME OUT AREA.
Time will not pass, for as long as you're in this zone.

Chapter Eight
Dreams

Sesh and Pip both shouted excitedly and rushed onward. Everything before the big sign was a deep void purple, then as sudden as the change from the webby portal to the darkness around, things changed.

Three steps past the sign a small circular white room appeared with only a single white couch off to one side. The room had a single door in it, opposite where Sesh stood with Pip sitting on his shoulder. Looking back, they could see the door he had come through fading away into the purple void. Shortly afterwards, the light from the room seemed to slowly eat away at the void, devouring the darkness into light.

This small couch was remarkably similar to the one Sesh had taken his short nap on before he had gotten his change of clothing and followed Saint Peter into the Rose Garden. He thought that this may possibly be just like that couch, a resting couch.

"Do you think this is a resting couch? Like the one I used in the resource building with Pat and Saint Peter?" He asked Pip.

"Yes, I do believe this is the same sort of couch. You nap, I will awaken you."

He had remembered, even without Pip telling him, that if he didn't have someone wake him, he would sleep forever. Pulling out his pack, Sesh decided that he would have a quick bite to eat from what was packed, then get a little bit of sleep. If he and Pip took turns waking the other, then they shouldn't have any issues. As he was about to take a bite of a piece of bread, slathered in olive spread, Sesh's stomach growled and twisted in hunger.

Pip charged forward to the food, grabbing a proportionately smaller piece, and devouring it. Pip encouraged Sesh again to get some rest, letting him know that he would awaken him when the time was right. "You go first Sesh, I slept a little when I was lounging in the web."

"Are you sure? Remember, you have to wake me up, or I will never wake up."

"Yes, yes, yes. I know I know. Now get you some rest! You're about to fall over as we speak."

"Ok! Thanks Pip!" Sesh limped slowly over to the couch and flopped down, and immediately spread out as best he could. The couch enveloped him in a soft, warm embrace. The very second his body came to rest; the darkness of sleep overtook him, and he fell into a deep, dream-filled sleep.

***

Sesh was a five-year-old little boy, running to catch up to his two older brothers. They were walking towards one of the last remaining ponds that used to be a lake, they liked to call, "Where'd it go" lake, in hopes of catching a couple of fish for their supper. His oldest brother Willard was carrying the three poles, while Sebastian, his second oldest brother, carried the tackle box and a small container of stink bait. They had to use artificial bait because anything that was edible was eaten, they just couldn't risk wasting good caloric intake on 'trying' to catch fish.

Willard and Sebastian had spent the previous evening putting together a foamy yet colorful and stinky, soft sticky bait, they could ball up and put on the little hooks. They had mixed in some of the bloody runoffs from a cow they helped slaughter at Mr. Fallows. If they got lucky, they would be able to catch four or five small fish, or even a big one or two.

Arriving at the "Where'd-it-go" lake, the three brothers set up a small spot off an inlet to cast their lines out. After getting his pole with bait and bobber attached, Sesh walked a few feet away from his brother and tried to cast over and over again, failing to get his line into the water.

"Seb can you help me?" he had asked in a tiny high-pitched voice.

"Sure, little brother, remember to leave it in the water, and reel like crazy if you see that bobber go under, okay?"

"Okay."

Sitting there quietly, intently staring at his bobber, it suddenly blooped right under the water. Sesh got so excited he forgot to reel the pole, and just jumped up and down.

"Reel it in quick!"

Sesh began reeling, feeling the fish fight and tug at the line, trying to escape. They would get to eat something tonight, he just had to get the fish to shore. He felt like this was a great white shark on the end of his line, fighting, pulling, and jumping. At last, he got the fish to the shore, and the three brothers whooped and hollered, excited that their trip was not going to be a failure.

They continued to cast their lines out, occasionally they would get bites, but nothing would be on the hook when they tried to set it. The three brothers enjoyed what peace and relaxation they could, while they fished.

They caught five fish that day, enough to feed their family for two days if they pushed it. They could filet the fish and get the steaks of meat out, then use the remaining parts of the fish to put into a stew or soup. No part of the fish would go to waste, as even the bones would be used to bait traps for small creatures that may possibly venture close enough for them to catch. Overall, it was a good day. Walking back home, Sesh suddenly realized he wasn't a five-year-old boy anymore. He was grown, trailing a little behind his brothers, he stared after them.

"Hey, hold up."

Turning, the two brothers smiled at him, clearly still seeing their little brother as he was that day. "Come on booger, you don't want to get left behind now."

Running forward, Sesh grabbed them both in a tight hug. They both hugged him back, the three of them standing in the middle of the carless potholed dirt covered road, in a setting sun, just holding each other.

"I miss you guys, so…so very much."

"We miss you too Sesh. We believe in you; you can do this."

"What? You…"

"Yea booger, just remember one thing, okay?"

"What's that?"

"It's time to wake up."

"Huh?"

"You've got to wake up."

"WAKE UP!"

"Sesh. Sesh. Sesh. Sesh. Sesh. Sesh, WAKE UP." Pip gently shook him awake, softly saying his name over and over again, occasionally raising his voice when he said, 'wake up.' "Wakey, Wakey, big guy."

"Mmmmmmmmmmmmmmmmmmmmmmmmmmmmmmmmmmmmmm mmmmm."

Smacking his lips in satisfaction and cracking his eyeballs just enough to see his little angel friend shaking his shoulder and speaking his name. "I'm up. What a wonderful nap. How long was I out?"

"Around 30 minutes, I know you told me to let you sleep for 10 minutes, but I felt like you could use a little more rest than the average person, so… there we have it." Pip said, with a huge smile, showing all of his teeth, from ear to ear. "Now one thing I want to tell you before I take my nap, is that sleep has a tendency of being a little harder on my kind than on humans, being that we weren't really designed to sleep. In fact, the only way I would be able to sleep, and recover strength, would be on a couch like this. We drain energy faster than we can make it while we are on 'guardian' duty instead of 'watch' duty. We usually just meditate to regenerate our strength. So, as I was saying, if I start tossing, turning, and growling or anything that gets to be too abnormal then please awaken me. I have never slept, let alone used one of these restful couches, but I have heard and read scrolls about this exact situation happening. It was said then that it is best not to know what an Angelic figure sees in his dreams."

"Gotcha, wake you up if you start throwing a hissy fit. I can do that." Sesh joked. "One more thing, before you go down, how long do you think this time stoppage will actually function?"

"Indefinitely, if you were to say, sleep alone on this couch, and not awaken, you would not require food, but slip into a trancelike state, similar to you human's comas, or stasis chambers for space travel. You would stay that way until someone came along and woke you up. Though, that being said, even couches like this have their peril. Time around you don't stop for everyone, just for you."

"Understood. Now get some sleep. I'll wake you in 30 minutes or earlier if necessary."

"Please awaken me in ten. I will require no more than that."

"Done."

Sesh watched as Sir Trilion eased off into a deep slumber. He suddenly had a strong feeling of sadness overtaking his emotional spectrum. He watched as his little guardian angel slept, and it reminded him of his baby sister, who was lost to those people who fell to the sickness that so many suffered. The baby was only two, but he remembered it like it was just yesterday... *Seshy? Seshy! I lub you, bubba."*

The 2-year-old was holding her arms out to her 10-year-old big brother from the car seat, they had just returned from the hospital for a checkup and a vitamin infusion. It was the day before her life was tragically taken by the family with the disease of the waking dead.

I love you too Eloise. I love you too little sister.

He planted a kiss on her forehead, then helped unbuckle her car seat and pull her free. He would take Eloise inside, lay her down and read her favorite book to her until she fell asleep. If he knew that this was the last time that he would put her down for a nap, or the last time he would get to witness her sleeping then he would have held her a little longer or read that book one more time.

As soon as little Eloise closed her big eyes, his mind quickly flashed to her funeral. He remembered the tiny little box that their father had pieced together from old pallets. They buried her in the hard unforgiving ground. He remembered the vacant look on his mother's face and the tear streaks in the dust that ran down all of their faces.

They all cried and held each other, his father comforting him. I know son, I know. I know. I know. There is nothing we can do. She is with Jesus now. They were all truly broken.

Tears rolling down their faces, they wept. They mourned and cried off and on until the sun came up the next day, until they were utterly spent. Mom and Dad had to go to work, he was left at the house all alone, to work in the garden. Left alone to deal with his own emotions, which was the way of the world.

Snapping out of his reminiscences, he noticed Pip was tossing, turning, growling, and shaking. The couch is soaked with sweat.

How long was I zoned out!?

Running over to the couch, Sesh began shaking Pip, shouting his name. "Pip! PIP! PIP! WAKE UP!"

"NOOOOOOOOOOOOOOOOOOOOOOOOOOOOOOOO!"

"What was that Pip? Are you OK?"

Eyes opening wide, he looked at Sesh for a moment in shock and fear, before shaking his head slightly and saying, "Yeah, I'm OK. That was the most intense vivid nightmare I have ever seen."

Pip began to wonder what exactly he had seen. He knew it was important, and from the tales he had heard from the elders, he also knew that to tell Sesh would be folly. At least, he could not tell Sesh ALL of it. Thinking back quickly, Pip remembered a little in fading flashes.

Flashes. A Giant cat standing regally, its huge imposing form, purple and fierce. Looking protectively at him and his charge, Sesh. Flashes. A graveyard filled with unholy beings and unsavory beings from the sky and night, each trying to suck a different part of them. One wanting the soul, the other wanting their blood. Flashes. Ferocious dogs, huge flaming jaws. Drool that looked like lava, trying to eat them in mind and body. Flashes. A huge battlefield full of corpses, Sesh and him standing in the center of it, scared. Flashes. Sesh holding his stomach and falling. The blood was seeping from between his fingers. Stabbed through by a flaming green shadow of a person, it was not clear. The person standing over him goes in to finish the kill, their fist still embedded in Sesh's stomach. Flashes. A Holy weapon is earned, revealed as to what is it by a huge golden light. Flashes. Pip could only watch in horror; he was being beaten down by a huge green flame. Flashes. Someone with small feminine hands, and blonde hair sat over Sesh, he was dying.

NOOOOOOOOOOOOOOOOOOOOOOOOOOOOOOOOOOOOOO!
NOOOOOOOOOOOOOOOOOOOOOOOOOOOOOOOOOOOOO!
NOOOOOOOOOOOOOOOOOOOOOOOOOOOOOOOOOOO!

Then Sesh woke him.

Chapter Nine
Hellhounds

Sesh watched Pip stretch his little body in silence for a few moments before asking, "What was that all about? Did you have a bad nightmare?"

"I don't want to talk about it." Pip finished stretching, then looked a little contemplative.

"Alright, well, let's head out, okay? I feel like we have a lot of ground to cover, and not a lot of time to get there."

"Okay."

Before taking off, they both had eaten their fill again, then filled Sesh's water canteen. Knowing they could not go backwards, and with only one door available, they exited and found a long corridor. It was a big, long hallway, which looked like it stretched directly forwards for miles. The walls were a dull gray brick-like substance, which was rough looking. It would not feel good to scrape against this wall. After they jogged for a good twenty minutes, Sesh came to a stop at a four-way intersection. Turning to Pip Sesh decided to ask on his well-being once again because he had a distant look on his face, as if in quiet contemplation, and was far quieter than he usually was.

"Are you sure that you're, OK? Do you want to talk about it or anything?"

"I am sure. I was just shaken up. I do not wish to partake in the sharing of my dream. Thank you." Pip knew if he began sharing, he would not want to stop, and he could not share it all, it would not be right, Sesh would not be able to continue on to do what needed to be done. It was also just flashes of memories, scenes from various times flickering in and out of his mind. He could not tell Sesh that when Angels dreamed, they dreamed of possible futures. He would not tell him because no future was set in stone, the Eternal one made sure of that. The simple fact that it was a possibility though, scared Pip to the bone. Dreams oftentimes turned out to be a little more than a possibility, but a probability. It would be unusual for his dreams not to come to pass. He also didn't want to tell Sesh, because if he did, then the small window he got a peek into would highly likely change. It could change into something much, much worse.

"Well OK then, let's go forward. Gabriel told me to just keep pressing forward." Looking forward, Sesh nodded to himself, then added, "So that's the way we will go!"

No sooner had the duo turned the first bend on the forward path than they began hearing the deep baying and cackling of hounds. It had to be hellhounds. The sound sent shivers up and down their spines and caused goose flesh to sprout all over their arms and necks.

"What is that!?" Sesh asked, already knowing, and dreading the answer.

"That sound is the mentally scarring sound of a hellhound Sesh. We need to run, immediately! If there are more than a few, we are dead."

The screams and frantic baying sounded like a woman screaming at the top of her lungs in the middle of the night, or a mountain lion scaring away intruders in its lair. The sound cracked through the air, vibrating the very bones inside both of their bodies. The first time Sesh heard the screams, he almost froze in fear. It brought him back to a time when he was a young boy, going to the market for the first time with his father.

He watched as a woman had her hand cut off, for trying to steal. The enforcer type police, at the time, went a bit Old Testament on thieves. When they punished someone who was caught stealing, they would do it publicly and make it a spectacle. His father had thought that it was a clever idea for his little boy, merely five years old, to watch it too. It is unclear if he knew that it was something that would be incredibly traumatizing for such a small child, that it would haunt him for most of his life. Sesh reasoned with himself, that his father was trying to teach him the consequences of stealing. He reasoned that his dad was just not thinking about everything all the way through. Sesh merely made excuses for the poor parenting that often happened for the few people he loved unconditionally.

Gasping, and forcing a word out between each breath, Sesh yelled over the sounds of his footsteps, "Why… would… we… have… hellhounds… chasing… us… through… this… maze!?"

Not breathing nearly as hard, because he was flying, zipping by Sesh's left ear, his wings flapping rapidly, "I don't know, it's one of the obstacles you have to overcome in order to surpass this maze. As a guardian angel, I am not privy to all the particulars surrounding the aspects of each trial. I have my thoughts, and I may have had a little knowledge passed to me, but I still don't know everything that will be thrown at us."

"I… will… trust… that… you… will… tell… me… when… you… figure… out… anything… particularly… important." Sesh gave a strained fear-filled smile to Pip, his air gushing back and forth between his teeth.

"Right now, you need to run, as fast as you can!"

Running as fast as they could, down the pathways of the maze, every fork in the road, or three or four-way split, was always decided immediately, and without questions. Each new corridor revealed a different looking set of walls and hallways. Some of the walls were covered with ivy and vines, with thin green curtains displaying lovely colorful flowers that released beckoning odors. Other walls were bare, showing the golden-brown bricks and small cracks that stretched all the way from the floor to the highest points on the wall they could see. On one particular occasion, they came to an intersection, and upon crossing it, saw a swarm of bats attacking a small rolling pile of insects. Neither of them wanted anything to do with the bats or the bugs. Fortunately, the bats and insects completely ignored the dashing duo as they ran and flew past them.

With the braying screaming hounds somewhere behind them, fading into the distance, they were able to slow the pace a little. They hoped they had lost them, but all their running didn't seem to be enough because the hellhounds could still be heard, so they kept going, even at a slower pace. Eventually, they felt a gentle change in the path they were running on. Ahead of them, the tunnel seemed to fade away, turning, and dropping in elevation. They couldn't stop to think about it, in fear the hellhounds behind them would catch up.

After coming around the particularly sharp turn, the slope was steeper than they expected, causing Sesh to stumble and fall down into a deep depression. Pip zipped down to his side, checking on his well-being. With the rounded off slopes the stumble was more of a log roll, so he didn't suffer more than a bruise or two. Assessing the flexibility of all of his limbs, Sesh worried for a second that he had broken something. Dismissing the thought and rising to his feet, he picked Pip up and tossed him into the air. As if in unspoken agreement, the small angel zipped back the direction they came from, checking on their unwanted followers. Meanwhile, Sesh looked around the depression and noticed that there are six different tunnels inside this one room.

The stumble gave the hellhounds the time they needed to find their scent again and begin the chase with renewed vigor. The sounds of their howls were sharp and clear, and rapidly approaching. Sesh wasn't sure what to do, with the many different tunnels, it was a crapshoot. They would have to try them one at a time, and hope they get lucky. Grabbing a small rock, he marked the ground near the center of the first hole on their right, with an arrow, pointing which way they were heading.

The deep baying of the hellhounds was even closer as they continued their frantic dash through the maze without a word said to each other. It was a short run before they found themselves at the lip of the same depression room where Sesh had fallen into. It seemed like the first tunnel made a loop, circling back in on itself. Sesh could see the mark he had made pointing at a different tunnel from the one they had just exited. They entered one hole, and came out of another, removing two of the six holes from consideration.

"We are two pathways down from the one we marked," Sesh stated, quickly marking an X on the ground in front of both tunnels. "That means those two are connected. We just have to keep doing trial and error and hope those beastly monsters don't catch up to us, I'm hoping they get lost in this maze."

"Well hope for something else! THEY'RE HERE!" Pip screamed.

Sesh turned just in time to see three exceptionally large, muscular beasts hop down the sloped depression. They slowed to a stop, growling deep, guttural growls while creating a small half-moon around the human and angel. The beasts looked terribly similar to the mount Simon had back in the Gateway Township.

The three dogs were noticeably smaller than the horse-dog that Simon mounted. These ones were roughly the size of small tigers, rippling with muscle, and glaring with their intense red eyes. One of the hellhounds was a tad bit smaller than the other two, this one being of a leaner more defined build. It also appeared to be the leader of the three.

The drool dripping from their fangs that hung out of their gaping maws was an orange color and it hissed and sizzled as it dripped steadily onto the maze floor. Without a question in his mind, Sesh knew just one bite from these beasts would mean incredible pain, and most likely death.

Whispering Pip said, "Sesh, Do NOT let them bite you. Try to distract one of the two in the back, throw rocks at it, or something. They will be confused when I take out their leader. I doubt there are, but if there are any more of them in the walkway, we will probably not make it out of this depression alive. Let us get it done, on the count of three..........one... two....... NOW!"

As Pip's voice, small as he was, rose to a mighty roar on the third count, Sesh stooped and grabbed a fist sized boulder. It seemed unusual that there were loose stones here, as if it were designed to be a defensive position within the Doomed Maze. Throwing the rock as fast and hard as he could, he didn't wait to see if he hit the dog or not. Stooping to grab another rock, he stood and threw the rock, then quickly had to roll away as one of the larger hounds lunged for him. Laying on his back, Sesh grabbed the hound by its shoulders, as it snapped and snarled in his face. Acid-like saliva burned into his shoulder and the side of his face. Sesh shoved the big dog back off of him for a quick second, grabbing another fist sized rock just before the hound lunged for his face again. Sesh swung the rock with all his might, smashing it directly into the glowing red eye-socket of the attacking hound. A different noise came as the hound yipped in pain, trying to get away, Sesh swung again, and again. When the hound fell to the ground and stopped moving, he looked up and saw an incredible scene unfolding.

Staring in disbelief, he saw Pip rush forward, a shadow of a giant mighty angel towering over the leading hound, touching him lightly on the snout, instantly turning it into stone. The large angel was covered head to toe in shimmering dusky gray armor that had large swooping angles and flexible joints. There were shining plates that covered the leading edge of the angels' wings. The gauntlets were sharp and angular, made for doing devastating damage with a single punch, but allowing the flexibility to hold the massive two-handed weapon he currently held.

Sesh watched as the angel swung the huge broadsword at the statue of a once living animal, shattering it into a million pieces. The smoking shards of the creature turned to stone flew like bullets into the side of the last remaining hound. Blood immediately sprouted from its pelt, as it yelped in pain. As the hound turned to flee, Pip hurled his sword at the dog, bisecting it in two. The maze instantly came to a quiet revocation of noise.

"HOLY COW! What on earth was that Pip? You were a giant angelic figure! You turned that hellhound into stone with a touch! How did you do that?"

"That… was my true form, or a shadow of it anyhow. I told you I was not a miniscule fairy sized angel; this is just my… current guardian angel form. That being said, be thankful, few humans get to see an angelic avatar turn into his true self. It is extremely demanding when not in heaven's boundaries to take on our true form. If I would have gone into my form completely, instead of just shadowing it, it most likely would have 'killed' me, or something similar to death. I would have ascended back to heaven, to report to the general. He would have asked me why I abandoned my post; I likely would be punished and if I weren't it would have been very difficult for me to return to you. That's even if I was even able to find you in this maze again. There are only two ways out of this maze Sesh. One way is to succeed, earn your holy item, accomplish your goal, and enter the levels. The other way is to die. At death you will be judged immediately. Simon and Gabriel would weigh your soul on the scales, and you would be sent to heaven or hell accordingly."

Sesh stared at Pip in awe, not knowing what to say. He felt like Pip had more to say about his guardian angel status, but he didn't want to push it, so he settled on giving his gratitude, "Thank you for showing that to me, and sharing some of your secrets with me."

"It is of no consequence, after you complete the seven levels of purgatory, you will lose all memory of this place itself, and everything you've faced in here. You will have a basic understanding of what you need to do to accomplish the true goal of your life, but that is it."

"I won't remember anything?"

"Very little."

"That's a bummer, I don't want to forget about you."

"We have a long way to go yet, to be worrying about such things right now. Let us continue towards our destination."

Sadly, Sesh nodded, "Okay."

Choosing to go down the next tunnel of the six, they kept an easy pace. After walking for a couple hundred yards, they both heard a sound that scared them to their cores. Hellhounds, hordes, and hordes of them. The baying was more like the sound of a tornado tearing through a subdivision.

It was absolutely terrifying to hear. Without speaking a word, Sesh broke into the fastest sprint he could maintain, with Pip hot on his heels flying. They rounded corner after corner, taking each sharply positioned turn, as fast as they could without falling over. They took a right, then a left, then came to a split in the road. Without hesitation, Sesh took them right again, then left, then right, then dead end.

"Oh no! Dead end." Sesh yelled, turning around. "Let us pray that those hellhounds haven't made it to our tunnel yet!"

Running hard, sweat pouring down his face, Sesh pressed on. The toll it took to destroy the previous two hounds was almost too much for Pip, and he was starting to flag. Sesh paused for a moment, grabbed his small guardian's form out of the air, and placed him on his shoulder, then took off again. Sesh was running, past the split in the road, and rounded another corner, falling face first down the depression sloped walls. They had come out of the last tunnel. The one directly to the left of the original tunnel they had started. Marking it, and the one they originally went into, Sesh charged into one of the final holes.

After running for a solid 20 minutes, with the baying and rumbling of the horde of hounds behind them, Sesh began noticing their racket was decreasing in volume. He and Pip were moving away from the hounds.

"We did it Pip! I think we made it past the hounds, we are moving away from them. I need to slow down and rest… I'm about to pass out with exhaustion." Sesh gushed, breathing extremely hard.

Falling to his knees, Sesh gently set pip on the ground, before falling face first onto the unforgiving ground. Sesh was resting his eyes for a few moments before Pip patted him lightly on the forehead.

"We must keep going, we don't have any time to rest."

Groaning, Sesh struggled to his feet, and began walking in the direction they were heading. The walls were made of a deep azure crystal, which was almost see through, but it gave off a faint glowing light, which seemed to prevent it from being transparent. Sesh thought it was curious that he hasn't once needed a light to guide his path, because the walls always emanated a little bit of light, making things visible.

Chapter Ten
Josephine

As the fantastic duo ventured deeper into the maze; they quickly came upon a dead end. The wall of the dead end had a great mosaic of a forest, with sparse undergrowth and evenly spaced bushes. The sunlight shown through the branches in streaks of golden light. It glistened off of damp brush leaves and drooping branches of the trees in an apparent coating of dew. Looking at the beautiful artwork, Sesh could almost hear the sounds of the wind blowing through the high branches, and reaching out, he could almost feel the warmth of those morning rays as they cut golden paths through the canopy to the forest floor. The only thing the mosaic lacked was wildlife, as there didn't seem to be any visible. It was the most realistic picture Sesh had ever seen, it was as if he was looking at the forest through a window.

"Great, another dead end," Pip muttered, not quite complaining, but verging on being a whiney child.

'Not all dead ends, are dead ends.' Standing there, Sesh thought for a second, back to what Gabriel was telling him about the maze. "Maybe this isn't actually a dead-end, Gabriel was telling me that not all dead ends were dead ends. I didn't know the entirety of what that meant then, but maybe…. Just maybe this is another portal!"

Contemplating Sesh's words for a second, Pip stared at the wall then said, "It is possible…. Let me test something."

Pip flew towards the mosaic, muttering and chanting a few words under his breath. He reached out and tapped the wall, causing a ripple and shimmer to present itself across the entirety of the picture. With a grin, Pip slowly eased his face towards one of the gaps between the trees. He pressed himself firmly against the wall until he just disappeared, then reappeared as a part of the picture. Sesh stood there for a moment, flabbergasted.

Waving his arms, he tried to see if Pip could react with him, while being inside the picture. Pip just stood there within the forest, grinning like a little schoolgirl who had just conquered the hop-scotch championship she held at recess every day during lunch. There was no reaction, it was as if Pip was now just a part of the mosaic.

After taking a deep breath, Sesh pressed himself against the same spot on the mosaic where Pip had been. Suddenly, an incredible sensation enveloped his entire body. It was as if every part of him had suddenly fallen asleep, replaced by a tingling, almost painful, feeling akin to sparklers igniting all over him. Then, after a few seconds, he felt a small pop ripple through his entire body, as feeling rushed back into his muscles and skin. He felt an urgent need to relieve himself but mostly held it back, letting out a small droplet of urine. The pop and urge to pee caused him to blink rapidly and suck in a deep breath. As he opened his eyes after his fourth blink in a row, he found himself standing in the heart of the forest, right beside a grinning miniature angel.

"Why are you grinning like that goofy?"

"Because I know exactly what you just felt, and that makes me happy. Did you wet yourself?" Pip said with a laugh.

Squinting his eyes at Pip, Sesh shot back, "Well, what I wanna know is why your small angel body looks so much different than your big angel body? Why is your baby fairy body, look like a little cherub?"

"I don't get to pick how I look in my small form." Pip replied with a huff.

Grinning in victory, Sesh walked over to a nearby brush and prevented himself from drowning in his own urine. He could have sworn that his vision was beginning to turn a slight yellow from how full his bladder was.

Washing his hands with his bottle of water, Sesh said, "Let's get through this forest, and continue on our journey."

Pip just nodded, then started flying lazily ahead of Sesh. Moving smoothly through the large open forest, they stumbled upon a curious sight nestled among the moss-covered roots of an ancient tree. Before them sat a small, cat-like creature with soft fur the color of a violet twilight. Its oversized, luminous eyes gleamed with a mischievous twinkle, reflecting the dappled light filtering through the canopy above.

Matching its small feline appearance, the creature also exuded an aura of innocence and curiosity rather than menace. It had delicate whiskers that twitched with every movement as it tilted its head, regarding the newcomers with a mixture of intrigue and cautiousness.

Pip landed softly on Sesh's shoulder, and he walked softly towards the cat, with his hand extended, palm down. With each gentle step closer, the creature's tufted ears perked up, and its tail, which was adorned with small fluffy puffs of fur, swished in anticipation. Sesh knew that when a cat's tail swished back and forth, it meant one of two things. It was either irritated, or ready to play. What followed encouraged Sesh that it was the latter. It emitted a soft, melodious purr, akin to the gentle hum of a summer breeze, as if welcoming Sesh and Pip into its hidden realm within the forest.

Though small in stature, the cat-like creature possessed an undeniable charm, its presence evoking a sense of warmth and comfort amidst the ancient trees. As they observed this enchanting being, they couldn't help but feel a stirring of wonder and affection for the mysterious creature of the woods. Stopping about ten feet away from the small cat, Sesh crouched down while Pip explained what they were looking at.

"That's... a sphynx. They are rare, even for purgatory and the heavens." Pip said.

Looking at the small cat, Sesh asked, "Aren't they supposed to be huge, and love riddles?"

"Oh piffle, that's an old-wives tale. A true sphynx is much smaller in stature than what your fables and legends would say. They are also sweet and cuddly in nature, instead of riddle loving. Unless threatened, they remain that way always. When threatened, they can be the most dangerous creatures in the land. This one is not quite fully grown, but she is very nearly there. You can tell by the puff balls on her tail. As she grows, they shrink, and when they are gone, she will cease growing. Her intelligence is, at the barest of minimum, on par with a human, but she only speaks rarely. When she does speak, it's telepathically. We must be courteous and kind to her and her lair. If we are not, she could see us as a threat to her home, or herself, which would be devastating. I would much rather face a pack of hell hounds than an angry sphynx."

'Curious, seeing a human and an angel fairy in my forest.'

They both heard soft female voice inside their head, it had a lightness to it, that felt young, playful, and sweet. If Sesh had to guess, he would have thought that the cat sounded like a teenager.

"Good day to you, young one, we would just like to pass through. Young Sesh here is on his journey to seek a holy weapon of sorts, so that he can enter and try to survive the seven levels of purgatory. Could you direct us the quickest way out of your forest, so that we may continue on in a hurry?"

'I could... but why should I?'

Pip eyed Sesh for a moment, and spoke quickly before Sesh could say anything, "Because Sesh is a good one, and we don't get many of those truly good ones coming through the Doomed Maze."

'True.'

After standing there staring at each other for a few moments, the sphynx began cleaning herself, licking her paw and wiping it over her face, repeatedly. Smiling, Sesh realized this was a very cat-like thing to see the sphynx doing. He hadn't seen a cat in a great many years, because most of them had been eaten, or ran off to die on their own. Every animal was food on Earth.

'I will go with you. My name is Josephine Amunet Ailurus.'

Josephine stood, stretched, then walked over to where Sesh stood, and hopped smoothly up to his left shoulder. She was the size of a small cat, so it was quite easy for Sesh to carry her. He thought about the sight the trio made, a tall human with a cat on one shoulder and a small fairy-sized angel on the other, one being dark, and the other light. It was almost as if he stood at the center of yin and yang.

"So, which way are we heading? Is there anything dangerous here that we should worry about? Have you lived here your entire life?" In typical Sesh fashion, he bombarded Josephine with questions. She decided to ambiguously answer them all at once.

'Out, yes, and yes.'

As Sesh, Josephine, and Pip ventured out of the forest's embrace, they found themselves amidst a realm of an ancient woodland forest. The towering trees had gnarled branches that reached skyward, which formed a majestic canopy overhead. The canopy filtered sunlight into dappled patterns that danced with the leaves upon the forest floor, in the midday breeze. Moss-covered rocks and ferns lined the path, while shafts of golden light pierced through the dense foliage, casting an ethereal glow upon their surroundings. The air was alive with the symphony of nature, as birdsong mingled with the rustle of leaves and the gentle burble of the nearby creek. The forest seemed to hum with an unseen energy, inviting the unique trio to explore its secrets and mysteries.

As they ventured deeper into the heart of the forest, the density of the trees began to diminish, their towering forms gradually giving way to scattered clusters of younger saplings. Shafts of sunlight grew more abundant, casting long shadows that stretched across the forest floor. The air carried a sense of openness, as if the forest itself was making way for the travelers' passage. Through the thinning veil of foliage, glimpses of the world beyond the forest's edge teased their senses, igniting a sense of anticipation for what lay ahead. Despite the fading canopy, the atmosphere remained charged with the same mystique and wonder that had guided them thus far, urging them onward toward the unknown layers of the Doomed Maze.

As they pressed onward, Josephine, the small twilight-colored cat, hopped down and led the way with a sense of purpose that belied her diminutive size. She moved like an experienced hunter, as each calculated step was fluid and assured, as if she had traversed this path countless times before. Indeed, it seemed that the creatures of the forest had parted ways for her, leaving only a scattering of songbirds to bear witness to their passage. With each step, the trio drew closer to a defining moment—the point where the ancient guardians of the forest yielded to the encroaching march of time. Here, where the towering trees gave way to a generation of saplings, they discovered another shimmering doorway, a portal beckoning them to venture forth into the next chapter of their journey. As they stood before it, the air thrummed with anticipation, the gateway a threshold to untold possibilities and adventures yet to unfold. Next to the portal stood an old, weathered, brown wooden sign, which read:

A new friend is a good sign indeed.
You're halfway through.
4 hours remain.

Chapter Eleven
The Dreadweaver

As Sesh, Pip, and Josephine stepped through the dark green portal into the expansive darkness of a cave, an eerie chill crept down each of their spines, setting every nerve on edge. The air hung heavy with a palpable sense of foreboding, punctuated by an ominous drip of water from stalactites overhead, each echoing like a sinister whisper in the cavern's depths. Misshapen shadows danced in the dim light, casting nightmarish shapes that seemed to move and shift with a life of their own.

The cave stretched out before them, its vast expanse littered with countless darkened alcoves and hidden recesses, each one a potential hiding place for unimaginable horrors. Sesh couldn't shake the feeling of being watched, of unseen eyes lurking in the shadows, waiting to pounce upon unsuspecting prey.

It wasn't until Sesh's gaze fell upon another weathered sign at the cave's low end that the true horror of their surroundings became apparent. With a sinking feeling in the pit of their stomachs, they realized that the worst creature of all was lurking within these depths, its presence looming like a malevolent shadow over the desolate landscape of the cave. The sign read:

The lair of the Dreadweaver

They found themselves deep within the darkest recesses of the Doomed Maze. Here lurked a creature so terrifying that even the bravest souls would quiver at the mere mention of its name—the Dreadweaver.

"No!" Pip exclaimed.

Josephine hissed in fright, her hair standing on end, and her claws gripped a little tighter on Sesh's shoulders. This wasn't a good thing. Sesh looked at Pip and asked him about the Dreadweaver. It was even worse than he had expected.

The Dreadweaver was a monstrous amalgamation of nightmares, a grotesque fusion of twisted limbs and jagged edges that seemed to defy all laws of nature. Its body was a blackened writhing mass of sinewy tentacles, each tipped with a razor-sharp claw that dripped with a toxic venom capable of inducing madness with a single scratch.

Its eyes, if they could be called such, glowed with a sickly green light, casting eerie shadows that danced and flickered across its grotesque form. Its mouth, lined with rows of jagged teeth, opened impossibly wide, and emitted a guttural hiss that sent chills down the spines of all who heard it.

Perhaps the most terrifying aspect of the Dreadweaver was its ability to warp reality itself, twisting the very fabric of space and time to suit its malevolent whims. It could summon forth nightmarish illusions, trapping its victims in a never-ending cycle of terror and despair. It fed on the fears and terror of its victims, granting it strength and empowerment.

Most people didn't know this, but when fear reached a certain pinnacle point, the soul is so terrified, that it actually leaves the body. At this moment, the Dreadweaver will imprison the soul, and devour the meat and juices of the body.

Those unlucky enough to cross paths with the Dreadweaver seldom lived to tell the tale. Its insatiable hunger for fear drove it to hunt relentlessly through the darkest corners of the maze, seeking out unsuspecting prey to add to its ever-growing collection of souls.

As Sesh and his companions ventured deeper into the heart of the Dreadweaver's lair, they knew that they would have to steel themselves against the horrors that awaited them, for the Dreadweaver itself, lurked in the shadows, waiting patiently for its next victim to stray too close.

Suddenly, a low rumble echoed through the maze, causing the ground to tremble beneath their feet. With a sinking feeling in the pit of his stomach, Sesh knew that their adversary was nearby. Looking around, he found himself in the midst of a larger, more open cavern. A grim sight greeted his eyes at every turn—piles of corpses, their lifeless forms twisted and contorted in agony, bearing witness to the Dreadweaver's insatiable hunger for fear. Some were fresh, their bloodied flesh still steaming in the chill air, while others lay in various stages of decay, their bones picked clean by the monstrous creature's relentless appetite. The stench of death hung heavy in the air, a haunting reminder of the horrors that lurked within the maze's dark embrace. The smell was palpable, gagging them, and overwhelming their senses. With each step he took, Sesh couldn't help but feel a deeper chill run down his spine, knowing that they were treading on ground tainted by the Dreadweaver's malevolent presence. Sesh wondered just how the Dreadweaver got all the people to consume. Were this many people actually trying the maze, or was someone intentionally feeding the Dreadweaver, because of its capability to stop most mazers.

Emerging from the shadows, the Dreadweaver slithered into view, its grotesque form twisting and writhing with unnatural grace. True to its description, its eyes glowed with that sickly green light as it fixed its gaze upon its now suspecting prey.

Sesh's heart pounded in his chest as he looked at Josephine and Pip, knowing that he was completely reliant on their courage and strength to survive. With a silent nod of understanding from Pip, and a low growl from Josephine, they sprang into action, moving to protect Sesh from the looming threat.

Josephine launched herself at the monster with a primal roar, her claws slashing through the air with deadly precision. Her flashing paw seemed to grow in size, with the power she put into the swing. She moved with a ferocity born of desperation. She was determined to keep the monstrous creature at bay, and to show the creature just what it meant to face a sphynx's power in battle. Josephine dashed and dodged the tentacles as they struck at her, missing her with each calculated movement.

Meanwhile, Pip darted around the Dreadweaver's flailing tentacles, his celestial energy crackling and popping with intensity as he unleashed blasts of holy power into the Dreadweaver's back. He danced through the shadows, a beacon of light amidst the darkness that threatened to consume them. Each strike he made, in his diminutive form, seemed to hold the power of his unique bloodline.

As Josephine and Pip battled fiercely against the Dreadweaver, Sesh frantically searched for a means of escape. His mind raced as he scanned their surroundings, looking for any sign of a way out of this portion of the Doomed Maze. He ran along the walls, prodding and feeling for a gape, or hidden entrance, to no avail. The Dreadweaver was relentless in its pursuit, its tentacles lashing out with deadly accuracy as it sought to overwhelm its adversaries.

Josephine seamlessly slipped through the shadows, appearing to vanish and reappear again in strategic positions, her movements synchronized with Pip's as they engaged in combat against the rampaging monster. Whenever a sharp tentacle threatened to strike Sesh's back, a timely blast of holy light from Pip would sever it, sending it harmlessly to the ground. At other moments, Josephine's razor-sharp claws tore through the air, effortlessly rending tentacles to shreds.

The battle flowed seamlessly until Pip endured a particularly brutal blow from a flailing tentacle, hurling him into the cave wall with bone-rattling force. The impact left small cracks spider-webbing from the point of collision, causing a couple of stalactites to fall onto the top of the Dreadweaver's head, and around Josephines' dodging body. While causing minimal harm to the creature, it did grant the Dreadweaver a brief respite from their onslaught. Josephine's attention shifted from dodging the falling stalactites toward Pip's prone form, tangled amidst the debris. She hesitated briefly, as she sought a way to aid her fallen comrade. Seizing the opportunity, the Dreadweaver lunged at Josephine, snipping off the tip of her tail with a vicious snap, eliciting a pained howl from her as she quickly dashed away. With Josephine momentarily incapacitated, the Dreadweaver redirected its focus toward Sesh, its malevolent gaze narrowing with predatory intent.

Tentacles stretched and slashed, smashing rocks and stalagmites alike. Sesh dodged and weaved between the narrow crevices and gaps between the tooth like stalagmites. Time and again, narrowly avoiding the creature's attacks, he desperately sought a way to turn the tide of battle in their favor. Just when all hope seemed lost, Sesh spotted it—a narrow opening in the cave wall, just wide enough for them to slip through to safety.

Glancing back, Sesh witnessed Josephine biting the clothing on Pip's back, picking up his small form, and swiftly bearing him toward safety with impeccable speed. With a surge of adrenaline coursing through his veins, Sesh's resolve hardened as he focused on the crack in the wall ahead. Darting forward, his companions hot on his heels, they made a daring escape from the clutches of the Dreadweaver, their hearts pounding with the exhilaration of narrowly evading death, or dismemberment.

As they emerged into the cool night air, their breath coming in ragged gasps, Sesh couldn't help but feel a sense of profound gratitude towards Josephine and Pip. Without their courage and sacrifice, they would surely have fallen victim to the Dreadweaver's insatiable hunger.

He watched and listened as the monstrous creature thrashed and writhed in frustration, its tentacles flailing wildly as it attempted to dig through the solid wall of the maze. Despite its best efforts, the Dreadweaver was unable to penetrate their makeshift escape route, and soon, its enraged hisses faded into the distance as it faded back into the shadow's waiting for another prey to come into its lair.

Gasping, Sesh rushed over to Pip, "Are you okay buddy?"

With a groan, and a small shudder, Pip gingerly sat up on the ground where Josephine had lain him down. "Yes, I do think I am going to be okay; I may just be sore for a while. That was incredible, I had no idea one of those was even in this maze. Those are from the deepest pits of hell. They are some of the Fallen's most powerful champions. We got very lucky."

Grabbing them both into a swift hug, Sesh held them close for a few moments before saying, "Thank you both for saving me."

Looking around the area they stood in, it appeared that they were back in the original style of walls they had started with. The back wall was again behind them, urging them to continue forward. Sesh picked Pip up, and set him on his shoulder, then looked at the only direction they had to go and continued his journey.

As they ventured forth into the unknown, their bond stronger than ever, they knew that no matter what trials lay ahead, as long as they stood together, they would always find a way to prevail against even the most daunting of challenges.

Chapter Twelve
The Desert Temple

It wasn't much further from the Dreadweaver's lair that Sesh, Josephine, and Pip came upon another door. This one was made of sandstone and had Sanskrit written very finely all over it, except for the very middle. In the center of the door, was a beautiful painting of an ancient temple in the middle of a desert oasis. There were crystal clear aqua ducts that seemed to shine and shimmer, even on the sandstone door. The sky was a deep blue, which seemed to stretch forever. The Temple seemed to stand in the center of a deep valley. Staring at the door for a few moments, Sesh marveled at the intricacies of the design. Someone must have spent an enormous amount of time working on this door and turning it into the amazing piece of artwork that it was.

There was no handle on this door, it appeared to slide into the wall like an abnormally large pocket door. Sesh looked at his companions and said, "What do you think? Shall we go through?"

"Where else are we going to go? Back in there with the Dreadweaver? I think I would rather not." Pip said sarcastically, with a slight chuckle.

'We should go forward into the desert. There's something about this painting, which seems very familiar to me.'

"You got it Josephine, let's do this."

Sesh reached out and placed his palm flat on the door, applying pressure until the door slowly began to slide into the left frame. As the door creaked open, warm dusty air came rushing out of the rapidly widening opening. It smelled of dirt, and old stone. The sunlight was bright, and the world that was beyond the door seemed to be vast.

When the door opened fully, a beautiful desert valley, not unlike the painting on the door, could be seen. A large waterfall off of a distant river crashed into the valley floor miles away. The mist from the basin rose into the air hundreds of feet, putting on display the raw power that water held when teaming up with gravity.

Sesh could see that in the heart of the vast desert valley, where the golden sands stretched from valley wall to valley wall, there stood a magnificent temple, its towering spires reaching toward the azure sky like fingers of stone. Carved from the very earth itself, the temple gleamed in the sunlight, its sandstone walls etched with delicate patterns and symbols of ancient wisdom.

The air was filled with the soothing sound of cascading water, which was a gentle soothing sound that echoed through the arid landscape. Crystal-clear aqueducts wound their way around the temple grounds, their cool waters flowed gracefully through channels carved into the sandstone, creating a mesmerizing network of shimmering streams and ponds.

The water glistened in the sunlight, catching the colors of the desert sky and the many-colored valley walls, casting dancing reflections upon the surrounding walls of the temple. Lush greenery thrived along the banks of the aqueducts, a stark contrast to the harsh desert landscape, offering a sanctuary of life and tranquility amidst the endless sea of sand.

From their elevated position, they could see that at the heart of the temple complex lay a grand courtyard, where a majestic fountain stands as the centerpiece, its waters sparkling with a brilliance unmatched by any gemstone. The sound of rushing water fills the air, a symphony of nature's beauty that resonates throughout the temple grounds.

Surrounding the courtyard are towering pillars adorned with swooping and finely drawn carvings and ancient hieroglyphics, their weathered surfaces bearing witness to the passage of countless generations. Beyond them, the temple's main entrance beckons, a grand gateway flanked by towering statues of ancient deities, their faces weathered by the sands of time but still radiating an aura of power and majesty.

In this oasis of serenity amidst the challenging desert landscape, the temple stood as a testament to the enduring power of beauty and the resilience of the human spirit. They stood there watching as the sun set over the horizon, casting the temple in a warm golden glow. Sesh could not help but feel a sense of awe and wonder at the beauty and mystery that lay within its sacred walls.

There was a visible path that led down the valley slope towards the temple, and the trio decided to take it. After going approximately a hundred feet, Sesh spotted another worn weathered wooden sign. Walking past it, it clearly read:

The Temple of Remembrance
Your time has been paused.
Rest. Recover. Remember.

As Pip and Sesh exchanged relieved smiles, Josephine was perched regally on Sesh's shoulder, her twilight-hued form a striking contrast against the desert backdrop. Despite the sense of relief that washed over her, Josephine couldn't shake the feeling of familiarity that enveloped her in the presence of the temple. It whispered to her of forgotten memories, of a past she could not quite grasp.

Try as she might, Josephine found herself unable to recall the details of her family or her origins. It was as if her past lay veiled in shadow, just beyond her reach. As she gazed upon the temple's majestic architecture and listened to the soothing sound of flowing water, she couldn't help but feel a glimmer of hope, and a distant memory, trying to come forward.

Perhaps, she thought, with time spent within the hallowed halls of the temple, memories long dormant would begin to stir. Maybe the ancient wisdom contained within its walls would unlock the secrets of her past, revealing the truth of who she was and where she came from.

As they stepped into the heart of the temple, Sesh's eyes widened in recognition as he spotted a familiar set of couches nestled in the corner, their plush cushions inviting weary travelers to rest and relax. Nearby, a table laden with an array of freshly baked bread and succulent meats beckoned enticingly, their tantalizing aromas filling the air with mouthwatering fragrance.

Cheering in delight, and even an excited lick of the lips from Josephine, the trio wasted no time in making their way towards the table, their hunger driving them forward with renewed vigor. As they drew closer, the sight and smells of the bountiful spread made their mouths water in anticipation of the feast that awaited them.

Eyes wide with joy, and bodies containing growling stomachs, they seated themselves at the table, their laughter ringing out like music in the temple's sacred halls. Together, they shared in the simple joy of tasty food and good company, their worries and cares momentarily forgotten in the warmth of the temple's embrace. As they savored each delicious bite, their spirits soared with the knowledge that they were safe and among friends, surrounded by the timeless beauty and tranquility of the temple sanctuary.

Having their bellies full, Sesh and Pip began to playfully argue about who got to take their rest first on the Restful Couches. While they went back and forth, Josephine sauntered over to the plush couch cushions and hopped onto the couch, curled up into a ball, and swiftly fell asleep

***

In the twilight-hued shadows of an ancient temple nestled amidst the sands of a forgotten desert valley, a young Josephine prowled at the heels of her mother, Bastet, the revered guardian of the feline warriors, Ra's chosen companion. As the last traces of sunlight faded into the horizon, casting the world in hues of deep indigo and violet, Bastet led her kitten through a series of complex training exercises, imparting upon her the skills and wisdom necessary to survive in a world fraught with danger.

'You must learn to fight in the ways of our forebearers, my daughter. I know it is difficult, but you are a mighty sphynx, you can do anything!'

'Yes mother.'

Nuzzling her young daughter after a successful combination bout in the makeshift arena, Bastet purred proudly at Josephine. Bastet was both loving and fierce, her golden eyes ablaze with a severe determination to prepare her daughter for the challenges that lay ahead. As Bastet performed each graceful movement, she demonstrated the art of combat, teaching Josephine to wield her claws and teeth with precision and purpose.

It was not just physical prowess that Bastet sought to instill in her young daughter; it was also a deep sense of courage and resilience that would serve her well in the trials to come. Through the ancient teachings passed down through generations, Bastet imbued within Josephine the knowledge that true strength came not just from physical might, but from an unwavering spirit that refused to yield in the face of adversity.

'Remember, that the dark is your ally. You are allowed to be afraid, but you should have the courage to face your fears, even when they are the most terrifying.'

As they trained beneath the watchful gaze of the desert stars, Josephine listened intently to her mother's teachings, absorbing every word like a sponge. She learned the importance of patience and discipline, of honing her instincts and trusting in her own abilities. With each passing day, she grew stronger and more confident, her bond with Bastet deepening with every shared moment.

'I love you Josie, remember that. Remember that sometimes you will feel out of control, you will feel like you don't have the time to accomplish the mission you were given. If you trust your instincts, and remember your training, you will have everything you need to accomplish what needs to be done.'

'I love you too mother. I will remember.'

Bastet taught her the wisdom of the ancients, the knowledge of the world beyond the confines of their desert home. Through stories passed down from generation to generation, Bastet painted vivid images of far-off lands and distant realms, igniting within Josephine a thirst for adventure and discovery.

'Your ancestors used to travel to the distant lands on the humans' planet. They would guide and teach those hairless primates. Humans would grow to love and revere our kind. Though, over time, our ancestors forgot their true calling, becoming nothing more than pets

to humans. Very few of our kind remain with the knowledge and remembrance of what they were.'

As the days turned into weeks and the weeks into months, Josephine grew from a curious kitten into a formidable warrior in her own right, her every movement a testament to the love and guidance of her mother. Though their time together was fleeting, the lessons learned, and memories shared would forever shape the path that lay ahead, guiding Josephine through the trials and tribulations of life with the strength and courage of a true warrior.

Within the celestial realm, Ra, the mighty sun god, summoned Bastet, the revered guardian of the feline warriors, to his side. With a voice that echoed like thunder across the heavens, Ra beseeched Bastet to go forth once more into battle on his behalf, to defend the realm against the encroaching forces of darkness.

Though Bastet's heart swelled with pride at the honor of being called upon by the great sun god himself, she couldn't shake the feeling of unease that gnawed at her from within. As she gazed upon her beloved daughter, Josephine, now a small adolescent on the cusp of adulthood, Bastet knew that she could not bear to leave her behind.

Ra's command was absolute and could only be over-ruled by The Eternal. So, with a heavy heart, Bastet bid farewell to Josephine, knowing that she must heed the call to battle and fulfill her duty to the realm.

'I must go to the front lines Josie.'

'Don't go mother... please don't go.'

'It has been commanded, only The Eternal is higher than Ra. I will do everything I can to return to you my sweet, sweet girl. Remember your training, trust your instincts. I love you with all my heart.'

Josephine wept as she watched her mother fade off into the distance, going to join the front line against their ancient foe. She wondered how long her mother would be gone. A nagging feeling in the pit of her stomach caused her to want to chase off her mother and try to stop her from leaving, but instead, she just wept.

Days turned into weeks, and weeks into months, yet Bastet did not return. With each passing day, Josephine's worry grew, her thoughts consumed by the fate of her beloved mother. As time wore on and still there was no sign of Bastet's return, Josephine's fears turned to despair. It was then that Ra appeared before Josephine, his countenance grave as he delivered the news that her mother had fallen in battle, her sacrifice forever etched in the annals of history. With tears streaming down her face, Josephine listened as Ra spoke of a new destiny that awaited her, one that would see her grow into the fierce warrior that her mother had always trained her to be.

'You will go and train in the Doomed Maze Forest. When I call upon you, you will come.'

Feeling heavy in heart and with determination burning bright within her, Josephine set forth into the depths of the Doomed Maze Forest, where she would undergo the trials of adulthood and emerge as a warrior worthy of her mother's legacy. For she knew that one day, when the realm was once again threatened by darkness, Ra would call upon her as he had called upon Bastet before her, and she would rise to meet the challenge with courage and strength, just as her mother had taught her. Little did she know that her memories would be taken, and she would forget her path, until a young human came along before she reached adulthood, to reawaken her fire, and reintroduce her to what it felt like, to have a family.

Chapter Thirteen
The Girl

Katie turned down Highway W, heading towards the market for her grandfather. He needed a replacement part for his gas-powered rototiller. It always surprised her at how people were still able to get fuel, considering no one was even making it anymore. Where the heck did it come from? Katie liked doing things for her grandfather, he was all she had left. Both of her parents, her grandmother, and both of her brothers were all shot and killed when they got the waking disease. It was incredibly tragic news when she found out what happened.

Ten years ago, while at the very same market she was headed towards, their waking disease suddenly manifested, which caused them to attack and eat a small child, in the middle of the street. They had nearly killed that child's mother in the process. Authorities had to put them down, for the safety of the public.

She was a short blonde girl, with stunningly straight white teeth, and dazzling green eyes. Her deep brown, perfectly shaped eyebrows set off the brightness of her eyes against the natural ruby red lips beneath her quaint little nose. She stood just over five foot tall, without any extra weight. Though, few people have a lot of extra weight nowadays anyway. She kept her teeth white by brushing with charcoal, like her grandfather taught her. He taught her a great many things about survival, including how to sing. She liked to sing while she did anything, and was currently singing along to an old country song from the 2020's. As she reached down to adjust the radio, she accidentally bumped the skip button on the small flat screen, changing the song.

"Damn."

Looking down at the screen, she quickly found the back button and put the song she was just singing back on. Her air conditioner didn't work, but her radio certainly did. A flash of something in her peripherals caught her attention, and she quickly flipped her eyes back to the road. An old pick-up truck was screaming down the highway in her lane, and she didn't have time to get out of the way. Katie lay on her horn while simultaneously jerking her wheel to the left, trying her best to get the other driver to change direction too.

Time seemed to slow down. She saw that he had his cell phone in his face, and tears running down his cheeks. Dropping his phone at the sound of her horn, he turned his eyes towards her, and she smiled.

It's all going to be okay.

Fast as lightning, thoughts of the result of this crash flew through her head. She knew that neither of them would make it, but it was okay. She wanted him to know that she had forgiven him the second he made the mistake. He had an innocent look to his face, and kind eyes. She always liked men with kind eyes.

Grampa won't get that part for his tiller now.

It was strange the thoughts that go through a person's head when they are about to die. It seems that the near-death experience causes adrenaline to course through her veins, bursting into her synapses, causing them to fire sporadically, which was enough to change the direction of her thoughts.

Their vehicles collided with the force of a small bomb. She had her seat belt on, but she didn't think it would matter. She watched as the man in the pick-up flew through the windshield, careening across his hood. As he flew through the air, he looked her way again, to which she sent back another smile.

Why in the hell am I smiling like a damn buffoon?

Katie had time for that one last thought before her head slammed painfully into the steering wheel, sending cracks across her skull, and bruising immediately sprouted on her brain as it vibrated, misfiring. The swelling was immediate to her brain inside her broken cranium. A blank emptiness overtook her mind instantly.

Unbeknownst to Katie, a powerful and beautiful angel gently reached up, and turned her chin, just before impact. It wasn't much, just a small amount to keep the damage caused by the steering wheel from actually killing her. The angel looked towards the man in the other vehicle, as his body rag dolled off of the vehicles. She watched for a moment, verified once again that her charge was still living, then winked back out of existence.

***

"What the heck happened!?" Katie screamed, jerking awake. She jumped to her feet immediately, looked around and noticed that she was standing in the middle of a bustling highway, heading directly into a grand shining city. Around her, walking quietly and peacefully towards the massive gates of the city, were people of every different type, race, and species. Katie noticed that some of the people looked very elflike, and some looked like dwarves. She began to wonder if she ended up in some medieval fairy-tail, or a renaissance fair. Ultimately, it was the two twenty-foot-tall giants that convinced her she was dreaming. There was just no way that anyone could have built a robot that large, just for a renaissance fair.

Even with all the unique types of people, and strange species she was witnessing, Katie's eyes were still drawn to the magnificent pillars and architecture that surrounded the gate. They were made of pearly-white stone, capped with golden gumdrop-shaped tops. The gateway gave off a feeling of being more than just a gate. It gave off the feeling of being a threshold between the mortal realm, and that of the divine. The gate was a threshold of transformation, granting each of the souls passing the gate, eternity within the celestial city. Katie didn't see any of the people passing through, getting turned away, it was almost as if they had already been judged, and were just now making their way into the celestial city.

Standing in front of the gate was a bright glorious angel. He seemed to see everything at once yet remained steadfast in his guardianship over the gateway. The angel was tall, well over fifteen feet, with huge powerful wings. He wore a beautiful white gown, with golden plate armor over his chest. A set of scales in one hand, and a large sword, almost as long as he was tall, strapped across his back.

Katie walked towards the gate, falling into line with the bustling creatures that entered the city. She noticed that the gateway covered more than just the stone road she walked on, but also a sparkling translucent river that flowed next to the road on either side. In the river, Katie could see large and small whale-like creatures, and others that appeared to be mermaids. The wide variety of life-forms really blew her mind, but she was nothing if not pliable to new experiences.

As Katie got up to the gate, and was about to pass through, a huge shining sword slammed into the ground in front of her, a shadow left where it was. Somehow the gate guardian had drawn his sword so fast and slammed it on the ground in front of her, that it left a sparkling hazy shadow behind where it once was. Yelping in fear, she hopped back, cowering in front of the giant angel that was leaning over in front of her. He had placed his piercing crystal blue eyes on her, entrapping her in his gaze. She did not feel a threatening aura from him but was afraid of his mere size and power that he exuded.

"You should not be here; it is not your time."

The flow of people continued to flow around her, ceaselessly pressing on into the magnificent city. Seemingly not noticing the scene that was unfolding. Katie didn't know what to do, so she just looked up at the Angel in fear. She just stared at him, believing with all her heart that at any instant, she would be cut down in the middle of the golden highway.

"My name is Gabriel, gatekeeper of Heaven. Only the souls who have passed judgement after their physical bodies have expired may enter. You should have been sent to The Gateway Township, instead of the gates of the Celestial City. Your body, girl, has not yet expired. Begone from here, to the Doomed Maze. There you must unite with the one who is responsible for your current predicament. Save him because he cannot save himself, and he is not ready for the trials that lie ahead of him."

With a powerful swing of his large sword, directly at Katie, she quickly closed her eyes and flinched back once again. Standing there for a few moments, and not feeling the impact of Gabriel's might, she slowly opened her eyes. She was no longer standing on the golden celestial road, but now stood within a dungeon cell. The damp air smelled of rat feces and decaying flesh. Shuddering, Katie looked around, and noticed the bones of a different prisoner lying wrapped in a single threadbare blanket, in the corner of the cell.

She thought about how the world of Earth had changed her perspective on things. She considered how it must be to be afraid of the dead, instead of accepting it as normal. It was not unusual for her to see the corpse of another person decaying in the streets. She thought back to her family, and how her grandfather and she had to go to the market, when she was just a young girl, to clean up their bodies. They could not abide leaving them without a proper burial. If they didn't clean them up, no one would ever have done it. There just weren't enough people left to do menial tasks like cleaning up the streets. It's not like there was enough water left to get poisoned by the decaying meat. The sun and heat alone were enough to dry out anything that would cause sickness. It was almost as if the entire world came to the silent acceptance that the carrion feeders would be the ones doing the work. Unfortunately, sometimes the carrion feeders, included some of the lower levels of humanity.

Walking over to the corpse, she grabbed the thread bare blanket, thinking back to some of the survival techniques that her grandfather had taught her. As she pulled the blanket away from the corpse, the smell grew. She noticed that there were small bone nubs in place of the full arms that used to be there. The teeth were also jagged and broken, as if they had clamped down on something and pulled, breaking, and tearing them from the gums. There was still decaying flesh and sinew holding some of the bones together. The rats had merely feasted on the poor soul's face and appendages. The flesh under the blanket was still fairly green. If Katie had to guess, she would say he, for it was a man, had been dead for a little more than week. She gave a quick cursory look across the spot where the corpse lay and found nothing.

Rolling the blanket up, Katie began to search the different corners of the cell, looking for weak points in the stone or the metal bars. Occasional screams of pain, and guttural howls of laughter could be heard. She thought they may have been a floor above her, so she was not too concerned about making noise, or moving slowly.

Katie felt a little give in the bars around a small door that was intended to feed prisoners. She started working the bar, twisting, and turning it. Each time she pulled on the bar, the entire door creaked, sending a sharp twang out into the darkness. Slowly, the bar began to spin, and move a little more freely. About the time Katie thought she just had to lift and pull, a pale green light spilled out from down the corridor towards her.

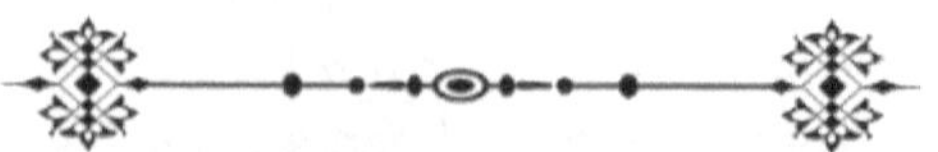

Chapter Fourteen
Demoness

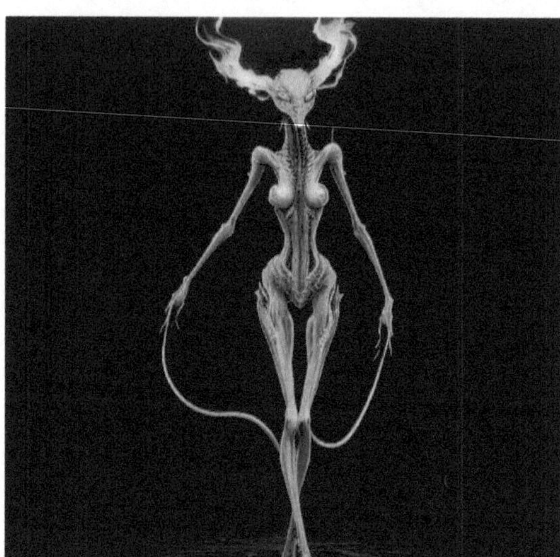

A sickly thin, pale green, tall figure came into view. It was slow and shuffling, moving with a purpose, directly towards Katie. The light was revealed to be coming from the creature itself. As it got closer, she could see that the creature was naked. It had skin that was torn in many places, flaking, and falling off in others. Green flames licked the deep crevasses of its body.

The skin was a pale green color, which was scaled like that of a serpent. As she looked a little closer, she could see steam, or smoke, rising off of its nightmarish body. She looked into its glowing red eyes that contained a bright yellow iris and felt like it pierced directly through her soul. The demon, for it had to be a demon, had two broken jagged horns on top of its hairless head, which seemed to flicker and wave, as if made of a green flame. It had a mouth that was far too large for its emaciated skinny face. It stretched, from ear to ear, open in a ghastly smile that was filled with blackened, sharp teeth.

The demon was very clearly female. It's sex drooping and decayed. Her full breasts sagged and flaked, occasionally a chunk would completely fall away. Katie watched as a particularly large piece fell away and was rapidly regrown with the same green decayed flesh. She had never felt this level of fear, as it approached her cell. The smell hit her like a freight train, completely obliterating the smell of the dead body she currently shared a cell with.

When the demon got to her cell, it stopped abruptly, continuing to face the direction it was originally striding, giving Katie a side profile view of the creature. Disappearing suddenly, then reappearing instantaneously in the same spot, rotated ninety degrees, the demon was suddenly looking directly at Katie, as she cowered in her cell.

In a raspy, gargling, feminine voice, the demon asked, "What do we have here?"

The door rattled and shook as the demon began to open the door. Snapping out of her cowering state, Katie desperately looked around, trying to find something that could hold the door closed, so she could gain just a few more moments of life. Looking down, she found an unattached broken femur bone from her unfortunate cellmate. She swiftly picked the bone up and dashed over to the door, shoving it in the gap where the cell door met the framed metal of the cage, wedging it in place, so the door could not open.

With a small sense of victory, and slight sigh of relief, Katie began to search her cell more, for another way to escape. As the demon hissed and shook the door in frustration, Katie rushed to the corner where the corpse lay, which was the last place remaining that she could possibly find a way to escape this nightmare. She didn't look here before, out of sanctity and respect for the deceased, but this time, she grabbed the corpse by the rib cage, throwing it towards the door, hoping against hope that when the demon finally came through, it would trip and fall. Just as she moved the last bone, she noticed that it lay on a circular bullring.

Hoping this was a way out, she snatched the ring and pulled with all her might. As the metal ring slowly pulled out, it was attached to an intricately woven metal cable, a spot under the window began to slowly fall away. The demon rattled and jerked at the door even more, desperately trying to get into the cell, to catch its prey. The second the opening in the wall was large enough for her small frame to squeeze through, two things happened simultaneously. The door to her cell began to melt, then exploded inwards, no longer stopping the demon from entering and seizing Katie. At the same time, Katie lurched through the small gap, which was just large enough for her to squeeze her hips through. She noticed that the drop out the hole in the wall, was not short. It fell nearly twenty feet into a scum filled moat.

'It is a castle, and why didn't the last guy use the damn bullring to escape?' She thought stupidly.

Katie screamed. The demon grabbed a hold of her ankle just as the rest of her body fell. Her screams of fear quickly changed into screams of pain, as the steaming decayed fingers of the Demon began to sizzle and burn the flesh on her ankle. She hung there, as her flesh cooked, and the top layers of skin began to loosen and slide off the muscle and veins beneath. Katie's screams were joined with those of a more guttural hissing, as the demon began to lose its grip. Slipping out of the demons' hands because the flesh on her ankle melted and slipped away, Katie fell into the sloshing muck of a moat.

The demon began to tear at the rock wall of the castle and cell. Its fingers tore and regenerated at a visible pace, getting nowhere. While the demon was incredibly thin, it's shoulders were too wide to go out the hole. Katie was fortunate that she was small in frame and size. For the first time in her life, she was actually grateful that food was hard to come by.

Crawling out of the brackish frogspawn and algae bloomed water, she tried to stand on her injured ankle. She was surprised to find that it held her weight well and did not hurt all that much to walk on. Hearing a splashing sound, she looked back over her shoulder and saw that a large gray brick fell into the water. The demon had managed to widen the hole a little and was now wriggling and working its large thin body through the hole. Katie ran, as fast as she could, towards a dark wall of trees that were a few hundred yards ahead of her. The ground was muddy and slippery as she placed her feet in precarious positions just to climb the slight incline towards the dark forest ahead of her.

"Please, Lord God, protect me from this evil. Save me from this valley of death and destruction I've found myself in. Grant me the strength I need to carry myself from this pit of despair."

Katie breathed in and out deeply, controlling her breathing as best as she could as she sprinted rapidly towards the tree line. Her grandfather always told her to remember to pray, because even when the times were good, praying kept her soul at peace. It would also mean she was more likely to be heard and have her prayers answered when she direly needed it, if she prayed at all times, instead of just when she needed it.

She chanced a look back, just in time to see the demon falling towards the water. She couldn't take her eyes away as she watched it hit the water, immediately the entirety of it steaming and bubbling, evaporating at a visible pace. The demon stood, looked directly at where Katie was running, and began to flicker towards her. It would disappear, then reappear several feet ahead of where it was previously standing. It was as if each step, would teleport the demon a short distance. She felt it's feral gaze directed at her, the aura of hate and consumption that came with it. Katie shrieked in desperate fear, turned back around, and tried to push herself even more, to a faster pace.

The forest was merely ten yards away when the demon finally reached within striking distance of where Katie continued to run. It hissed and growled, reaching towards her. Katie looked back just in time to duck the out-stretched arms of the terrifying creature. She noticed the ground behind them was on fire, clearly from the heat the demon was putting off.

Howling in frustration as Katie dove into the tree line the forest making a wall due to the very closely spaced trees. She knew if she made it into the tree line, she would very likely be safe from the thing behind her. As her hips hit two trees and began to slow her progression into the forest, the demon reached once again for her ankles, this time merely grabbing a shoe. The rubber from her shoe swiftly melted off, causing the demon to lose her once again. The acrid smell of burned rubber combined with the sour stench of burnt flesh and hair was almost enough to cause Katie to vomit uncontrollably. She choked back a bit of sour bile, then fell backwards, gasping for air.

Laying on her back inside the forest, with the tree wall firmly between her and the demon, she continued catching her breath. Katie looked around, knowing the demon was trying to burn the trees down, she had to keep moving forward into the forest. She stood, looked back at the glaring monster, it didn't appear to be trying very hard to get to her, just standing there looking at her with hate and hunger.

"You.... May.... Run.... Little... One...... I have tasted you now, you... can.... not.... escape.... Me." The demon spoke in a slow whispering voice. It seemed to vibrate the air, coming from a different direction with each syllable.

Katie turned on her melted heel and ran, deeper into the forest. She found that she was on a pathway of sorts, which wound and twisted through the trees. At every fork in the winding path, Katie went right, knowing it was the quickest way out of the forest. Eventually she came upon a thick sign made of weathered hardwood.

Welcome to the Doomed Maze
Katie
Pick a door!

In front of her were two doorways, standing inside two very thick and large trees. It was almost as if the doors grew inside of the trees, instead of being cut into them. One door was as green as freshly cut grass, and the other was black as the darkest night, with white sparkling stars twinkling here and there. She initially leaned towards the starlight black door, but her intuition and gut told her that was a terrible idea.

Deciding on the bright green door, Katie reached for it, opening the door, and seeing a swirling portal. The portal was spinning greens and blues, it reminded her of a beautiful summer day, full of life and possibilities. Without hesitating further, Katie stepped through the portal.

***

From the deepest shadows of the towering trees, the demon with green fire, stepped out just as Katie stepped into the portal. It watched her leave, knowing the direction she went was actually down, as it sensed it through the flesh that its body was slowly consuming within its many stomachs. The demon had a stomach in place of each of its major organs. They were made to consume every

90

bit of energy living flesh contained, as it broke it down to atomic levels. As it approached the doors, a weathered wooden sign appeared, which the demon ignored. Reaching for the green door, it turned the handle and entered the portal. If the demon would have read the sign, it may have given it pause.

You have no further place here.
Go back to your forgotten castle.
You will not survive if you continue.
This is your only warning.

Chapter Fifteen
Buffalo-Storm

The first thing Katie did when she stepped out of the portal, was remove the remaining whole shoe and the partially melted fabric and plastic of the ruined shoe. She tucked it away in a makeshift pouch, that she had made out of her shirt, and the shoelace. It was awkward running through that forest with only one shoe, but it couldn't be helped, time was not her friend in there.

Afterwards, standing up and stretching, feeling the dirt and grass between her toes, she looked out into a wide-open plain of grass, stretched as far as she could see in every direction. The grass was a beautiful dark verdant green, teaming with life of all kinds. She could see herds of animals in the distance, whether they were buffalo, deer, or another grass-eating herbivore, she wasn't sure. The sky was cloudless, and the deepest blue she had ever seen, far into the horizon.

Katie remembered reading back in a history book, before she stopped going to school, about how the great plains of the United States used to be. It was miles and miles of wild grass, rolling hills, and herds of large animals, until the mass extinction and desecration of the land caused by global warming and humanities unerring desire for war and bloodshed.

She remembered how the northern part of the old United States used to be called "Big Sky Country." She assumed this was because of how big and blue the sky looked as one spun in a circle, following the horizon with their eyes. It had to deal with the full unobstructed views of the big blue vastness and openness of the sky. Now the great plains and mountains are more akin to dead rock and sand covered deserts, where not even cacti grew. The big skies are full of hazy dust clouds, with the occasional lightning storm that didn't drop a single drop of water. Scientists said that there was indeed moisture in the clouds, it's just that it was evaporating before it hit the ground, or being absorbed by the elevated parts per million of dust particles that were in the atmosphere.

Katie just smiled, taking in the huge expanse she could see. She imagined building a cabin on one of the distant rolling hills, imaging that there was a spring fed creek or lake just on the other side, out of view. With a satisfied sigh, she began walking towards the herd of grazing creatures in the distance. The pain in her ankle was a little more prominent after the adrenaline of the chase faded. She felt a shooting pain blazing up her leg with each step, starting at the lower edge of her burned flesh, skipping over the charred flesh of her ankle, then beginning again at the top edge of her burnt flesh. She knew she had third degree burns on her ankle, even so, Katie wondered just how long she would have to get it cleaned, until infection would begin to set in. She was grateful that none of the tendons or ligaments were damaged to the point where she couldn't use them.

In her shuffling, pain-riddled gait, she made surprisingly substantial progress into the gently rolling hills of the great plains. After close to two miles, she came across a wooden weathered sign in the middle of a particularly low spot, it read:

A great danger has made her choice,
The portals will randomly place you inside their destination,
Seek below the center of the herd,
There you will find your path.

Katie considered the sign for a moment and didn't understand some of it. "What did it mean that a great danger has made her choice? I assume the portal it speaks of is the door… and I hope that the herd it speaks of is that one… but what does it mean below it? In the dirt and grass? I guess I'll continue heading that way and find out."

*****

"I… can taste you… in the air…human girl. You cannot escape me, for I am Morana, the demoness of fire and death, and first daughter of Lilith, she who was the first demoness. I have never allowed my prey to escape, and I will not do so now."

Morana was delivered nearly forty miles away from Katie by the door portal. She slinked off into the plains, immediately setting fire to the grasslands. Her inner sense of hunting allowed her to know immediately the direction that Katie was in from her. Facing the direction where Katie could be found, Morana began to teleport walk, at an unprecedented pace.

The fields of green blackened and caught fire, spreading indiscriminately across the rolling hills. Soon, huge clouds of smoke rose into the air behind the demoness Morana. Like the grand engine of a long black train, she was leading the raging flaming clouds. Morana was on an undeterrable tract for the human called Katie.

*****

Katie made it to the outside edge of the herd; it turned out to be made up of large docile buffalo. She smiled as they looked at her in a dumb curious way, that only a bovine could pull off. They were not afraid of her presence, as she walked slowly amongst them. Occasionally reaching out and scratching and patting a buffalo here and there. With all the adorable creatures around her, she had trouble keeping her eyes to the ground. Occasionally, a curious calf would bounce at her, braying happily, as it encouraged her to play with it. A cow would then snort at her small child, as if scolding the calf, causing it to return back to the safe space between its mother's legs. The calf would return, only to turn around and look at Katie, as if telling her that the safe space would be welcome to her too.

All at once, all the buffalo turned and faced the setting sun. On the horizon was a large swath of billowing white clouds, which seemed to be slowly expanding. Katie noticed that it was growing at an exponential rate, to the point where she recognized that it was not clouds, but smoke. The great plains were on fire, and it was rapidly approaching her location. Quickly putting her eyes back to the ground, she began to frantically search for the path below the herd. Almost panicking, she began to wonder if this was even the herd the mysterious sign was talking about.

When she was just about to give up, she spotted a wide oblong oval of mud, with the circumference of around fifty feet. All the buffalo were casually standing around the pit, disallowing any curious calves from playing in the mud.

"That has to be it!"

Katie excitedly ran towards the mud circle, and the buffalo smoothly stepped aside, granting her a path. The edges of the mud pit were slimy, and algae covered. It squished and gushed between the toes of her shoeless feet. She looked down and could tell that the deep mahogany colored dirt and clay would be dying her skin a darker tone. The further she walked out into the thick mud, the deeper it became. It was never really super wet, or liquid, but more of a slow-moving thick goo. She was well past the point of no return when she realized that no matter what, she had to go through with this, because she was not pulling herself out of the grasping, sucking mud.

As the mud had held her body, from the neck down, she began to panic. Frantic thoughts raced through her mind, *'What do I do!? What do I DO!? I CAN'T ESCAPE! This is the end...'* She thought about her grandfather, and his words of wisdom he always told her, 'Always remain calm in the face of danger. It will save your life more than you would ever consider.' A calm acceptance came over her mind, as she embraced her fate. 'I'd rather suffocate in mud than burn to death in a raging grass fire. So be it, I accept my fate.'

Katie began to wiggle her body, moving her legs a fraction of a centimeter, but every little bit sank her lower and lower. First her mouth was under, then her nose. Right after her nose went under, the rest practically sank as fast as an anchor in water. She closed her eyes, and imagined herself falling, slowly off to sleep. She fell, gaining speed, her stomach doing somersaults, and the wind blasting past her face, practically blowing the mud off of her. She had been holding her breath for what felt like minutes, and they were burning. Upon feeling the wind, her mouth gaped open, and she took a huge gasping, gratifying breath. Like creaking open an old dusty book, her synapses fired with the fresh intake of oxygen, immediately she realized she wasn't in the mud anymore, she was falling through open air, or something close to it.

Katie was high up in the sky, falling towards a towering landscape that seemed to be filled with every sort of environment she could ever imagine. She could see fiery volcanoes, raging seas, huge waterfalls, and deep valleys. In one of the valleys, she swore she could see a beautiful sandstone temple. As she reached terminal velocity, she noticed she was falling towards a large tube, with a huge funnel at the top. As she hit it, she landed smoothly on very sharply inclined tube walls, speeding her way towards the ground. Like riding on a several mile long slide, she zipped in spiraling circles, getting closer and closer to the ground, and lying more and more horizontally on the slide. She was safely deposited at the top of a large desert valley, overlooking a stunning sandstone temple.

***

Morana blinked her way towards the thousand strong buffalo herd. As she approached, she noticed the buffalo stirring, shuffling around. She thought with a grim sense of humor, 'It appears they are moving their strong to the front, probably hoping I will just pass them by, and not kill them all.'

Their hopes were for naught, the demoness slaughtered them all. She dashed from buffalo to buffalo, blinking in and out of reality, each time she flickered in, she would kill. With each kill, she would consume their essences, granting her a little bit more strength. She placed the best parts of them into one of her many stomachs, to slowly devour and break down the flesh into a constant stream of energy and fuel for her ever-burning body. As she approached the mud pit, she lashed out at a final fleeing calf, slicing the small creature directly in twain. The burbling guts from a thousand sliced and burnt buffalo left the area smelling of burnt hair and cooked meat. The fire's raged on, leaving the entire terrain as an ash covered desolate landscape.

Morana stepped towards the mud, in which it sizzled and cracked as the mud dried rapidly. She could not sink into this dirt, as the heat from her smoldering body worked against her when it came to quicksand. It evaporated all the moisture that gave the quicksand its namesake, turning it into plain old sand. So, she dug. She heaved hundreds of pounds of blackened stained sand out of her hole with each movement of her arms. When she finally revealed the spinning dark portal, she didn't hesitate to dive into it, continuing her chase of the human girl.

Chapter Sixteen
The Central Hub

*T*he small SUV hurtled at him.... The sound of the two vehicles crunching and smashing together... The last flash of a beautiful smiling blonde woman having her head smashed open by the rapid contact, which forced her forehead into the steering wheel.... Pain... his skin was flayed, busted open, and he was bleeding profusely.... Why was his face shaking?

"Wake up Sesh, not to be a pain, but we really must continue our journey."

Pip was shaking Sesh as much as his tiny little arms could. "Wake up!" Pip shoved two of his little fingers directly into Sesh's nose, grabbed ahold of a couple of small hairs, and jerked them out.

"AACHOOO!"

Pip went flying away from Sesh's face, his sneeze causing his head to jerk forward, creating a catapult for the little fairy sized angel. Josephine sat near the couches cleaning herself and watching the boys be idiots. She winced as Pip's little body hurtled backwards into the table of foodstuffs, sending bread and meat flying.

'Wake up human, we must go.' Josephine was proud of her memories of her mother. She decided that she would not share them with anyone just yet, as they were near and dear to her heart, and wanted them only for herself.

"I'm up, I'm up. Man, that couch is awesome. I've never slept so good in my entire life."

Rising from the food table, pulling at a slice of aged cheese that was stuck to the side of his head, Pip frowned at Sesh. "Of course you haven't, those are the resting couches remember?"

"Well yeah, I remember, I'm just commenting on how awesome it makes me feel."

"I'm glad. You ready to continue on through the Doomed Maze?"

"Yes, though I don't see why it is called the 'Doomed Maze.' I can see why it's doomed, this stuff has been pretty dang terrifying so far, but why is it called a maze? We have run into very few options for changing direction or location."

"I will consider how best to answer you, while I do that, fill your satchel up with some of this bread and dried meats. We do not know when our next resting area will be, or even if there will be one."

Sesh filled up the satchel as best he could. Josephine had slowly sauntered over, pawed a small piece of meat over to herself, and was licking it to 'death.' Sesh smiled a little at the adorable cat. As the basics were completed, they began walking towards the southern end of the valley, past the beautiful scenery that the temple held.

"So, the Doomed Maze… It is a maze, in a lot of ways. The main way is the randomness of the portals. Some of the choices of portals made were not the only choices available. It was just the portal that you had the most obvious access to. For instance, when we went into the cave system portal, which turned us into the Dreadweaver's cave, we likely had another option, which was down the path, or behind a secret tunnel wall. Surely, if we would have searched a little harder, we may have found it… or we may not have and would have ended up caught by the hounds, or the Dreadweaver. This… realm, has a way of making a person go exactly where it they are meant to."

"I don't even know how much time we have left, the last sign that said anything about it, said we had four hours left, but I swear that was many hours ago."

"It's quite likely you still have plenty of time. As I told you before, as long as you're pushing forward, you're going as fast as you need to be, to complete your mission. The real danger isn't in running out of time, that's just to tell you that this isn't a treasure hunt. The real danger is the obstacles that were put in your path, which are here to prevent you from being able to complete your mission, or goal."

"How come we haven't seen anyone else in the maze, other than the nightmare fuel, and Josephine?"

"That is strange to me as well, I'm not sure. Potentially, there are thousands of souls in the maze, or as few as just you, me, and Josephine. I would have thought that we would have seen at least a couple since we got in here, but who knows. I don't have all the answers, just a few."

They walked on briskly for a little while in silence, climbing out of the valley. As they approached the top of the ridgeline, Sesh stopped for a moment and turned around, looking out towards the grand temple, and the wide valley below. He caught a glimpse of movement, trekking down the switchbacks, towards the temple below. It was just a flash, almost too fast for him to be absolutely certain that he actually saw someone or something. Thinking little of it, Sesh, Pip, and Josephine crested the ridgeline, and expected to see a wide expanse of desert land and terrain ahead of them. Instead, they were faced with a giant central hub of pathways and tunnels. All of the pathways and tunnels had a low, slowly moving fog rolling out of their entryways. Some of the pathways were tightly clustered trees and brush, pressed seamlessly into the walls that all seemed to be made of a beige textured brick. Other tunnels were made of stone, and disappeared downward into the earth, as if the one who entered, would be beginning a great spelunking adventure. The rocks and stone would grow in size then set smoothly against the walls. All while the towering walls of the maze stretched their mighty bodies to the skies, disappearing out of view into the heavens above. For the first time, Sesh felt like he genuinely was inside a maze.

"Wow."

"Yeah, I didn't expect that coming out of that valley. Pip, where did those walls come from? How come we didn't see them while we were down in the valley?"

Josephine spoke up for the first time since telling Sesh to wake up, 'Things are different here, in this realm. You can have nothing three feet ahead of you, then take a step, and something would appear.

One cannot trust their eyes here, as an individual's eyes, will lie to them.'

"Josie is right, Sesh. It's quite likely those walls weren't there but sprouted when we stepped on the top of the ridgeline. It's also just as likely that they were there the entire time, and the mysticism of this environment just hid them from our eyes."

"I understand."

"Good. Now which option should we go? Trust your instincts, allow them to guide you to your destination."

"Let's get a little closer and see if there's any particular hole that gives us the heebie-jeebies, so we know which ones to avoid."

'That is an excellent idea.'

"Yep!"

The trio walked towards the center of the hub, and nearly tripped over a large weathered wooden sign that was lying down in the middle of the room. It was not clear how the sign got knocked over. In small bold print, the sign read:

The Central Hub
Congratulations, you made it to the central hub of the
Doomed Maze.
Choose a path that speaks to you most.
One portal leads you to your destination.
One portal leads you to instant death.
Many portals lead you to various routes that will result in one
or both the previous options.
Choose.

Sesh shuddered reading the sign. I would hate to choose wrong. Let me get a feel for the tunnel entrances. They walked towards the far-right tunnel, which just so happened to be a crystal riddled cave entrance.

They could see the gentle slope of the cave, going upwards, and disappearing into an otherwise bland maze wall. The crystals inside were beautiful, refracting rainbow light in every direction. Sesh felt that this cave would be a wonderful adventure, but it didn't sit quite right with his innards.

The next entrance was a beautiful forest path, it was wide, and well lit. It felt safe. Sesh could almost hear a beckoning song coming from the pathway, and he wanted to choose this path immediately. Suddenly, Pip was zipping around in his face, saying some sort of mumbo-jumbo that Sesh couldn't understand.

With a pop, Sesh could hear clearly again. "What was that?"

"Those are Sireni. A beautiful and dangerous creature that binds to giant trees and lures in unsuspecting creatures with a blissful tone of serendipity. You would have been strangled to death by the roots of their bonded tree, or outright slaughtered by the humanoid creature itself, and then left to give nutrients to their bonded tree, allowing it to grow and increase in size. They are close cousins to the more water-bound Siren's you may know from your planet. They are incredibly dangerous."

"I don't think we have siren on planet Earth. At least I've never heard of them."

"The fables of your people would have taught you about them, I'm afraid those fables have died out with the people of old."

Nodding in understanding, Sesh guided them towards the next tunnel, finding no true calling amongst the next four options. It was the fifth tunnel entrance that Sesh felt like he was at the right one. The pathway led to a slow moving, gently burbling creek. Sesh walked into the entryway of this path a bit, and noticed that next to the low swooping trees, and quiet tranquil water, sat a canoe. Looking at his partners in crime, Sesh smiled and walked into the tunnel, grabbing ahold of the canoe, maneuvering it into the shallow water of the creek, and hopping in.

"This is it, guys. This is our path. Come on now, hop in! Float Trip!"

Josephine did not want to get into the canoe, and arched her back, digging her claws into the soft soil at the edge of the creek. Sesh hopped back out of the canoe, bent down, and picked up the scared cat. She clung to his arms as if her life depended on it, absolutely terrified. Climbing back into the canoe, he placed her down on the floor of the canoe. She immediately dashed to a safe spot, between his legs. She sat tensely between Sesh's feet; her tail wrapped tightly around his leg to support herself. Sesh grabbed the oar and shoved the canoe off the bank. The rocking of the small craft caused the terrified cat to scramble quickly to Sesh's right shoe, where she said, claws digging into his pants leg, and her tail wrapped even more tightly around his ankle. She would eventually get comfortable enough to sit up in the middle seat, but for now, she was afraid. Pip settled down in the front of the canoe, at the point, and stuck his arms out wide, with a huge smile on his tiny face. The unusual trio floated off into the low hanging branches of the willow trees that lined the edges of the long winding creek.

Chapter Seventeen
Carmen

Katie walked casually into the temple after stepping off of the last switchback, her mindset being one of calm and solitude. The serene temple around her reminded her of an old desert oasis that she would occasionally read about in her ancient history books, back when she went to elementary school.

She intentionally looked to cross all of the bridges, just taking in the peacefulness of her surroundings. The sounds of the gently lapping and flowing waters brought a level of ease to her mind. All of the chaos from the past couple of days has really put a twister of angst throughout her being.

Katie paused and watched as the multicolored coy swam around in the pristine water. Eventually, she ran out of aqueduct bridges to cross, and rainbowy colored fish to watch, so she left the waterways behind and walked towards a central square, near the big, towering temple. The towering temple was awe inspiring, as she gaped up at the huge sandstone building.

Entering the courtyard, Katie noticed a beautiful white sofa, sitting across the area from a table that had various breads, meats, and cheeses scattered about. It looked as if a child had sat on top the table and was tossing the foodstuffs to family pet. She walked over to the scattered, messy table, feeling her stomach growl and twist in hunger. Picking through the less damaged items, she was able to make herself a makeshift sandwich. Deciding that this was a good spot to take a break, she made her way over to the large white sofa and sat down to eat her food.

With a full stomach, Katie lay back on the sofa, and closed her eyes, feeling like this would be a good spot to take a short nap. She fell asleep quickly, not knowing what the resting couch was, and not knowing that she wouldn't awaken without assistance.

***

The spawn of Lillith, Morana, landed gracefully in the desert. There were rolling sands and dunes as far as she could see in every direction. She knew which direction Katie was, but felt that at the distance of her landing, it would take her several days to reach her. Without further delay, Morana began her journey across the cold, unforgiving desert.

***

Katie dreamed.

"We don't have enough food mom. We have just enough to give to grampa and Katie, but the rest of us will have to go without."

"It's okay son, Katie is so little, we have to give her food, and with grampa being sick, I don't know if it would be wise for us not to feed him, he would die without food. We will make it; we just have to head to the market tomorrow and see if we can find some food... we will have to do anything we can to find it... I mean anything."

105

Eight-year-old Katie watched from the dark corner where she liked to hide and play with her little Raggedy-Ann doll. Every time she sat in this corner, everyone else seemed to ignore her, or forget that she was even there. She didn't quite understand the different implications of what her older brother and mommy were talking about, but she still thought it was a good thing, she liked going to the market, and began to get excited that she would get to go tomorrow.

"Take this to grampa, make sure he drinks the broth and eats the bits. It's the only thing that will keep him going."

"Yes mother." Katie's big brother Jeff responded, and took the bowl of liquid carefully, not spilling a drop, to the back room where their grandfather was sitting up, coughing.

Grampa had been sick for a while, he was weak, which caused his production in their garden and at work to be non-existent. They had no more food, and nothing producing in their garden. The plants were growing, they just weren't producing yet, it was in between harvests. Jeff and Cale, Katies big brothers, worked where they could, but it was a comparable situation for everyone, they had money, but nothing to spend it on. They had everything they needed in their home, except for food. A person could last a long time on water, salt, and whatever bits they could put in it.

"Here baby girl, eat this soup. You have to keep your strength up."

"Thank you, mommy."

Katie got up and ate the soup without question, the bits of green and brown were likely from a dead or dying tree outside, just to get a few extra calories for her small body to burn. The flavor was bland, and watery, but Katie didn't mind, because it helped fill the ever-growing hole in her empty stomach.

The next day, Katie stood on the porch crying, watching as her grandma, mom, and two brothers walked towards the market. She had been so excited to get to go to the market, only for them to be so firm with not allowing her to go.

"You have to stay here and take care of grampa, make sure he eats something, even if it's bugs you find under the logs outside. You have to eat, we will be back as soon as possible, when we find food. I love you baby girl."

Her mom and dad had hugged her weakly as they slowly began shuffling towards the market, catching up with the rest of their family. Katie wept, she wanted to go to the market too. She didn't like being left alone with sick Grampa. She didn't want to dig up bugs to put in soup for Grampa. She wanted to go to the market and smell the good smells and see the people and other kids.

Katie didn't know that this would be the last time she saw her family alive. She didn't know that in just three weeks, grampa would have enough strength to take her to the market, get a wagon, gather up the decayed, bone-picked corpses of her grandmother, mom, dad, and two brothers, so they could bury them in the yard.

Katie didn't know that this day was the first day of her new life. It was the day where her real adventure began, and her grandfather would teach her survival techniques. She would learn how to outlast the many of the trials that this chaotic world would throw at her.

***

A stunning angel stood over Katie, in full blown glory. She was tall and lithe, like a mountain lion in human form. Her glorious wings were a pristine white, that seemed to radiate her majestic aura. She had shoulder length silver hair, which waved in a space with no wind. Her perfectly proportional face, stared impassively at the blonde human girl, lying on the couch, sleeping soundly.

"Oh dear."

An ethereal voice spoke from everywhere, and nowhere all at once. It was rich, deep, and disembodied.

"Yes, I am going to have to awaken her, soon. She has slept for nearly two days. She did not know that this couch was the resting couch, and she does not know of the dangers that are quickly approaching. Though, there's a chance, in the next cycle of choices, she can find a little reprieve from Lillith's spawn."

"Be careful of revealing yourself to her, Carmen. She may not be ready to handle the truth of reality."

"I am aware, Gabriel. Thank you for your concern." She did not say this unkindly.

"Good. I will leave you to it. The boy is quickly advancing, no mortal could have predicted he would gain the allies he did, but it seems to be working well for him. I think a part of him still believes this is all a dream, which is allowing him to be more accepting."

"If only they knew how tightly their paths are twisted together. I would genuinely like to see my love, Pip again."

"Yes, it is truly a sad thing that while performing your duty, you are not allowed to see any potential distractions, which may cause you to neglect that duty. I believe we have all learned the lesson, from the last time that issues arose."

"I will always heed the rules, even if I do not agree with them."

"Good. I will allow you to do your duty again, the time approaches that she must continue on her journey. The window is nigh."

"Good day, Gabriel."

"Good day, Carmen."

Gliding over slowly to where Katie slept on the couch, Carmen reached down, and lightly tapped Katie on the tip of her nose. When she didn't stir, Carmen grabbed her shoulder, and gave her a gentle shake. She didn't expect Katie's eyes to fly open at the speed they did, but she was prepared regardless.

The second her eyes flew open, Katie lurched to her feet, ready to fight or flee. Katie looked in every direction and without seeing anything alarming, she took a long slow breath, stretched a little, and calmed herself down. Katie had never felt so rested in her life and had no idea how long she had been sleeping. Looking around, Katie grabbed the small couch pillow that rested on the cushion, and began to tear at it, ripping the cover off. She needed a bag that would be a makeshift satchel to carry some food with her. Her torn shirt and ratty blanket just weren't cutting it. She didn't know when she would be able to eat again, so she stowed every bit of food she could find, including the food that was lying on the ground. It turned out that much of the food had begun to become stale and smell bad, but not looking a gift horse in the mouth, she took it all, anyway. She had eaten worse things in her life and will likely eat even worse things again. She then looked towards the opposite end of the valley from which she had come in and started walking in that direction.

Never in her life did she feel as good as she felt right then, Katie walked with a little more pep in her step. She nibbled on a hastily put together, nearly spoiled sandwich and hummed quietly to herself. Errant thoughts thanking her body for having a cast iron stomach from all the disgusting things she's put into it, in her life. As she broached the top of the valley ridgeline, she was greeted with the majesty that was the central hub. A small sign was standing in front of her, directly in her path, it read:

The Central Hub
Choose your path!

Walking to the left side of the hub which, unbeknownst to her, was the opposite side of the hub that Sesh and friends had started on. Katie walked to the first tunnel, finding that it was very similar to the tree path that she had been in, when she ran from the Demon.

She was immediately against going in this one, as she wanted nothing to do with that big green demon. Moving on to the next tunnel, she found a hole in the ground, surrounded by bronze-colored stalagmites sprouting around the hole, like four-foot-tall teeth. The hole gave off a golden glow that emitted a warm sensation, which was almost beckoning. Katie considered this one for a moment, then decided that the jagged stalagmites that looked like teeth, were enough to convince her not to choose this path.

The last path Katie came to turned out to be the one she chose. She didn't even need to look into all of the remaining paths, this one was calling her name. It was a smooth walking trail that disappeared into a brightly lit glade of bright purple flowers. The smell that emitted from the walking trail gave her a feeling of peace and resolution. Katie stepped off down the trail, humming incoherently.

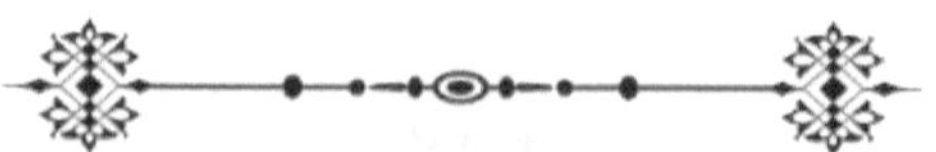

Chapter Eighteen
Sireni

Morana walked towards a distant valley, following the feeling of Katie, like a bloodhound would follow the scent of a deer. Suddenly, the direction shifted to almost directly behind her. Stopping in her ground charring tracks, Morana had to consider the area and situation. She knew about the Doomed Maze and its blasted tricky portals. She knew that if she turned around and walked into the desert after the feeling of the human, there's a good chance she would never find her. She also knew that she would likely end up just walking in circles, chasing the direction, because the portals teleported her all over the damned maze.

After deep consideration, for nearly twenty minutes, Morana decided to continue on in a direction that was against her nature. She went opposite of the way her sense was telling her to go, pressing on towards the valley. Morana knew, by the simple fact of Katie's extreme change in position, that there had to be a portal in the temple, so that was where she would go.

A day later, Morana crested the top of the valley wall. She looked with disgust into the valley where the hideous human-made buildings resided. Glaring at the building, seeing that they were made of stone, instead of wood, she spat a globule of flaming goo.

"Its… too… bad… I would have liked to burn it all down."

Flickering down the switchbacks, Morana came to the clear aqueducts where the coy swam in lazy circles. Smirking to herself lightly, her sharp teeth grinding quietly, Morana stuck her hand into the water and watched the area around her hand sizzle and come to a boil. The fish tried as best they could to escape the rising water temperatures, swimming to the far end of the aqueduct, near the waterfall.

Frustration at the escaping fish, Morana leapt full body into the water, pushing out her burning aura in a rage. The water went from merely boiling, to evaporating at a visible speed. With the waterfall steadily pushing water into the aqueduct, it became a race between the demon and the natural power of a distant spring.

The spring lost. Morana watched as the coy lay dead in the steaming brick of the aqueduct. The waterfall evaporated the instant it hit the piping hot stone of the aqueduct floor. With a rare feeling of glee, the demon flickered out of the ditch, and walked towards a courtyard a few hundred yards ahead. As she passed the green growth that was growing near the constant supply of water, she would run her hand along the branches, igniting them. Everywhere she walked, she left a burning swath of destruction behind her.

Flickering into the courtyard, Morana saw the sofa and an empty table, with nothing else of note in the area. She flashed quickly to the sofa, yearning to see it burn. She could see and feel the power that the sofa held. The demoness would not be swayed, grinning, she kicked the side of it and set the couch on fire. Immediately, the budding fire squelched, sputtered, then went out.

"Not even you have the power to destroy a Resting Couch, Morana."

Hissing loudly, she flickered back, raising her hands in preparation for battle. Her flames grew slightly in the recesses of her body, and the steam got thicker. Her mouth pulled back, exposing the bulk of her sharpened teeth. Large chunks of flesh and skin molted away, just to be regrown, at a much more visible pace.

"Gabriel." She hissed lowly, almost a growl.

Gabriel appeared before Morana, looking back behind her, at the destruction she caused on her way into the temple courtyard. In disgust, he said, "This temple is as old as your mother. Not even she would have dared cause the destruction here that you did. You are like a child with a toy slingshot in a glass house."

"What… do… you… want…?" She forced through gritted teeth.

"I have come to warn you, one last time, as you refused to heed the last one. The Eternal wanted to give you one last chance, due to your blatant disregard of the sign. They do not want to see the death of a long-lived soul, even one as callous and evil as yours."

"The Eternal cares not for my kind, Angel."

"Yet, They still love Their granddaughter."

"I refuse to acknowledge them as my Grandparent."

"Your acknowledgement does not change anything of the fact. Turn back and live, return to the forgotten castle, feed on the undeserving, leave the innocent you chase to her journey. This is the only way you survive. You will not be cautioned or warned again. What say you?"

"I… will… not… allow… the… human… to… escape."

"I will take that as your answer." Gabriel spat in disgust, "You are a fool, and cannot see that she has already escaped you."

With a flash, the mighty angel disappeared into nothingness, the feeling of his presence departing with him. Morana smirked, the whispered to herself, "You know nothing, Angel. You are old and your mind has wasted away."

Looking at the sofa once again, she scoffed then turned towards the northern end of the valley, and started her strange flicker walk rapidly towards the exit of the temple. As she topped the ridgeline, she saw her options. This was going to be difficult, she would have to trust her sense, and choose the direction that the human girl went.

There was no sign to warn or instruct Morana. There was no sign to give her advice, or to tell her the location name. The pathway for her was entirely up to her, without guidance or direction. Morana walked straight to the first few pathways, ignoring each of them rapidly, until she came to a pathway that was wide open, and called to her. She stood in front of a very inviting pathway, which had distant singing and a sense of longing emanating from it. Her sense of where the human girl had gone was now confused and difficult to decipher. Something from this path was interrupting her intuition.

Stepping down the path where the singing and beckoning had come from, Morana started walking slowly, the only flickering being her feet, as they changed location one step at a time. She would find the girl after she removed the nuisance of the meddlesome Sireni that were down this pathway. She had never seen them before, but she learned about them through the different creatures that she came across in her torture chambers, deep within her forgotten castle.

The feeling of being teleported unwillingly made Morana's flesh tingle, which was unusual, because usually she felt nothing, with all the flame and burning going on. The cycling of meat and flesh, a constant for her body. All of the regeneration and the teleporting she did with her flickering gate, usually meant she would feel nothing. She turned immediately after feeling the tingling, seeing that the way back was still open, which caused her to smirk in satisfaction. She knew that her plan would work. Turning back towards the annoying sounds coming from the distant Sireni, Morana flickered rapidly towards her target. She needed to eat anyway, her aura had been tainted and fading a little since the buffalo, especially with all the digging.

A large trio of trees stood at the end of the pathway, which was completely riddled with bones all over the ground. The trees were all the same species, which a human would have identified as a giant redwood. To Morana, it was simply a product that would burn.

She flickered towards the trees and began flickering between the three, running her hands along the lower edges of the tree, scratching the bark, and scorching the mighty trees, causing small red and green flames to flicker to life. Smoldering, acrid smoke began to billow from around the trees. Turning her head skywards, Morana grinned, seeing her prey present themselves to her.

With screams of pain, a scaled humanoid flew down the tree, crashing into Morana. The humanoid creature had grey scaley skin, with sharp yellow jagged teeth. It was clearly female, with an apelike face, and bright yellow spikes for eyebrows above her sickly orange eyes. Her large full breasts were covered and plated with a dark metallic armor that stretched down and covered her lower torso and seamlessly formed into a hanging skirt. Her shoulders were bare, showing leathery skin. She had five curved spikes atop her scaled bald head. They were hard and hornlike structures, and each looked like a thick strand of hair. The back of her head was full of yellow spikes, which oozed with a venomous liquid. All the spikes combined to look like a mullet of death. The creature exuded power, yet the power paled in comparison to the daughter of Lillith.

Morana grabbed the first Sireni by her throat, burning directly through the flesh and bone, completely severing the head in an instant of contact. Allowing the lifeless corpse to fall to the ground, its head coming to rest near the growing puddle of cytoplasmic blood. The middle redwood tree began to crumble, brown leaves dropping from the sky hundreds of feet above, like a torrential downpour. It died instantly, with its bonded siren. She turned to face the remaining two Sireni. They screamed and howled at the death of their sister. Sireni are always born in threes, and they can only grow together. With the death of one of the sisters, the remaining two would never be able to grow anymore, the total height of their tree and their lives has just been limited. When the middle tree died, the intertwined root system crumbled, weakening the ground below. It didn't kill the other two trees, but it severely dampened their capability for supporting such incredible weight.

Smirking at their despair, Morana flickered forward and struck out with her claws, stabbing through the chest of the leftmost Sireni, completely removing her heart in one fell swoop. Tossing the charred meat into her mouth, Morana smiled at the last remaining Sireni, as it stood directly in front of a crumbling redwood tree. Choosing to survive instead of facing the overwhelming force that was Morana, the last sister turned and tried to flee up the final living redwood tree.

Flickering upwards into the sky, Morana appeared above the fleeing sister. She flipped her body, putting her head towards the ground. Morana stabbed the last sister through the chest with her flaming horns, plowing her into the ground, ending the sister's life, and removing three giants from the doomed maze, forever.

After consuming the strength of the three Sireni, Morana turned back towards the portal, she had prey that was still trying to escape. That was unacceptable. Moving as quickly as she could, she raced back towards the central hub. She had spent far too much time dealing with the angel and these disgusting tree rats.

Chapter Nineteen
The Gazebo

The two boys started the journey goofing off, splashing water at each other, and just generally enjoying the sunlight and peaceful ride. Josephine would growl and occasionally scold them through their mental connection, calling them children. She was not an enthusiastic fan of water. After a couple of hours, they each settled down, and relaxed.

The canoe glided silently down the still creek, the occasional droplet of water off the oar, and the gentle rustle of the willow branches whispering to the wind, was the only sound. The world felt to Sesh like it was holding its breath, waiting for something extraordinary to happen. Josephine would occasionally turn her head back, wide eyed, looking to Sesh as the canoe would rock with his rowing. Pip just smiled, staring off the bow, eager to see what the next portion of their journey would hold. As the canoe made a final bend in the creek, they could see that it slowed, and pooled into a large round pond. An outlet on another end held a waterfall that fell into a small rocky creek, not floatable via canoe, trailing off into the forest beyond the glade. The pond was peacefully sitting inside a large beam of sunlight, perfectly framed in the beautiful, serene willow forest. Off to the side of the pond, was a pristine white gazebo, with white benches lining the inside, near the rails. The gazebo immediately caught the gaze of the three travelers, enchanting their minds with wonder, thinking about what types of magical memories were made at such a beautiful place.

Sesh, Pip, and Josephine all seemed to hold their breath with the silence that surrounded the pond centered glade. Looking at Sesh, Josephine said, 'I think we should stop the canoe, and find out what the gazebo is all about. I feel like this place holds something extraordinary.'

"I agree, I think we should go see the gazebo too."

As the canoe entered the pond from the creek, the sound of the forest seemed to let out its breath, exhaling a cacophony of wild singing and musical melodies. The frogs croaked, birds chirped, and insects buzzed. The muted sounds of the waterfall were a curtain, surrounding the hidden musical symphony of the forest, keeping it enclosed in its dull roar. These very sounds of tranquility, in a glade such as this, brought a smile to the two humanoids, Sesh and Pip, and a quiet purr to the young cat, Josephine. They all felt the relaxation and calmness that came from the startlingly white gazebo.

Josephine pounced from insect to frog, occasionally crunching one between her teeth, if she found it particularly juicy. She was showing her true youthful age, as she played with the smaller things of the glade. Pip would flit from firefly to firefly, catching them one at a time, then flying them back to Sesh just to release them in his face, their little blinking glow shining a soft yellow light on his smile that stretched fully from ear to ear. Occasionally, Sesh would join each of his two companions, in trying to catch frogs, or fireflies.

They all took their time, relishing the relaxing environment, as they slowly made their way to the gazebo.

When they got to the gazebo, Sesh noticed that it was not empty. Pulling up short of the entrance of the gazebo, Sesh stood there dumbfounded, staring at the semi-translucent man sitting on the bench, furthest from the exit. The man sat there, staring at Sesh with a grand smile on his face. Sesh immediately recognized him, which is why he was so surprised. It was his oldest brother, Willard.

Pip nudged Josephine softly with his small elbow, and jerked his chin away, towards the grass. He was hinting to her, that they should allow the two family members a moment of privacy. She eagerly leapt back into the grass, taking the hint. Willard had the same sandy-brown hair and general face shape as Sesh. He was a little bit shorter than his younger brother, but where Sesh was thin and tall; Willard was broad and muscular. Willard stood as Sesh approached slowly.

"Willy?"

"Yes, baby brother, it is I."

"WILLY!" Sesh rushed forward and wrapped his arms tightly around his subtly translucent older brother. "I missed you so much." Sesh wept in joy at the small family reunion while Pip and Josephine continued to play amongst the grass, chasing the frogs and insects with glee.

"I missed you too. How are mom and dad? How are the girls?"

Wincing, Sesh told him about mom and dad, and how much they were struggling now. He also broke the news of how their sisters passed into the void, and how hard it was burying everyone. After they shared a moment of silence, and retrospect of their lost family members, Sesh continued to explain how life on earth had further deteriorated since Willard had died. Just trying to survive every day was the trickiest thing he had ever experienced, until he came to the Doomed Maze.

"How did you get here Willy?"

"Well little bro, I was sent to the Doomed Maze because I felt my soul would not pass the judgement, so I requested an opportunity to right my scales. I made many mistakes in my life, and most of them I never atoned for, or confessed. Since I was not baptized, I must earn my place in the celestial city, by balancing my scales."

"I didn't even know that was possible, there really should be a manual of this somewhere."

"Ha! There have been many manuals written, how many religious scriptures are out in the world? How many different religions with the same generalized statements and meanings behind the words? More than both you and I could count, even if we had the next ten years to count them."

"But... Those scriptures and religious texts, never mentioned anything about being able to have a chance to right the scales of judgement after death."

"They did, but likely it was lost in translation as the countless ages passed. More than once, the Eternal is mentioned, and it is stated that his love for humanity is without end. What kind of love wants to see the object of love burning eternally or being devoured by the flames of the demon kin?"

"Where did you learn all of this?"

"I learned much of it from Gabriel, and even more from the petitioners of this here Doomed Maze. I take it you have run into some of the other patrons of the maze?"

"I haven't, I've only come across my guardian angel, Sir Trillion Pippenstein..."

"The third!" Pip yelled from somewhere in the grass surrounding the gazebo.

"Right, the third, and I have come across Miss Josephine Amunet Ailuros. I don't know if you know this or not Will, but she's a sphynx. Did you know that the Sphynx we know from ancient Egypt, is completely wrong? The Sphynx is closer to a common housecat, than a huge riddle loving creature of the desert. She is mighty, don't get me wrong, just not quite the one we were led to believe."

"Curious indeed. That is some excellent information about the Sphynx, thank you for sharing that with me. Tell me about how you came to find and see your guardian angel. It was my understanding that they are not supposed to be visible by their charges, ever. Yet, here you are, having yours play in the grass with another creature of legend."

"Oh, that's an interesting story. Let me get a little food out of my bag here, and I'll tell you all about it."

Sesh told Willard all about how he ended up in the Doomed Maze, in purgatory because he was in a coma. He told him how he found Pip stuck in the webbing of the large blind spider. He also shared how he had found Josephine and their battle with the Dreamweaver. Willard was the perfect audience, gasping and raising his eyebrows at all the appropriate times. Josephine and Pip had come into the gazebo and settled in for a bite to eat and a nap while they listened to the story, adding in parts of the story occasionally, where appropriate.

After the story was told, they sat in silence for a long five minutes, just enjoying each other's company. It was not long before Sesh began to wonder just why he found his brother in this doomed maze. He remembered how Saint Peter was telling him about spirits and how they would slowly fade away, until they were nothing but sprites, unable to move forward or backward, stuck eternally as lights for the wary soul.

"Willard… Why are you here?"

"I told you that already Sesh, don't you remember?"

"Not that, I mean really, why are you still here? Why haven't you completed your task yet?"

Sighing, Willard looked at Sesh for a long moment, "Well, it is because I need your help little brother."

"What do you need my help with? I will gladly help you with anything."

"I am stuck here, a piece of my soul, the piece I need that can balance my scales, was stolen by a swarm of smoke crows. They are a black wispy crow that can vanish into the shadows, unseen by the eyes of any spirit. Only a living mortal can see them at all times...at least while it's daylight. You… You could see them at all times during the day baby brother. It is in the shape of a small marble. The center of which swirls with a white fog, which is the goodness that should be within my soul. Will you help me? I beg of you."

"Of course I will, Willy. You are my brother. I will do anything for you. Where are these darn birds? Josephine really likes to eat birds."

"These birds are… probably not edible, as they are made of a dark smoke, like the burned black wisps of Styrofoam, when you toss it into a campfire."

"I see, well, either way, we will help you, right guys?"

Josephine and Pip nodded, and hopped to their feet, and the three of them followed Willard out of the gazebo, and into the forest. They followed a tight little rock-strewn trail, that gradually climbed away from the creek. Occasionally, through the thick canopies, Sesh could catch a glimpse of tall cliffs, on which were hundreds of humungous bird-nests. Stepping out into a sandy cliff bottom, the four of them stared upwards at the exceptionally large bird nests. Occasionally, they could catch a glimpse of a towering black bird, zipping from one nest to another. Seeing a small pathway to the top, Sesh pointed it out. Josephine eagerly rushed to the wall and began climbing.

Taking a deep breath, Sesh headed to the base of the cliff where Josephine started up, then whispered, "Whelp, this is going to be an adventure."

Chapter Twenty
A Good Goodbye

Josephine jumped smoothly from one dangling stone, grabbing ahold of a soft section of moss that clung tightly to the cliff edge. Dangling there for a moment, hanging on by just her protruding claws, she glanced down towards Sesh, before climbing up to the top of the rock, gracefully.

They were making their way up the side of the cliff, trying as hard as they could to reach the top where the crow nests resided. Josephine had been occasionally looking back, checking to see how her chosen human struggled as he climbed from ledge to ledge, up the steep cliff. She could clearly see the pathway he had to take, it was obvious, and plain as day. She scoffed, then thought to herself, *'Humans are terrible at climbing things.'*

Pip flapped and fluttered his wings behind Sesh, as he climbed. Constant words of encouragement spewing from his mouth. Willard was right below Sesh, climbing as well, but since he had taken so long to complete his task, his spirit was not very tangible, so his climbing a bit easier. It was clear he had truly little weight to his spirit, so if he slipped, he would fall so slowly, he would practically just float in one spot.

"You got this Sesh! Right there, yes, yes, no, not there, it's above your right shoulder. Yes, that is the next grab hole. You should be able to get to the top of that boulder, and then when you get there, you will be able to easily see how to get onto the next ledge so you can take a breather."

Sesh grunted, looking up towards his next grab spot. He wished he had some of that tacky powder he heard about rock climbers using, to help with his grip. Looking at the next spot to grab hold of, he saw the bright eyes of Josephine, looking down at him from, what seemed like, a vast distance. He could almost feel her judging him for taking so long to climb.

"I'm coming Josie, hold your horses. You probably are up there thinking that humans can't climb at all." Sesh grunted, as he climbed onto the ledge, which was about halfway up the cliff-face. He was fortunate that the cliff face wasn't a sheer wall, straight up and down. It did have a very slight gradual incline to it, like climbing a wall that was eighty percent incline. Those ten percents of angle, really have influence on the difficulty.

"Good job Sesh. You're doing well." The constant cheerleader encouraged.

"Th..." gasp for breath, followed by a small coughing fit, "Thanks."

"What? You act like you've been climbing the side of a sheer cliff or something."

Sesh rolled his eyes at the small angel flying next to him, then looked over at Willard who had just sat down on the ledge. Willard wasn't out of breath at all, it was almost like he was out for a leisurely stroll. His spirit seemed much dimmer up here, in the bright beaming light of the afternoon sun. The thought of his brother fading out into oblivion, becoming a mindless wisp really made Sesh more worried about their time requirement, how much time did Willard have left?

"Easy climb for you, big brother?"

"Not terrible."

"How come you aren't exhausted like I am?"

"Because I'm more spirit and ghost than I am a tangible solid person, I weigh very little. I pretty much just have to guide myself up the hill and give little pushes. Imagine if we had little to no gravity. Just a little moon-climb."

"Wait, aren't I technically a spirit too? My tangible body is in a coma on earth. How come I am not an intangible spirit too?"

"Well, I believe it is because your soul has yet to begin to lose the will to hold itself together. You are steadily on your task, striving for your goal."

"Technically, I'm not though, right? I strayed from it so I could help you with yours."

"Hmm, well the maze has a way of making sure you have enough time to complete your task, have no fear. It also may be the will of the Eternal for you to help me in this task. No one utterly understands the happenings."

"He's right Sesh, it's possible that you helping to your big brother, was actually a designed side 'quest' if you will, for you to complete your task. Even though you haven't been judged, that doesn't mean you aren't being tested. The Eternal likes to evaluate your inner balance, not because They don't already know it, but because we, as individuals, should know the metal of our own inner soul."

"That's good, because I was wondering if I already had lost, because I chose to help. I would have helped either way, but I still wondered."

Pip spoke up quickly, "No one loses time in the Doomed Maze for helping another in a moment of great need."

Nodding, Willard said, "True. I also completely understand your concern, but you should understand this, if I thought you would be at risk of failing your task, I would have not allowed you to find me in the gazebo. I would have dashed into the forest and hidden until you and your companions moved on. You are my baby brother, and I would die for you a million times, before I allowed you to die for me just once." After looking at Sesh for a moment, with pride on his face, he finished with, "Well, how about it? Are you ready to finish this climb?"

Smiling like a goober, Sesh said, "Yes, let's go."

Pip took to the air, as Sesh stretched one more time and began to climb the side of the cliff slowly and steadily towards where Josephine was cleaning herself while patiently waiting for him. After another fifteen grueling minutes, he finally placed a hand on the ledge where Josephine lay basking in the sunlight. When he got to the top, he rolled onto his back next to the languid sunbathing cat, gasping for air.

"Sometimes, I wish I could be a cat."

"You certainly would climb better. And Faster."

"It would be easier if you just had wings."

"Well, I don't have wings now do I, Pip?"

Grinning, Pip said, "No, but I could have changed to my full size, and flown you up here, so in a way, you could have borrowed mine."

Staring at Pip, Sesh wasn't sure how to respond. Until finally he said, "Wait… Seriously?"

"Nope."

They looked at each other for a few moments before bursting out in laughter. That would have been a wild sight, Pip, a mighty angel, carrying a human piggy-back, and flying up the side of a mountain towards a sun-bathing cat. They roared with laughter, causing them all, including Willard to be completely out of air.

After things began to settle down, Sesh stood next to Willard, looking at the hundreds of Crow nests that were absolutely brimming with smoke-emitting birds, roughly the size of a large turkeys. There were so many of them, and so many nests, Sesh wasn't sure how they were ever going to find the marble.

"How are we going to do this? Just dive right in?" Sesh questioned.

"Like this!"

After her telepathic shout, Josephine excitedly jumped into the first nest, swatting at a smoking crow, her paw nearly passing through it, before gaining friction and sending the bird flying in squawks.

"CAH CAH CAH!"

The birds yelled at them, as they dug through each nest, finding mostly bones and detritus. Occasionally, they would find a small silver coin, or a piece of jewelry. Crows loved collecting small shining objects, and since these crows were so large, many of the shiny objects were a little larger.

Halfway through searching the nests, Sesh looked out of a particularly large one, and saw the many crows were flying and flapping everywhere. They were beginning to circle overhead. He climbed out of the big nest and stood on the edge. The crows began diving into the invaders, trying to push them out and off of the nests and cliff. Sesh covered his head, as a crow plowed into him. He was still standing in a precarious position on the edge of the large nest. As he started tilting towards the edge, Sesh realized that if he fell here, he would fall all the way to the ground, off the cliff. It would mean the end of his journey, the end of his opportunity to save his family, and his planet. As he leaned ever more over the edge of the nest, his arms spun in a tight circle, trying to correct his balance, to no avail. He was not a bird, not an angel.

Suddenly, Pip was there, large and commanding. He rested his full-sized angelic hand lightly on Sesh's back, and gently pushed him back into the center of the nest. Sesh slid and rolled down the sloped side of the nest, ending up facedown, when he came to a stop. The ammonia from the bird excrement smelled sharp and overwhelming, in his nostrils. He pushed himself to his hands and knees, looking down directly in front of him, and there it was, covered in bird poop and pieces of dried bone. A purple marble swirling internally with a white spinning mist. If one looked closely, a faint sparkle of light could be seen flickering from time to time, like small lightning bolts amongst the swirling clouds of a thunderstorm.

Reaching for it, Sesh was going to secure it when a crow swooped in and snatched it up. Flapping its wings vigorously, the shadow crow began rising into the air, only to be knocked out of the sky by a large twilight colored cat. Josephine wrapped the bird in all four legs, and bore it to the bottom of the nest, right in front of Sesh.

"GREAT JOB JOSIE!"

Leaning forward, Sesh plucked the soul marble out of the grasp of the crow's powerful talons. He swiftly deposited the marble into his pocket, then turned and started climbing back out of the crow city.

Running and dodging the dive-bombing crows, he made rapid progress towards the outskirts of the nest conglomeration. Looking back, he could see the others were hot on his heels, following closely. The closer they got to the edge of the clusters of nests, the less the crows harassed them. They hadn't been able to get close to injuring any of them since Sir Trillion Pippenstein the Third went into full angel mode. His presence alone was enough to frighten many of the shadow crows into hiding. The ones that didn't, circled and kept a close eye on the invaders, ready to protect their young and nests if necessary.

On top of the cliff, there was a tree line that the small group rushed into. They each celebrated in their own way, one smiled, two whooped in joy, and another merely sauntering and sashaying her cattail magnanimously. Clearly, it was she who saved the day. They all celebrated and cheered the near disastrous victory.

"We got it Willy!"

"YES!!! Thank the Eternal!"

Grinning, Sesh asked, "What is next? What does this mean?"

"It means the second you hand that to me, my soul will begin its judgement, so that I can pass on, into the celestial city of Heaven."

"I… I don't want you to go yet, though."

"I know baby brother, but this is what must be done. I do not have much longer as a fading spirit, soon I will become a sprite, stuck in the middle, unable to press on, or to fail out."

"I know, I'm just really enjoying having you back in my life, if even for a little while, it will be like losing you all over again."

Smiling, Willard leaned in and hugged his little brother, squeezing him tightly. "I love you Seshy. You were always the best of us."

"I love you too Willy. I love you so much." Dropping the small marble into his hand, he released his brother from the hug. Immediately, they could see the changes taking place in Willy's body. His body initially gained substance, becoming more tangible in the universe. Then immediately, it started fading, becoming transparent again. Willard seeing and feeling how quickly the process was going, spoke quickly.

"Give my love to mom and dad. If you run into the girls, or Sebastian, please tell them I love them too, and help them anyway you can. If you don't see them, I'll look for them in Heaven, and tell them that you love them and miss them terribly. Be safe and know that I love you. I'm so immensely proud of you little brother."

As his words faded, so did his spirit. It faded into a light, which rose as fast as it faded, disappearing into the atmosphere. Sesh stared after him, in quiet sadness, tears running down his face. It was hard to see his brother go, but he knew that Willard would be in a better place, and that it would last for eternity.

"I love you, Willard, good-bye, I'll miss you."

Josephine stood watching, with Pip back in his small form, sitting on her back, like he was riding a feline horse. They knew there was nothing they could do to help ease the pain that Sesh was feeling right now. Still, they offered companionship as Josie walked a little closer to where he stood and nuzzled him softly against his leg. They shared the silent comradery in the stillness of the moment.

Chapter Twenty-One
Lightning and Bugs

Sighing, Sesh said, "Let's get a move on. I'd like to get home and tell my mom and dad about seeing Willy."

"Yes, let's get you home."

They headed further into the woods, finding a small deer trail, and following it. After a mile of easy hiking, they came across a fork in the trail. One looked to be heading back towards the cliff, and the others off into the forest. The three friends decided the best path to take was the one of the ones through the woods. It was another old deer trail, which went through several low brushes, and thorny paths but was still a far cry better than trying to descend the cliff. If they tried that, they could head back towards the gazebo, and their canoe. It didn't seem like there was much further they could go with that canoe, anyway, considering the waterfall and rocks that riddled the creek bed. It just reinforced the idea that forward was the best option, even with Gabriels's advice.

"I wonder how much time we have left to get to where we are supposed to go. I'm supposed to find a holy weapon of some sort, as Gabriel said, and I quote, 'possibly not unlike mine.' I don't know if he is being figurative, because his weapon is holy, or if he were meaning that what I would find is a mighty sword, that I don't know how to use, that looks just like his."

"I don't know Sesh, I would imagine it's going to be pretty obvious, when we do find it. A holy weapon, just that description alone, can literally classify as anything."

"Anything?"

"Yes, in fact, anything, or anyone. I guess what that means is what you're looking for, is something that is from heaven, or blessed by heaven, which could be used as a weapon for your journey into purgatory."

"It's just wild to me, to think that I haven't even actually been in purgatory. I've been in this maze for what feels like ages."

"I totally understand that, just remember that it's incredibly rare that anyone actually makes it out of this maze."

"Wait, couldn't you be my holy weapon?"

"No, not technically. You didn't find me; I've been with you since your birth."

"That's right, I just didn't see you. Well, technically we found Josephine here, could she classify as a holy weapon?"

"In a sense, she could… though I sense she was not blessed by Heaven. A Sphynx who remembers their heritage are usually not all that altruistic, usually- they are quite 'fur'- ocious."

'The fairy speaks the truth, I am a warrior of Ra, the sun god. While the Eternal is the ultimate power that is, Ra is in my chain of command.'

Squinting at Josephine, scowling, Pip said, "You know I'm not a fairy. Are you a housecat?"

Ignoring them both, Sesh questioned, "Ra? He's real?"

'Indeed. He is not the almighty God, but he is a god still. All gods are subordinate to the one and only Eternal.'

"How many gods are there? I know the bible says that it was a commandment not to put any god before the one true God…."

"That's because there is no god that's before the one true God. It doesn't mean that there aren't other gods."

'The infant bird is correct again. I was taught that your world has a vast number of gods recognized by its people. There was a rather bloody religion that came out of a boot shaped country, that really suppressed the recognition of the other deities. That was a designed plan, the Eternal did warn that no other god should be put before Them. They were punished, and he utilized his faithful as a catalyst to deliver said punishment.'

Pip was visibly shaking, and glaring at Josephine, but because of the seriousness of the subject, he didn't interrupt her. The moment she finished speaking, he practically shouted, "INFANT BIRD!? Listen here you kitten…."

Josephine just stared at him, then began cleaning herself by licking her twilight-colored paw and rubbing it across her face. She was clearly unphased by the small angel's fury. Sesh laughed at the antics of the two friends.

"So, are all the deities that I've learned about real?"

Calming down a little but still shaking, Pip responded, "Most of them, I'm sure. Regardless of how many there are they are merely tools and subordinates of the Eternal. The Eternal utilizes the other gods to run the finer intricacies of the planet. It's not like They aren't capable, it's just that They like to relax like everyone else. In fact, the true absolute meaning of life is to seek out the most comfort possible. Everyone has their own version of comfort, and we should all find out what that is."

They walked along the forest deer trail for several more minutes without speaking, just in quiet contemplation. When they came to a fork in the trail, they took the right fork without even thinking, like they were out for a casual walk through the woods, looking for the perfect picnic spot. After travelling like this for several miles, occasionally sharing a small exchange of words, they came across a weathered wooden sign, in the middle of the trail. They would have to walk off of the trail, or climb over the sign, in order to continue on their path. The sign read:

One Hour Remaining.
Hurry Sesh, Death Approaches.
Dead End.

"Do you think this is one of those signs I'm not supposed to read?"

"Hmm… Could be. I definitely see a trail ahead. What do you want to do?"

'Continue the direction we are going.'

"Okay."

They scooted around the sign and continued walking down the deer trail. It wasn't much further; they came to a dead end."

"I guess that sign was telling the truth."

"Oh, the signs cannot lie. They are divine messages. They can mislead, but not lie. For instance, if it said: Dead End, and we happened to find a passageway through the dead end, it doesn't mean that the sign lied, it merely means that the road here has dead ended. We just forged our own path. It's like I said before, since the beginning, the Eternal gave humanity the right to choose."

"I understand. Let's look around and see if there's a route through this dead end."

'I have found a path.'

Josephine was sitting with her front paws placed inside an exceedingly small rabbit hole through the underbrush. Her hind haunches were in the air, and her tail wagged back and forth in excitement. She could smell the small rodents that have used this trail. Sesh walked over and got down on both of his knees, leaning forward to stick his head into the hole, next to Josephine.

"Yea Josie, I don't know if I'm going to be able to fit into this tiny rabbit path."

'You can fit, just wiggle like a worm.'

"I tell you what, go through that, and see if it widens up. If it goes more than one hundred feet without getting bigger, we will have to find another path."

'Okay.' Josephine could walk with her head in line with her back, without hitting the brush branches above her. After thirty seconds, Josephine came back. *'It is clear after twenty feet.'*

"Okay, let's do this. Pip, come along behind me, in case you have to pull me out."

Sesh got on his belly and slithered like a serpent through the small tunnel through the brush. After twenty feet, just like Josephine said, the whole trail widened up, and opened up. He was able to climb to his feet, still surrounded completely by brush.

Smiling, Sesh looked around, and walked forward through the beautiful brush tunnel that surrounded him. The brightness inside the tunnel was fading quickly, as the brightness outside began to dim rapidly, with the setting sun.

"We aren't going to be able to see each other very soon. It will be very dark."

'*I will be able to see just fine…*' Josephine's words trailed off, as they all noticed the happenings. The instant he said the word 'dark' Sesh witnessed the first firefly light its bum and glow brightly for a few moments, before winking back out. As if the first firefly was the conductor, the chorus of fireflies lit the tunnel like a flickering candle. There were millions of lightning bugs, flickering on and off, but granting enough light for Sesh to see. He walked slowly through the mass of insects, being careful where he stepped, so as not to kill too many.

As they walked through the lit tunnel, Sesh saw the top of a wooden sign, completely covered with fireflies. He looked over at Pip and made eye contact.

"I think we ignore that sign there and press onwards."

"I agree."

'Yes. There is a portal ahead, I can see it. It is swirling with lightning."

"Let's go!"

Pip zipped forward, his little wings a blur, as a hummingbirds' wings are, when in flight. Josephine was right behind him, leaping from a dark spot on the ground, to a different dark spot on the ground, so as not to injure any of the bugs. Sesh did his best to follow them, but the bugs were beginning to swirl and swarm. There were so many that Sesh lost visibility, only being able to see the glow of the bugs as they swarmed his face and body.

Sesh pulled his shirt up over his eyes, so that he wouldn't get bugs climbing all over his face. He stopped worrying about smashing the insects with his footsteps, and just plowed through in the direction he last saw Pip and Josephine, towards the lightning portal. These portals always showed what the generalized theme was inside. This one was lightning, inside the swirling cloud.

"I hope it's not a portal inside a lightning storm, which would be incredibly difficult to dodge and make it through unscathed. Guys, I can't see anything, I had to cover my face because of the sheer quantity of lightning bugs."

'Just keep walking forward, you are about thirty feet away from a clear spot. The bugs are not coming near the portal, so there is a five-to-ten-foot circle surrounding it.'

"Thank you, Josie."

Sesh busted through the bug swarm, and felt a weight rapidly lift off of his clothes and body. It was surprising how much millions of fireflies weighed when they all landed and crawled all over one's clothing. Sesh stood there, staring into the portal, which was sparkling with streaks of lightning across its surface. Occasionally, a bolt of lightning would strike the center, then fork out in every direction. As he watched in silence, he kept waiting for the thunder that never came. The only sound he could hear was the buzz and hum of billions of lightning bugs behind him.

"Are we sure we want to go through this one? Can we see if there's another one, I am not sure how a lightning storm is going to be easier than this tunnel to get through. Perhaps we can find another portal further on."

"Well, it's possible that what you need, is actually inside there. Just because lightning is striking, does not mean that lightning will actually be striking inside there. I do not think we have a choice."

'I just did a quick look around the rest of this area, I am confident that there was nothing else here except the bugs.'

Sighing, Sesh said, "I guess we go in then."

"Yes."

Taking a deep breath, then nodding at both Josephine and Pip, Sesh slowly stuck a tentative hand into the portal. The instant he did the portal acted like a super powered vacuum. His hand was held tight, sucking him quickly into the portal. Pip and Josephine quickly followed.

Chapter Twenty-Two
Beans

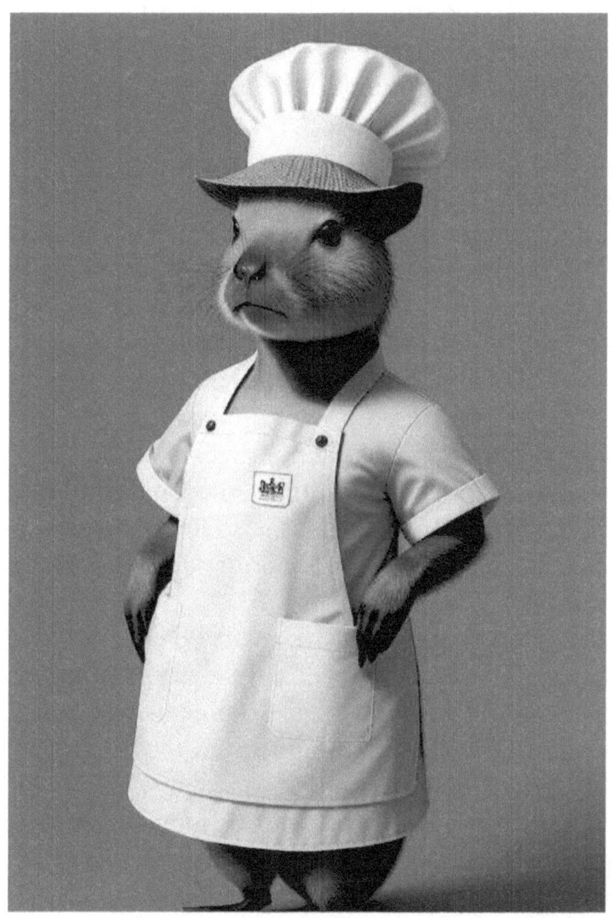

The trail into the bright purple flowers switched back and forth on itself over and over again, like a chef folding dough for pizza. It never gained altitude, or dropped any, just simply zigged and zagged back and forth through the dense forest. Without losing her good mood, Katie just pressed on singing when she wasn't humming.

When the smell of baking bread tickled her nose, she paused in the path for a moment. A huge grin spread across her face, because compared to the spoiled fare in her homemade satchel, a meal of freshly baked bread would be absolutely divine. Katie hurried and followed the wonderful smell of freshly baked bread down the trail that twisted and turned a little more before suddenly opening up into a large wide glade, with a quaint little cottage, pressed tightly against the tree line at the far end. The cottage had a little bit of wood smoke coming from the chimney, and a cheery yellow light shining out of the window, in the rapidly dimming light from the sun.

The fireflies flickered and sputtered in the evening glow, along the tall grass, just before the low brush that grew along the trail, the cottage, and the tree line. Katie edged her way closer to the cottage, still smelling that wonderful aromatic smell of freshly baked wheat bread. It was as if she was being pulled along by the smoke, like an old fashioned black and white cartoon character. As she approached the cottage, she could occasionally catch the higher pitched squeaking sound of someone singing in the small building.

"Freeeeessssssshhhh Breaaaaaaaaaad! OOOH how you maaaaake the woooooorld goooo roooounnnddd! FREEESSSSHHH BREAAAAAD!!!"

So close to the building, she worried her muffled shoeless footsteps would be heard, but at least she could finally see through the window. Standing in front of a fireplace, with a large cast iron Dutch oven placed in the cooking position, in front of it, was a large capybara, the size of a short woman, or a large child. This capybara was wearing a frilly white apron with a light gray undershirt, and a large white chef's hat. The adorable capybara had a light brew, coffee colored fur that covered its entire body, and huge black eyes that matched its happy mouse face perfectly. The capybara gave the illusion of extreme joy and happiness, and Katie wanted nothing more than to likewise squeal in joy and give the large creature a hug and a snuggle.

"Freshly BAAAAAKEDDDD BREEEAAAAAAAAAAAAAAAAAD! GET IN MYYYY BEEELLLLLYYYYY!!!" The creature pulled the cast iron Dutch oven from the fire with a matching set of white frilly oven-mitts. When the lid was removed, a far more intense smell was released, that seemed to wind up and flick the inside of Katie's nose.

Katie's stomach growled at the thought of putting some of that heavenly looking bread into her stomach. She decided then, that she would knock on the door, and see if she could get some. Afterall, what kind of capybara was ever mean?

KNOCK, KNOCK, KNOCK

"Ooh! Company?!? On a day like today!?" The high-pitched childlike voice from the human-sized capybara came from the other side of the door.

The door creaked open, and the capybara peaked one of its large black eyes through the crack that was made.

"Oh dear! What is this? A human girl? What in the world?"

"Hi… I'm Katie, I smelled your bread, and… I'm really hungry."

"Oh Dear! Oh Dear! Indeed. Come here, sweet child. Get some of this freshly baked bread, oh dear. I just pulled it out of the oven. I just love freshly baked bread!" The capybara said the last three words almost singingly, as it flung the door open wide, and ushered Katie in quickly.

"My name is Beans. Oh dear. Please share some of my fresh bread with me. I just pulled it from the oven. Oh dear. Oh, dear indeed. I just said that didn't I? Oh dear."

"Thank you, Beans, it's super nice to meet you."

"Oh dear. Yes, yes, come, eat some of this bread, try some of my bean paste, yes dear, it is quite lovely."

"Thank you so much."

Katie devoured two slices of bean spread on fresh bread. The flavor exploded in her mouth. It was rich in spices and was as smooth as lightly melted butter. It was truly a flavor Katie would seek out, for the rest of her life.

"This is the best thing I've ever tasted Beans. It is utterly amazing, how did you get out here, in the middle of this place?"

"Oh dear, the Doomed Maze? It has been my home for many, many years. Oh dear, are you passing through or stuck here?"

"I'm passing through, I've been given a task to save a stranger, but I don't even know how to save myself, let alone him."

"Oh dear, it will be okay, yes, yes. These things have a way of figuring themselves out along the way. Yes, yes. Have some more freshly baked bread with bean paste. Oh dear."

Beans shuffled around and cleaned up the very tidy kitchen in the corner of this little cottage. Katie noticed a comfortable-looking chair in one corner, and a small bed along the opposite wall. The center of the floor was covered by an intricately designed rug, which looked hand woven. The color scheme of the entire room was a beautiful burgundy and a deep forest green. The rug had geometric shapes, each shape's color alternating between burgundy and green. The blanket on the bed was burgundy and green squares.

"Beans, I really like your cottage, it is really pretty, and peaceful."

"Oh dear, yes, yes, I built it myself. I had help from my dear Greggory, he is truly kind. Oh dear, Greggory has not been here for a long time, I wonder how he is doing, yes, yes. Greggory is a half-giant, he has been here longer than I, yes, yes."

"A real giant?"

"Oh dear, yes, yes. He was slain by a human who became king for doing so. The Quran said so. Greggory is a Phillistine giant, formerly known as the Goliath. They gave him that nickname because he was so big and mighty. Yes, yes."

"The Quran? Are you Muslim Beans?"

"Oh dear, yes, yes."

"That's really neat. It's always inspiring to me to see all the many religions, and how they come together."

"Oh dear, yes, yes, all religions have merit here. This is the crossroads for all. Oh dear. I do wonder where Greggory has been."

Feeling like she may be making the large, adorable capybara uncomfortable, Katie decided to switch subjects, "Is it okay if I take a small nap here? I am genuinely exhausted."

"Oh dear, yes, yes, sweet child, sleep on my bed. I will watch over you. Oh dear."

Katie was suddenly onset with far more exhaustion and weary than her adrenaline riddled body had on her way into the forest. It was as if the relaxing environment, with a full stomach, soothed her mind towards a sleeping state. She stood, and walked over to the small bed, then lay down on top of the blankets. She fell fast into a deep, dreamless sleep. Beans stood vigil over an unknowing Katie as she slept, without moving, without speaking, just standing, facing the door as her steadfast guardian.

Eight hours later, Katie awoke, feeling fully rested. The first thing she saw was the large plump cake factory of back side attached to a capybara, as it stood still as a statue, facing the door. The kind creature meant what he said, when he said he would watch over her while she slept. This brought tears brimming in her eyes, because no one had been so kind to her in a great many years. She stretched, feeling the muscles in her back and arms burn, it was a good feeling. Her gentle rustling caught the attention of the steadfast Beans.

"Oh dear, yes, yes, did you sleep well?"

"Yes, I did, thank you for allowing me to rest."

"Yes, yes."

"I am going to continue on my journey, what is the best way through the forest? Maybe towards another door or portal of some sort?"

"Oh dear, eat first, I will draw a map for you. Yes, yes."

"Thank you."

"Yes, yes, I will make you large shadow crow eggs for your bread, not freshly cooked, oh dear, not freshly cooked at all, still good though. Yes, yes."

"I don't know what a shadow crow is, but it sounds delicious."

As Beans went about getting breakfast ready for both of them, he seemed saddened by something. Big, thick, droplets of water welled up in his eyes, and fell from his face. Beans began to cry silently, as he cooked.

"Are you okay Beans? What's the matter?"

"Oh dear, I was once a young, spry, capybara. I loved to romp around and play with everything. One early morning, I was cooking breakfast... I was making bean spread, eggs, and fresh bread for my family and me. Oh dear, we were attacked by a pack of burning hell hounds. I watched, as they chased us down. I watched them... oh dear, oh dear, oh dear." Beans stopped speaking and cried uncontrollably for a few minutes. He continued cooking through the tears, making sure not to burn the eggs, or the bean spread he was heating.

"Oh dear, oh dear. I escaped. My father sacrificed himself, oh dear, they all did, for me to escape."

Katie watched as Beans cried softly for a little longer, then took a deep breath, and began to dab his eyes with the hem of his apron. She stood and walked towards the capybara, lightly putting her hand on the creature's shoulder. He turned, looked her in the face, then embraced her. They held each other for five full minutes, until Beans pulled away, and nudged the top of her head with his nose.

"Oh dear, your food is getting cold. Oh dear, come eat, come eat."

"Thank you, Beans."

"Oh dear, it is nothing. Pardon my sadness, whenever I make beans and eggs, the memories jerk my tears out. Yes, yes."

Katie ate what may have been the greatest breakfast of her life. The eggs had a perfect creamy texture and the exact amount of savoriness. They coupled flawlessly with the creamy, lightly lumpy beans, and the fried, textured bread.

"Oh dear, yes, yes, come see."

Katie saw the map that Beans had drawn on a small, flat board. It was crudely drawn, but easily decipherable. Katie could see the cottage, and the trail she came in on. It clearly showed the way back towards the central hub where the portals were. The other direction showed another trail, which seemed to twist and turn, splitting off in many different directions, most of which led to dead ends. Katie saw four distinct circles, with spirals drawn inside the center of them. Looking towards the capybara, she decided to ask, "Those are portals, right?"

"Oh dear, yes, yes."

"Which is the best one to take?"

"Oh dear, I do not know, not at all. Yes, yes."

Looking at the portals, Katie saw one that had a heart drawn in the center of the spiral, another that had a beetle of some sort. Looking closely at the remaining two, she saw that one had a fish, and the other a lightning bolt. After thinking about the difference in the four portals, Katie decided to pick randomly, since she didn't know anything further about them. She labeled them one through four in her mind, then asked Beans, "Pick a number between one and four."

"Oh dear, hmm, I pick two, yes, yes."

"Two? Okay! Lightning portal it is!"

The next hour consisted of Beans adding some sacked lunches to Katie's satchel. Upon opening the satchel, he found some old stale bread, moldy meats, and cheese that had gone blue. With an appalled look, he swiftly threw the entirety of the foods Katie had found in the desert temple into the fire. He deemed it unfit to be consumed.

"I didn't know they had gotten that bad, it seems like such a long time ago that I even collected them."

"Oh dear, not good to eat, no, no. Make you very sick. Yes, yes."

With a freshly packed satchel, Katie was certain not to forget, she headed out the door. After hugging Beans goodbye, she walked into the woods, and followed the complex trail to the portal with the lightning swirl. With a sense of finality rumbling deep within her body, Katie felt like she would be coming to the end of her journey soon.

When she got to the portal, it crackled and sparkled as lightning swirled and spread out from the center to the outside edges of the frame. Taking a deep breath, she thought about Beans, and his lonely existence there in the glade. She hopped Greggory would come visit him soon, as everyone needed companionship and a friend. Then with a deep breath, Katie stepped off into the lightning portal, excited to see what was next.

Chapter Twenty-Three
Greggory

Beans watched as the blonde human called Katie walked into the wilderness, her eyes planted firmly on the wooden tablet that he had produced for her. He stared after her, feeling a peculiar feeling in the deepest parts of his bowels. Not knowing if it was fear and dread, or the simple need to defecate, he hurried off to his restroom location on the other side of the cottage, just past a sandy hill.

"Oh dear, maybe I must do the poo. Yes, yes."

After dropping off his waste, then burying it, Beans headed back to his cottage. He never understood how so many of his kind would be so inconsiderate and disgusting with their waste. Cleanliness was the key to a happy life, and fresh bread. He decided that would go prepare his next loaf of bread. Afterall, most of his bread had gotten eaten the previous day and that morning. It also helped that he really did love fresh bread. He thought about that human girl, and how sweet and nice she was. She had knowing eyes, for one so young. What a tough journey she was on.

KNOCK…KNOCK!

The shaking of the entire cottage, and the rattling of the dishes that came with the two hard knocks at the door told Beans exactly who was there. Only one person would ever knock that hard, and to do it twice. It had to be Greggory the Goliath. Beans bounced with excitement, and quickly waddled to the door, throwing it open to reveal a towering man.

"Oh dear! Greggory! You have returned, after so long. Yes, yes!"

Standing in the doorway was a giant of a man. He stood at well over eight feet tall, with a huge bushy black beard, streaked with grey. His long dark curly hair fell past his shoulders. He had penetrating eyes that seemed to bore into a person and rippling muscular arms that were capable of tearing a person apart, limb from limb. The giant wore a large bear skin rug as a tunic, with a handwoven beige undercoat that looked like a rug that belonged on a kitchen floor. He also wore what looked like handmade pants and leather shoes. Looking closely at the clothing, it was clear that the stitching was made with clumsy hands, likely those that are far too large to be able to properly manage a needle and thread.

"Hello my dear Capy friend. How I missed thee."

Greggory spoke in a very deep, slow voice, which seemed to rumble and roll as a mudslide would fall down a rocky precipice. It crackled and churned in the air, as if a storm were brewing. Though it was rough and deep, it gave off the presence of pure kindness. The giant was truly a softy at heart.

"Oh dear, please come in, yes, yes."

"I see you have taken up your anxious mutterings of 'oh dear,' and 'yes, yes,' again. Did something happen, Beans, which would cause you that level of stress?"

"Oh dear, I certainly did not even realize I was speaking that way again." Beans' childlike high-pitched voice seemed to gain strength, as he looked inwards and listened to the words he was uttering.

"You have."

"Oh dear, well, yes…. yes… erm… eh hem. I mean, yes, I did have a strange visitor, just yesterday, and she left today, in fact. It seems that this is the time for visitors, indeed, now that you've come too."

"Truly? Who was this girl? A new lady love perchance?"

"Oh dear, no, no!" Beans fur took on a flushed, deeper cocoa appearance, "She was a human girl, Greggory!"

"A human girl? In the doomed maze? Was she one of the forsaken?"

"Oh de… eh hem. No, she was on a task, a journey of some sort to save a stranger, she said. She gave me a sense of ease and brought me back to a simpler time when I was a young capybara."

"Truly? And you did not sob all over her like a withering mewling little babe?"

"I did no such thing," Beans lied, with a wink.

Chuckling in a way only Greggory the Goliath could, he just nodded appreciatively. They sat in silence for a little while, enjoying each other's company. Until Greggory decided to ask more questions.

"Which way did she go? Back towards the central hub?"

"Oh dear, no, no… She went towards the portal of electricity. She picked randomly; I drew her a map."

"Interesting."

"Greggory, do you know what is in that portal? I have not dared enter."

"Yes. It is a place where she will have to face her deepest, darkest, fears. A place where she must come to recognition of who she is on the inside. It is not easy for anyone, but I believe it is possible for everyone, so they then can find out their true nature, or at least a piece of it."

"Oh dear, that sounds terrifying indeed. I hope she does well, she really was very kind, she had the most awful decrepit food stuff in her satchel. I was so disturbed that I threw it into the fire in a fit of rage."

"A fit of rage huh?"

"Well, no, but I did throw it in the fire, it was all rotten and spoiled."

"Yes, well, time does move strangely in the Doomed Maze. It does not surprise me her food was spoiled and rotten. What could have been gathered as soon as yesterday, may have actually been last week. Time is not controlled by anyone but the Eternal, and They have deemed it to be sporadic at best in this place."

Rubbing his large round belly, Beans shudders a little. "Oh dear, would you like to go for a walk with me, my dear Greggory? My innards have been a dastardly unsettling thing of late."

"You feel it too then?"

"Oh dear, Yes, yes."

The two friends, one half the size of the other, walked outside and towards the trails that led into the forest. They both walked in silence for a little while, analyzing the feeling they felt inside their bowels. How was it possible that they were both feeling the same sick feeling of dread and fear? Beans really wanted to know.

"How come we both feel dread and fear in our innards Greggory?"

"I do not know, my dear Beans. I have not felt this feeling since I faced the musician king. It was the last time I had this feeling, staring at him across the battlefield. The single fateful fight that would determine the fate of millions. In retrospect, I am glad I lost for I fear I would have been far worse off when trying to balance my scales. I was fortunate enough to have been given the opportunity to stay in the Doomed Maze as a caregiver of the gardens and trees."

"Yes, yes. I am glad too, because I would not have ever met you, and never have gained you as my best friend. I love you my dear Greggory."

"I love you too Beans."

They walked around the forest trails for an hour, talking about the unimportant things here and there, until they found themselves facing the lightning portal. Staring at it, not getting within twenty feet of the transportation device, they both began thinking about the girl that went through. One of them had never met her, but his closest friend had, and he thought very highly of her.

"Katie was her name, oh dear. I do hope she is going to be okay, yes, yes."

"Katie will be fine, Beans." Greggory said calmly, trying to calm his friend in turn, "Let's head on back and get us some of your bean spread and freshly baked bread, shall we?"

"Oh yes, yes! I just looooove fresssssssshhlyyy baaaaaaaked Breaaaaaaaaad!"

Greggory chuckled a little as he followed the swiftly waddling capybara back to his cottage. Beans was a pure creature, full of kindness and love. He wondered how Beans ended up in the Doomed Maze, for he had never been killed. It probably had something to do with his celestial nature, being one of the creatures of the in-between. Beans had told Greggory how he had run for his life from the hellhounds, his family sacrificing themselves so that he, the youngest, could escape. The kindest thing a person could do was to give their life for the wellbeing of another. He was happy that he had his best friend here in the maze, for the afterlife would be a lot slower and harder without him, even if it were sometimes a long time between visits.

Back at the cottage, Beans whipped up some bread dough, kneading it and pressing it like a professional baker. Indeed, he was as close to a professional baker as any in the entirety of the in-between lands. He just specialized in baking bread, instead of cakes and treats. Beans decided to cook up a little bit of the eggs in a soup of chicken broth, to go with the bread. He did not know where his supplies came from, they just stayed stocked in his small cabinet. When he used some, they would be replaced after he closed the door. It was his never-ending giver of food. He would never test the boundaries of that, as his level of gratitude towards the free food stuff was beyond reproach.

Beans and Greggory ate their fill, enjoying the company and succulent meal together. After supper they sat out on the front porch. Greggory sat on a large tree stump, and Beans on a small three-legged stool. The feeling of dread inside their stomachs only seemed to grow, as time pressed on.

"This feeling is not going away, Beans."

"Oh dear, no, no, it is most definitely not."

"We should depart this area, Beans."

"Oh dear, I cannot Greggory. You know as well as I, that if I depart from this area, it will no longer be protected from the senses of those of ill intent. I cannot leave, this is my place until I depart from this existence, and when I do, the sensory magic will remain. Oh dear, you must go Greggory, yes, yes. I feel it too, and you must go, so you do not face what I must."

"I will not leave you to face what's coming alone, Beans."

Reaching forward, and grabbing the big man's hand, Beans looked to his greatest friend and smiled, large tears rolling down his face.

Without anxiety and full of conviction, Beans said confidently, "Thank you, Greggory. You really are the best friend a lowly capybara could ask for."

"And you are mine."

The dreadful feeling reached a crescendo as they smelt the smoke before they could see what was coming towards them. Turning towards the central hub, they began to see a flickering green light. Together, they stared off towards the approaching green flames, which ignited the surrounding forest, like so much tinder.

Chapter Twenty-Four
Blackened Heart

Morana left the Sireni path in disgust. She hated having to be deterred from her true goal, which is not allowing that human to escape. Walking down the wide trail towards the central hub, she began tasting the air, wondering if her more physical senses would enable her to follow the girl, when her mental ones, her aura-based ones, were being fooled. She primarily used her mental senses to follow the girl, like when she was in the desert, but this time, Morana did not truly know where the girl went, so she would have to go with a more basic form of tracking. Taste.

In the central hub, Morana began tasting the air, and smelling the different areas for the scent of the human girl. She was like a bloodhound, tracking a racoon. Stopping at each and every pathway, Morana would give it a thorough inspection, finding she liked the flavor of two paths more than all of the others. Bouncing back and forth between a path containing a creek, and one containing a long winding trail, Morana decided the one with the creek tasted a bit too much like an angel and a sphynx, then it did a human girl, so she went the other direction. Perhaps, after dealing with the pesky rodent of a girl, she would return and tackle the angel and sphynx.

"I found your trail little girl."

Morana began her strange flickering gait down the winding trail, igniting everything that would burn. If it didn't catch fire by her mere closeness, she would scratch a nail across the surface of whatever it was, just to set it aflame. She felt the magic as the environment changed as if the world itself changed around her. She had crossed the invisible barrier that was the portal, into this new area. The moment she did, the flavor of the air changed as well. It was full of smoke and roasted wheat grain. She spat in disgust, then tasted the air again for the other flavors. She found that there was also the underlying taste of a giant and a rodent. The taste of the girl was here, but there was no direction to it, it seemed to swirl and twist in the atmosphere, hidden and suppressed by those of the stronger smells.

She continued her destructive path down the switchback trail burning everything. The once beautiful vibrant purple flower lined pathway was now a blackened and charred wasteland. The pathway opened up into a large glade in front of her. She was surprised to be greeted with an unusual sight. There, sitting on a log and a small three-legged chair were the giant and the rodent, staring at her as she approached. She noticed that this giant had to only be half, because he was far too small to be a full giant. Morana looked around, not seeing the girl anywhere. Perhaps she was inside the small building these creatures would call home.

Stopping around fifty feet from the giant and rodent, Morana stared at them, as they both got to their feet. The giant stepped in front of the large capybara, as if in defense. She stared a bit longer before speaking in her demanding hissing gargle, "Bring… Me…. The…. Human…. Girl."

"Oh dear, oh dear, oh dear, oh dear."

Glancing down at his best friend, Greggory looked at the demon, "You will find no human here. Be gone demon, you are not welcome here."

"You… do… not… command… me."

Beans cowered behind Greggory, uttering over, and over again his anxiety driven words, "Oh dear, oh dear, oh dear, no, no, no, no, oh dear."

"Be gone demon!" Greggory shouted, his voice a mountain crumbling into pieces. He hoisted a large metal club, brandishing it at the demoness. Beans did not know where Greggory got the club, as he did not have it moments ago.

Practically whispering, but with all the venom and vehemence in the world, Morana pointed at the half-giant and said, "Dieeee…."

Large green flames erupted from the ground a Greggory's feet, engulfing him completely. His clothing quickly burnt away, leaving behind only the charred leather that was stripped of all fur and hair. Shouting in pain and anger, Greggory stepped out of the green eruption of flames, and towards Morana. She was surprised, as the giant began to charge her.

"Giants have an innate affinity for fire, Demon!"

He reared back with his metal club to strike his dangerous foe, but the demoness was quicker. Morana flickered forward, slamming a flaming fist into the chest of the charging Giant, sending him flying back into the nearby trees. His club went flying, lost forever in the forest around the glade. She flickered closer, trying to capitalize on his slow rise, and lack of a weapon, only to find him plunging a large bolder sized fist into the thin flaking flesh of her ribs. He had erupted out of the tall brush like a rocket, hoping to deal devastating damage to the frightening green demon. The strike sent her sliding backwards in the dirt, lighting the lower brush on fire, and causing her anger to spike. Her flaming horns burned brighter as she flickered forward once more, appearing behind the giant, and grabbing him by his swinging arm.

She twisted, showing incredible strength for having a body that was both decaying, burning, and thin, as she launched the giant back across the small glade, over near the cowering Beans. Greggory once again, rose to his feet bringing with him a large boulder from the ground. He launched it with incredible speed and accuracy at the demon but was dismayed to see that the rock melted into magma and slag as it approached her intense blaze.

Smirking, Morana reveled in the feeling of battle. Giants were resilient, but ultimately, they were a one trick pony. He could handle the strength of her heat, and being thrown around, but his capability to do her harm was nearly non-existent. She flickered towards the giant once more.

"Where... is... the... human girl? Tell me!"

"Never!"

Greggory moved and met Morana halfway across the glade, throwing wild punches, but hitting nothing but air. The heat was causing his skin to blister, and turn a dark red, almost black in places. He knew there was no winning this battle, but hopefully he could distract her enough for Beans to escape.

"Beans, run!"

Morana did not bother attacking anymore at this moment, allowing the Giant to cook and exhaust himself by throwing pointlessly slow punches and jabs. He stepped back, grabbing another rock and hurled it at her, only for the result to be the same, slag and magma.

Beans just watched and wept loudly. A large puddle formed beneath his feet as he lost control of his bladder. The truest fear he had ever experienced was watching his best friend face the demon, Morana. He watched as Morana reached out, grabbed Greggory by one of his arms as he swung his rapidly weakening and slowing punches. Beans watched in horror as he could visibly see her heat diminish, so she could prolong the pain that Greggory was going through. Morana put a hand on the shoulder of Greggory, the smoke and smell of burnt meat and flesh came off his burning flesh. Then, Beans screamed, his vision going black for a moment, as he watched Morana give a quick jerk with the hand holding Greggory's wrist and pulled his arm free from his torso. She stuck a burning hand to the gaping hole that was his shoulder socket and cauterized the wound. She would make his suffering last. She had countless centuries fine tuning the art of her torture.

Beans fell to the ground, burying his tear and snot covered face in the dirt. He begged for Morana to stop, to no avail.

"Oh dear, please stop! Oh dear, oh dear."

Greggory fell to his knees and then just looked at his closest friend, the best friend he had ever had. The one he loved more than he loved anything in his entire existence. Greggory whispered just loud enough for Beans to hear over the snapping and popping of cooking meat, "It's okay Beans. I love you."

With those words, Morana placed her hands on the gentle giants' neck, causing the flesh to cook and burn immediately. Suddenly, she let go, as Beans spoke in a resigned anxiety free voice just loud enough for her to hear.

"The human girl left, many hours ago. She went through the electrical portal, just please don't hurt Greggory anymore… he is the gentlest of us… of all of us."

"Beans…. No…."

With those words of betrayal, tears fell down the giant's cheeks. His heart broke at the sadness that the entirety of Beans' being was lost because of his love for his best friend. Beans betrayed his mission, his purpose, and he will suffer because of it. One cannot simply break the pact of an innate purpose and not feel the backlash.

Morana smiled her ghastly flaming smile, with her mouth too large and teeth too plentiful. After hearing this utterance, she turned swiftly, snatched each side of the giant's head, then violently ripped it from his neck and shoulders. As his now headless and one-armed body fell to the ground, in a quickly widening pool of blood, Morana tossed the head at the rapidly aging capybara. She had no need to kill the rodent, he betrayed his meaning. He would face the punishment of one who does such and face the ravages of time from his entire existence. His last thoughts before blackness overtook him, were of his best friend, his love, Greggory the Goliath.

Morana stood still, pulling in her heat so she didn't speed up the process. She watched as the rodent rapidly grayed, thinned, and shriveled. His death was apparent moments ago, but the punishment of time was not to be diminished, even by death. He very quickly turned into a dried-out husk, of a once happy vibrant and bread loving capybara.

Morana could sense where the girl went again, the magics of this sanctuary gone with the betrayal of Beans the bread eating capybara. As she turned, she decided that the disgusting building these creatures called home, was unfit to remain. She burned it to the ground, then flickered towards the forest, catching everything on fire as she went.

As the fires raged around her, Morana came to each portal individually, first was the beetle portal, a place where she would undoubtedly find many insects to devour and eat, possibly growing her power even more. This was not going to be the case, because she was only after one thing, and that was the yellow headed human girl. Perhaps on her return, she will be able to come back through here. If so, she will enter this portal and consume it all.

The second portal was one with a heart. She considered that it was likely one with some quaint little village full of happy little fairies or garden gnomes. Things with hearts always led to some twisted little pure spirited village. She spit in disgust into the portal, watching the flaming liquid fly into the portal, and disappear. She watched as a curious reaction occurred after her flames entered the portal, a blemish appeared on the heart. It was small but black and cancerous. Thinking that this could only mean one thing, she laughed in glee. Morana then began to spit more globules of flaming goo into the portal, until the entire heart turned black, then crumbled to dust. The portal, no longer having a purpose, flickered twice, then winked out of existence. She loved the feeling of complete destruction. It complimented her purpose to life.

Coming to the third portal, still with the entirety of the forest ablaze around her, Morana saw that this portal had a fish on it. Swiftly pulling away from this portal in a rare case of fear, she knew if she entered it, there was a good chance she would be unable to continue her journey, likely even resulting in her death. Water was a natural obstacle for one such as her. In smaller quantities, such as the moat around her forgotten castle, she could desecrate the entirety of it with her heat alone, evaporating every particle of water and turning the many species living within, into small burnt corpses. This circumstance though, with the fish being the epitome of the portal, it was likely under or within a sea. Not even Hades himself had the power to evaporate an entire sea.

As Morana approached the final portal, she knew it was the one that would take her to her prey. She felt the culmination of her journey rapidly approaching. It was time she reminded the human, just from whom she tried to escape. As the first daughter of Lillith, Morana would not be denied. She stepped into the portal with electricity swirling out from the center, a lightning bolt glowing.

Chapter Twenty-Five
The Walking Dead

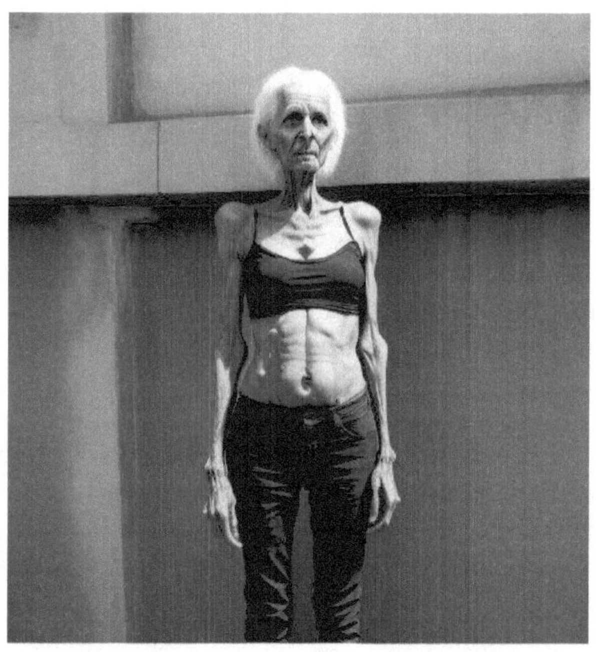

Sesh, Josephine, and Pip stepped through the lightning portal, feeling a surge of electricity that caused their hair and fur to stand on end. The moment they stepped foot on the grass of an impossibly large open field, Sesh felt an odd sensation. His entire body seemed to be tingling, and full of constantly stabbing needles. It was as if every muscle and layer of skin fell asleep all at once.

Turning to where Pip and Josephine were standing, he said, "Hey, do you guys feel—."

Stopping midsentence, he noticed that his two greatest friends and companions were completely still, hovering several feet off the ground. They did not look to be in pain, but they also did not look to be entirely alive. Their expressions were completely blank, without movement or sign of life. Rushing over, Sesh went to shake Pip, but his hands passed completely through his unmoving body. Testing it on Josephine, he got the same results. Both of their bodies were in suspended animation.

"What… is going on….?"

Sesh noticed something out of the corner of his eye. It was his own body, with the same blank expression, hovering a few feet off the ground in a standing position. It was at this point that he realized there was more to what was going on here than he originally believed. He also briefly considered the humor in being in a dreamlike state in an intangible dimension, while floating in a tangible dimension, while also being in a coma in another tangible dimension. The whole thing was just surreal.

"Truly is, turtles all the way down."

The time of day felt like mid-morning, with the sun around ten o'clock in the sky. Looking around, Sesh noticed that he stood in what he would guess was the center of an expansive, and impossibly flat grass field. The grass was cut incredibly short, almost as if he was standing on a golf green. There were very little changes to the environment, in any direction. He learned about those in history class and remembered laughing with the two other people in the class, that people actually mowed their grass for decoration and status symbols, instead of tilling up that part of their yard for their garden.

Suddenly, an immensely powerful voice spoke from every direction. It was as if the voice rumbled from every blade of grass and permeated from every molecule of air. It said, "Watch, and learn."

The pressure from the voice's power forced Sesh to his knees as the entire world changed. The grass rapidly turned brown, and withered, crumbling away with a small breeze that picked up. The heat was visible to the naked eye, with the wavering rays stretching and skewing everything in the distance, creating mirage like hazes of great seas. Tree's sprouted, and then burst into flame as the uncontrolled global warming killed the very things that were trying to consume the greenhouse gasses. Nature looked to be possibly catching up, or at least slowing the decline of the death of everything, until suddenly streaks from rockets, covered the skyline.

Then there was a series of large flashes, and hundreds of mountainous mushroom clouds climbed the sky. The winds picked up again, blowing the clouds away at a rapid pace, with the dirt turning a burnt orange. After-images of trees that were not there before, were blown away with the wind, like dust.

Suddenly, the planet beneath his feet rolled, twisting, and spinning. It only stopped when he was standing in a city. The dust covered everything, no vehicles moved, and the buildings were crumbling and empty. Half of them were broken and had fallen, and the other half were fragile guardians of the skyline, awaiting a good strong wind, to finish the job of returning this city to the desert landscape. There was no sign of life.

The planet under his feet whirled once again, to a small midwestern town. It was his town, Sparkstown. Sesh saw his happy mom, and his hardworking father. He saw his baby sister Eloise, playing in the dirt that was their front yard. His father was using a garden hoe to churn up the dirt in their barely surviving garden. There was little greenery, but the sprouts that fought bravely through the dirt gave a dirty brownish green to the environment around them proclaiming their existence, telling the world that they had not given up, and were still alive.

He watched as he himself as a small child came outside, picked up the small toddler, then put her in the car, for a trip to town. His father turned to him, holding out the hoe, sweat dripping down his face in roiling streams. Young Sesh rushed forward and grabbed the hoe, quickly chopping between the rows of dirty potatoes and other tuber style plants that were nearly the only thing able to be grown. He remembered thinking that it would be amazing to have a piece of fruit, as he hadn't had one in years. All they had to eat was potatoes and turnips, and the occasional piece of stringy meat from an unknown beast.

The vision swam a little, not changing completely, just advancing the time. He was in the car with his mother, but only as a viewer. He noticed that his younger self stayed with his father, working in the garden. There was a lot of work to do, after all. The car ride was quick, and his mother sang happily to the tiny Eloise in the back. Sesh couldn't remember the last time he had seen his mother this happy. She was such a broken woman now.

The vision flashed and sparkled again, then there was his mother and little sister returning to their barely able to run car from the public market. Mom needed to get some diapers and cleaning products for the little one. It was a mixed bag, because of all the death that happened to the younger children, and the overall stagnant birthrates, it created a market deficit for the need of the very items she got. He watched in horror, as five people stepped out of a nearby darkened alleyway, looking at his mom and baby sister. The elderly woman was the first to advance, a furious hunger on her face.

Knowing what was about to happen, Sesh screamed, "NO!"

He rushed forward, trying to stop the atrocity from happening, to no avail. He was unable to influence anything that the past contained. The vision flickered, and it started over as the people stepped out of the alleyway, again. Sesh stopped, and stared at them, tears rolling down his face, not wanting to watch, but unable to look away. He saw their faces, their human, sane faces. They were not of the waking dead.

Then like a light switch, the old lady's face changed, darkening, and angering. Her scowl scrunched her face up, as she let loose a bone chilling scream, then charged the unknowing mother and small child. The four people with the elderly lady ran after her, trying to stop her. The old lady was surprisingly fast, as she reached his mother and baby sister first. She shouldered into Sesh's mom, knocking her to the ground, where her head slammed painfully off the crumbling asphalt. She stood, trying to get to her daughter, when the old lady bent and grabbed the toddler, biting into her small arm. The arterial spray of the upper arm caused a warm sickly-sweet smell to invade the nostrils of everyone present.

Like a switch, the other people with the old lady also darkened visibly, their anger and hunger becoming uncontrolled. The distended bellies of each of them showed that they have not eaten anything in weeks. The kwashiorkor visibly present in their protein deficient bodies. The large dark hollows under their eyes showed they hadn't slept in weeks either and showed a significant lack of fluid and electrolyte intake. A woman, who looked to be the daughter of the old lady, grabbed the other arm of the screaming toddler, pulling and biting by the armpit. The amount of force between the two women, caused the weakened joint to separate from the shoulder, tearing the arm free. As the screams began to slow from the toddler as she quickly ran out of blood, Sesh's mom was screaming, trying to get to her feet to stop them, but the injury she took upon the initial shove had damaged something in her brain. Watching her daughter being eaten alive damaged something more within her mind and spirit. The largest man of the group turned to her as she moved to save her baby. He leapt at her, driving her back to the ground. He swung a large hammer fist into her face, three separate times, knocking her entirely unconscious.

Sesh wept. He did not know why the large man decided to attack his mom, but not try to consume her. He did not know why they targeted the young child over anything else in the area. Perhaps it was the base instincts of an animal predator preying on the young of other animals. He had imagined this situation a great many times since the day it happened, but it was never to this level of tragic chaos.

The world spun again, showing the funeral he had put on for his baby sister. He was the last child his parents had now. His mother's sunken face, one of defeat and unconscionable pain. His father's helpless look, not knowing what to do to save what was left of the woman he loved, knowing that it was never, ever going to be the same.

Sesh began to see, it wasn't just him that hurt, everyone hurt. He had to be strong, for all of them, so that he could end the chaos that overtook the planet he loved. Sesh had to accept that sometimes things were out of his control.

The same booming all-encompassing voice came again, "What did you learn?"

Crying, and breathing hard, Sesh said nothing for a few moments, just thinking in silence to himself. The voice patiently waited, not demanding it again, until Sesh finally spoke, "That sometimes things are out of my control, that I must continue this journey, so I can change the world for the better, for everyone."

"Acceptable."

Blackness checkered the world around him, until nothing remained but his own inner turmoil. Disassociating, Sesh felt like he was alone again, that not even Josephine or Pip were at his side anymore, even though they were merely feet away from him. They were facing their own inner demons, and he could only wish them the best, and wait for them to come through the darkness, to rejoin him at his side.

The green world of eternal grass faded back into view. Sesh stood around fifty feet away from where Josephine and Pip were hovering above the ground. He could no longer see his own body there and concluded that after he got his 'acceptable' he returned to his shell. Falling to his knees, he cried long deep sobbing cries of loss. It would be a long time, if ever, for him to be able to forget the memory of seeing his baby sister devoured in front of him.

Chapter Twenty-Six
Execution

Katie placed her foot down on a beautiful green open grassland. She could see miles and miles in every direction, with absolutely no change in the landscape. It was flat and empty, the only thing visible was grass. Walking in a large circle, and spinning, she suddenly noticed something. She saw herself, standing in midair, several feet off the ground. Her face was all slack-jawed and witless. She walked closer to her body and reached out to grab her own hand.

Her hand passed through her shells hand. She immediately realized that this was not a typical place, that she was in a dream state of sorts. Feeling the pressure of something all encompassing, Katie settled down into a low crouch, as if bracing herself for a strike from any direction. Then she heard an incredibly powerful voice, that seemed to be a vibration within her very soul. It was masculine and deep, with a slight accent that she could not place.

"Watch and learn."

Her vision of the world spun, as if inside a tornado. She saw the ice caps melt in the southern seas. The land masses on the continents shrank with the increase fluids in the oceans. The melted snow from the huge increase in global temperatures, left thousands and thousands of square miles of fertile farmable land in Antarctica. It has become a green oasis of life, on the swiftly browning planet, called Earth. Katie watched as the snow melted, all the way to the highest peaks of the many mountain ranges that the mightiest continent held. The raging rivers of pure untainted snow water flowed and created deep valleys and gorges. They ultimately flowed into tributaries that emptied into the green, brown sea.

As time moved in fast forward, Katie stared in wonder as buildings sprouted up from the ground. Thousands of people rushed around to create an existence in one of the last remaining viable places to live on the planet. She watched as large fertile plains became enormous farms for many diverse types of plants. Humanity seemed to grasp ahold of their last chance to survive on this planet. Time continued to be in fast forward, as the sea browned even more, the rivers and creeks began to dry up, as there was no more snow to melt. The rocks and shorelines around the southernmost continent became tainted with disease and death as millions of fish and sea life died. Soon, the encroaching decay of life pressed inwards, slowly turning the green continent of Antarctica into another barely survivable desert.

The world spun again, and Katie saw a familiar little city. Time slowed as the spinning world stopped and what she was seeing was her own home. There she was, as a little girl, crying and staring after her family as they walked down the road towards the city. She remembered wishing with all her might that she would be able to go with them, but they told her to take care of grampa. She didn't know at the time that this was the last time she would ever see them alive, ever again.

A ripple in the scene showed her something she had never seen before. Her family was there, walking into the city. They had a slow, unsteady gait. Skirting around the edges of town, they searched every trash can, and every gutter for anything to eat, finding nothing. Ultimately, ending up in a dirty dark alleyway, which came out onto the street near one of the last remaining markets that food may be able to be found. There in front of them was a woman and a small toddler. The woman was carrying a basket of diapers and cleaning items, while holding the hand of the toddler, smiling down at her.

Katie watched as her grandmother's face went from a cautious look, to one of pure anger, bile, and hunger. She charged forward, her face changed into one of the waking dead. She closed her eyes not wanting to see what she knew would happen, instead feeling the rippling shift in time and the scene once again. Creaking her eyes open it was almost like the initial conflict was cut out. She was unable to look away as she watched in horror as her grandmother, mother, father, and older brothers sat on their knees, leaning over the body of a lifeless child, eating. The puddle of blood surrounding the child, and the unconscious woman lying mere feet away put a surrealness to the entire situation. The blood that was smeared on their hands and clothes also covered their faces. All of their eyes were blank and empty, like hollowed out demons from old horror films. She saw what had become of them, all of them became the waking dead. Moments later, the peacekeepers showed up.

Katie screamed and cried as she watched her family being put down like rabid dogs in front of her. They didn't try to run or try to fight back. They merely sat there, tearing small strips of meat off of little appendages, with what little teeth they had remaining. The two peacekeepers had looked at each other, walked forward slowly, placing the barrels of their guns directly on their skulls, and pulled the trigger one at a time. There ended the bulk of her family, all that remained was her grandfather and her.

Katie wept.

This is a common occurrence now, on this dying planet. The two peacekeepers were likely the only ones of their profession left in the entire town, and they only did it because no one else would. They feared their own families would be next, so they had originally come together as a community, and many of the workers would take turns doing patrols during the day. This helped keep the community a little safer than if no one did anything, and let the waking dead just run around attempting to eat everyone and everything.

Katie wept.

She knew in her heart of hearts that was the only thing that could be done for them. She knew that when they came out of the heart of darkness and placed eyes on that small defenseless child, that there was no turning back, no stopping the inevitable. Life on this planet has gotten to be too hard.

She was relieved that their deaths were quick, and painless. She understood that there was no other option sometimes. At this moment, Katie accepted that sometimes things were out of her control, and sometimes death was the only answer. She didn't know if that was what the entity wanted her to learn, but that was what she had gathered from witnessing one of the most atrocious heartbreaking things she had ever seen.

"What did you learn?"

The all-encompassing voice was back, and Katie was furious. She stood tall, staring defiantly into the sky, and screamed incoherently. In her scream, she put all the vehemence and anger that one could possibly feel, after being forced to watch their family be executed. She didn't answer.

"What did you learn?"

The voice seemed a little softer this time, as if in understanding. Though it persisted, in wanting to know. It did help and had allowed her to get her anger under control. Drying her tears and glaring at nothing in particular, Katie forced out what she had learned, "I learned that I have to accept that some things are out of my control. I have also learned that sometimes, the best and kindest answer, is death."

"Acceptable."

She physically felt the entity leave her presence. The second it did, she fell to her knees, vomiting. Who or what would make someone watch that? Why would they do such a thing? To teach a lesson that seemed like it would be easier told than shown? Placing her forehead on the soft grass, she tried to calm herself, as she cried.

She was suddenly surprised by a gentle voice that came from behind her.

"Did you watch your family die too?"

Turning rapidly, Katie saw a young man, close to her own age, sitting on the grass around fifteen feet away from her. His face was dirt streaked and eyes red and puffy. It was clear he had been crying, just as she had been. The vanity part of her mind wondered if she herself looked like she had been crying too, but she squashed it with absolution. Of course it was.

"Who are you? How did you get here?"

"I'm Sesh. I walked here with two of the greatest souls I've ever met. I would ask *you* how you got here, but I just saw you appear."

Looking around, Katie said, "What two souls? I'm Katie by the way."

"They are still getting their 'Watch and learn' session," Sesh said with disgust. "Do I know you?"

"I don't know, you do look familiar."

She saw that he had king eyes, and a handsome face. He saw that she had a sweet smile to her, one that he knew. It was at this moment they both recognized each other immediately. Their eyes widened in shock as they said simultaneously, "You!"

Sesh quickly began apologizing, "I'm so sorry Katie, I should have been paying attention."

"It's okay Sesh, I have already forgiven you. These kinds of things happen."

"Yea but normally I'm a very thoughtful driver. It was just a very hard day for me, which sounds like an excuse. There's no excuse, I messed up, I really am sorry."

"I—" She started to utter but was interrupted by an angry little angel popping into existence, right between the two of them.

Chapter Twenty-Seven
Samson

Pip knew exactly what was going on the moment he floated into the central part of the Doomed Maze. He didn't even bother to look around at the floating bodies of his companions, because he knew who was in charge of this central abode. Looking to the expansive sky, Pip glared. Afterall, it was his natural born feeling of disgust and hatred towards the one who betrayed Yeshua.

"JUDAH!"

"Sir Trillion, you must watch and learn."

Before Judah could send Pip into a spiraling vision, he shouted once more, "Do not send me to my greatest failure Judah!"

The world spun. It was not the same as with Sesh and Katie, this was more akin to the changing of channels on a television. Pip fumed as he waited for the vision he fully expected to see. It was the vision of his first charge, and his last charge before Sesh, Samson.

Coming into focus was Samson, asleep in his bed with a beautiful Hebrew woman, that he knew was named Delilah lying next to him. While they slept, Pip watched as a pale skinned Philistine snuck into the room, with a pair of sheep shears in hand. Pip reached forward, having been there when this happened, but was unable to stop the situation. He knew that the result of the cutting of Samsons hair, was entirely Samsons fault. Samson put his trust in the wrong person and told her his secret.

As the Philistine reached out and sheared away a goodly portion of Samsons hair, Pip watched as Samson turned in his sleep, not noticing the loss of his strength.

"Delilah, I know you cannot hear me, but I do dearly wish you to stub your toe. I hope you stumble when you climb out of bed in the middle of the night, to use the pot, and spill it all over your freshly stubbed toe."

The scene flickered. Pip was supposed to be watching out for Samson, but was instead chatting it up with Carmen, his love. Carmen was a beautiful silver-haired Angel, and they had fallen in love many, many years ago.

Most people did not know or understand that Angels loved and felt as much as any human, if not more. Pip and Carmen were soulmates. The moment they had each set their eyes on each other, they fell deeply into one of the purest forms of love any two souls could find. They would often find themselves sneaking away from their charges, to steal a quick moment with each other. Both of them were young, in terms of the ages of Angels.

Like many creatures across all the universes, Angels connected with their mates, for life. If they were separated, they would never seek out the comforts of another, nor would they hint at any sort of betrayal of their other part. They would have their futures and paths completely, and unbreakably intertwined. Pip and Carmen had given their oaths to each other, under supervision of the Eternal, and had their souls intertwined for all of existence. If one should perish, the other would perish as well.

Pip had noticed that Samson was not doing well. After he was betrayed by his lover, Delilah, he was taken prisoner. There, he had his eyes gouged out, so that he would be easier to control. Again, Pip was unable to intervene, as Samson had put his trust in the wrong person and must therefore reap what he had sown. Such is the way of the Eternal. It was around this time that Pip saw Samson was a prisoner, and was not going to be going anywhere, anytime soon, that he decided to take a quick visit to his soul's partner, Carmen.

The vision flickered again, and Pip was embracing Carmen, whispering to each other.

"I missed you, my love."

"And I you. You should be at your charge Pip. You should not leave him alone; you are his guardian."

"He is a prisoner, betrayed by the love of his life. She did not reciprocate him. It is not my place to question the will of the Eternal, though I do not understand why these humans would be allowed so much leeway in their decisions."

"It is because the Eternal gave them the power of choice. To choose the correct path, such as with us Angels. We have far less inclination to steer away from our task at hand though." She eyed him seriously for a second, "It is really good to see you though."

The rest of his conversation with Carmen, and what happened afterwards, was not caught, as the world twisted and spun. Pip was shown what he had only seen the aftermath of. While he was intertwined with Carmen, he was shown what Samson was going through as a prisoner. In front of him was Samson, in chains and marching towards a temple of a lesser god. The philistines worshiped Dagon, which Pip didn't quite understand. Dagon was just a very free spirit, who liked to spread his seed. He was the father of a great many lesser gods, which were equally destitute and squashed by the Eternal. They were merely afterthoughts in the grand scheme of things.

When the multitude of Philistines entered the temple, they had Samson shackled to a pillar and told him to worship their gods. Pip watched, knowing that Samson was a true believer in the Eternal, the highest of all gods. It was here that Pip knew his greatest failure happened. Samson prayed to the Eternal for his great strength to return to him, so that he could end the lives of all of those who put another god before the one true God, and repay those who took his eyes, in kind. He knew that the Eternal was a loving God, but also a vengeful one.

"Eternal God! Please grant me the strength I once had. For I would seek vengeance from these false worshipers, for taking my eyes."

Pip hyper focused as the Eternal granted the prayer to one of his most faithful. Samsons strength was returned, and he pushed with all of his might against the two pillars that he was chained to. Pip watched in horror as the pillars fell, the building coming down, and crushing every living person inside the temple.

He had a moment of clarity, where time seemed to slow down, that he should have stepped in and save his charge from the falling pillars. He should have pulled him away from the pillars, so that he could die fighting the army of philistines that were outside the temple. Since Pip was not there to save Samson, Samson had ended up committing one of the cardinal sins. He had committed suicide. This had allowed a great many of people who would have been slain in the battle afterwards, to live on. Their habits spread to their offspring, creating a slew of heretical misguided sinners.

Pip knew that shirking his duties meant that Samson was unable to die in battle, and that he was forced to take his own life. In result, the Eternal had forgiven Pip's charge of the cardinal sin, allowing him to have balanced scales and to enter the celestial city. Unfortunately, Pip was not as lucky, as shirking one's duty to a charge was a grave mistake.

The world flickered once more. Pip was on his knees in front of the Eternal, which he could not see. It was merely the power from the presence of Eternal that forced Pip to take to his knees.

"You have failed in your duties young Trillion. As such, you shall be punished. Do know that everyone must face the consequences of their actions, and Angels, even with the intentions of one guided by love, cannot escape that fate."

Knowing he was at fault, and accepting responsibility, Pip uttered with his head bowed, "Yes Eternal."

"You will not have another charge for three thousand years. You will lose the power of a true Angel, until the day returns that you deserve it back. The only time you may use the true power, is when you are saving a future charge from a premature death, or other irreparable situation. Lastly, I forbid you from seeing your intertwined soul, until circumstances warrant your connection to be reignited. That time may be as little as a year from now, or it may be as great as a hundred thousand years from now. Arise, and be dismissed, Sir Trillion Pippenstein the Third."

The world flickered and twisted once more. He was back in the central glade, staring at the sky once more. Pip knew he was at fault. That was the first time he saw the entirety of what happened. The presence of Judah pressed in, and spoke, "What did you learn?"

"Judah, I know why you're here. You do not get to ask me what I learned. What did you learn from betraying Yeshua? What did you learn from throwing your best friend to the wolves? Who are you to ask me what I learned?"

"Sir Trillion, I must insist. What did you learn?"

"I will not answer you traitor!"

"It is not I, asking the question, but the Eternal. What… did… you… learn?"

Sighing loudly, and practically gritting his teeth, Pip said, "I learned that I must never shirk my duties, even for the sake of the purest form of power in all existence, Love. My duties resulted in the misrepresented suicide of another soul, which is a cardinal sin."

He knew that he was acting like a petulant child, but his anger was strong and billowing. It was primarily anger at himself, for failing Samson in such a way. He was still considered young, for an angel. He did not have the capability to temper his own temperament, like Gabriel did. If only Carmen was here, she would always have a sound reason and responsibility. She knew exactly what to say and do, to soothe his soul.

"Acceptable."

"Judah, before you send me back, I want you to know that forever is not long enough for what you did."

"I have been punished by the Eternal; it is not anyone's place to question my punishment. Return to your body."

"Judah!"

Things flickered, and Pip popped into existence, fuming, and glaring up at the sky. He vaguely noticed a blond girl and Sesh sitting on either side of him. His anger was palpable, as he fumed at what Judah had said to him. He was absolutely right, which made Pip even more angry. It wasn't Pip's place to question the will of Heaven's Eternal.

Chapter Twenty-Eight
Introductions

"**P**ip's back!" Sesh exclaimed.

Katie eyed the small fairy-like creature for a moment, noticing his small pristine white wings, and obviously angry face. She couldn't help but compare him and a particular grand angelic figure that was guarding that massive celestial city. Gabriel was mighty and had a strong power that permeated from his being. This little Pip was nothing like that, he was diminutive and sweet looking. His presence gave off a comfortable feeling, which made her relax a little bit more.

"Pip?" she asked, gesturing with her chin towards the small angel.

"Yes, Pip is my guardian angel. His full name is Sir Trillion Pippenstein the Third, but everyone just calls him Pip. He's been the absolute best friend someone could ever ask for. Super knowledgeable too."

"I wish Judah would have been damned. He's a blasted traitor." Pip was muttering things under his breath, but loud enough for Sesh and Katie to hear. "But I'm not questioning the Heavenly Eternal, oh no, definitely not."

"Who's Judah buddy?"

"Judah is who, many of you, humans would know as Judas Iscariot. The man who betrayed the Eternals Gift. He is in charge of this central glade. He was put here as punishment for his betrayal. Now, he must be the over watcher in perpetuity." Scowling, he added, "In this glade, he is almost all-powerful. It was to lessen the punishment a little, even though he is never able to leave." Glancing around and noticing Katie for the first time, Pip asked the girl, "So, you did end up in here after all." It wasn't a question, but a statement. "I was wondering if you were going to die or not, your guardian angel must have changed something, just a bit. That was a nasty impact to your skull."

"Do…. Do you know me?"

"Of course I do, I was there when this dingle-hopper here was texting and driving then plowed into your vehicle. Though, I don't know your name, I'm Pip, pleasure to meet you."

"Katie. Nice to meet you too." She stuck her hand out, before quickly grinning, then changed it to an individual finger, to shake Pip's outstretched little hand.

"Awesome, glad everyone is acquainted now. So, I saw the most horrifying thing ever… I understand that there was a lesson to be learned from it, but why… just WHY did it have to be that… that… vision." Sesh said, staring off into the never-ending glade.

"Yeah, I agree with Sesh, that was profoundly disturbing. If I never have to see that again, it will be too soon." Katie said.

Concern crossed Pip's small face, "Do you guys want to talk about what you've seen?"

Shaking his head, Sesh said, "Maybe…. Someday…. But not today."

Katie just shook her head 'no.'

"Well then, let's talk about what led us all here. Katie, how did you end up in the central glade the same time we did? If I knew you ended up in the Doomed Maze as well, I would have guessed we would cross paths at some point, but it's also fair to assume that there are many, many, entrances to this central glade." Pip questioned.

"Well, I was originally walking down a really long bridge into this beautiful golden city, with a huge angel outside of it."

Pip interrupted, "You went to the celestial city of Heaven? You must have been closer to death than I thought. Whoever your guardian angel is, they cut it awfully close."

Continuing, Katie said, "Well, I think it was a mistake, because he said, 'You shouldn't be here.' Then told me to do something and teleported me into a dirty old castle with a flaming green demon in it. That demon was very definitely eating people. I escaped, and ran, finally making my way here. I did run into the best capybara ever before coming here. He made some really good bread, and sandwiches. Do you guys want one?"

Their eyes lit up, and they both grinned at each other. Food that wasn't rotten was definitely going to make the mood better. Katie pulled her sack over to her lap, then began pulling out a bit of food to eat, handing a sandwich to Sesh, who then tore a little piece off and gave it to Pip.

"What about you guys?"

Sesh told her the story of how they got to this location, with all the scary and exciting details. He told her of the heroics from Pip and Josephine at the Dreadweaver's lair. That led him to discuss Josephine a little more, which was noted that she wasn't finished with her visions yet. After mention of the visions, the three people got quiet, sinking into their own thoughts of what they had been forced to bear witness to.

Wanting to break the uncomfortable silence, and change the subject, Katie thought for a second then asked, "You had signs telling you where to go, too?"

"Sort of, didn't you?"

"Just a few, but they didn't really tell me where to go… they just told me generalized advise, except in the buffalo herd, that one told me the portal was beneath all the buffalo... and I guess it was, because it was under a quicksand pit. Which was terrifying to say the least, I thought I was going to drown."

"I imagine that would be terrifying! I think dying in a cave collapse or a rockslide would be the most horrible way to die. Why do the signs even tell us anything about what's going on?" Sesh asked.

"So, that's something I do know. The signs appear and disappear according to the path of each individual. For instance, Katie, since you never really questioned your path, you didn't need much assistance on finding your way, so you got only a couple of the signs. While Sesh here, came across many paths, he sometimes needed direction. So, the observer of the Doomed Maze would drop a sign for him. He didn't read all of them, which is fortunate, because it was said early on that not all the signs gave viable information. Possibly, a little trickery afoot. There are some sneaky little maze gnomes that run through the maze, making mischief, which includes making false signs for people. We luckily did not run across any."

Sesh chuckled then muttered, "Gnomes rule."

Katie just looked at Pip and nodded, "I understand, that's strange but I do understand."

"Yep. My question is now, what is your task that you were given? I am searching for a heavenly weapon of sorts. It could literally be anything, but I don't have much of a clue, other than— 'Go forward.'"

"I…" She looked at Sesh for a moment, knowing he was the one she was supposed to save, she just didn't know when. She didn't know if it would change things if she told him. Sort of like a time travelers' paradox. Deciding, that it would be best not to say anything, and just keep close to the man she had just met, she said, "I am not going to say right now. There are things in the work that I must keep to myself. When the time is right, I will tell you what my task is. I do have a question though; do I have a guardian angel too? If you have one…, why wouldn't I have one too right?"

"Fair enough, on your task, as for the guardian angel thing, I would figure you probably did too, but the better person to ask would be Pip here."

"Well, yes, you most definitely have a guardian angel, but they are very much likely not visible because they haven't been forced into visibility yet. You two can only see me because I was forced to reveal myself to Sesh here and have then since been allowed to retain my visibility. There are very elegantly written rules when it comes to guardian angels, I just… I guess I can say I was lucky that I was able to be trapped by that spider. Though when I think about it, I wonder how come he didn't come and try to eat me while I was entangled in the web. It's almost like we had a little help and assistance, but I could not even begin to guess by who. Either way, if you do have a guardian angel, they can see us, but we won't be able to see them, just yet." Pip looked at Sesh and smiled.

***

Carmen watched as the three people discussed who Katie's guardian angel was. She wanted more than anything to reveal herself to them, to rush forward into the tiny arms of her love. The punishment he received made it to where he cannot even sense where she is anymore. She was not punished, but there were still rules that must be followed.

She did not get a vision of her own because she was a non-visible guardian angel, which meant she was in between reality, or not technically a part of the Doomed Maze. She was linked to Katie's soul, and since Katie was within and a part of the Doomed Maze, Carmen had to follow her soul. So, she did get to stand by and watch the horrible things that happened to Katie's family and the atrocities that they committed before their souls were sent for judgement. That being said, when Pip became visible to Sesh, he became a part of the maze as well as linked to Sesh's soul. Therefore, he became subjected to the rules of the Doomed Maze. The magics of the central glade were strong enough to temporarily overcome the bond between guardian angel and ward.

She wondered what her vision would have been if she was to have one. Curious as to whether it would be when Pip got punished, and she had to follow the rules and deal with the ramifications of his actions. It was truly a difficult period for her, it's been over three thousand years since she had seen or held her beloved. While, when it comes to the lives of angels, three thousand years is not a long time but only when considering they live for eternity, if not slain in the line of duty. If eternity is not considered, three thousand years seems like an eternity itself.

The other option was that it could be when she watched her father, the most beautiful, and favorite angel of The Eternal, fall from heaven. He became too ambitious and began to question the ideals of

175

The Eternal. It was a strictly written rule of law to not question the wisdom and guidance of Them. She would sometimes wonder about how her father was, being that he had become the most infamous and evil entity known to all of humanity. His absence made her mother's death hit even harder. Everyone recognized that her father was the fallen angel, known as Moloch. Even the angelic providence leaders knew and recognized him as a fallen. She had actually been thinking about that more often, since seeing her half-sister in that dreadful forgotten castle. She doubted whether Morana even knew that she existed. Carmen knew it was a good possibility, because she had been born thousands of years before Morana.

***

"How much longer do you think Josephine will be?" Sesh questioned Pip.

"I don't know, but I hope it's not too traumatic for her, she's just a little bitty sphynx after all."

Katie smiled, "I am really looking forward to meeting Josephine, cats have always been my very favorite."

"I wish we could get something to drink. None of us have any liquids."

"Me too, my grandfather would always tell me of how his grandfather would drink nothing but some kind of black leaf tea, whatever that is. He said that his grandpa would never, ever, disgrace the tea by adding any sugar or honey to it, that it was the absolute best by drinking it pure and cold."

"I've never had any kind of tea, heck, I don't even know what it is… but it does sound super good."

"Tea is a leaf from a particular tree from your planet, that when steeped in hot water, would produce a sometimes bitter or herbal flavored liquid. The tannins in the tea would change the color of the water, and one could sometimes get a little energy from said tea as well. Consider it a less bitter, less caffeinated coffee." Pip was explaining the type of tea when suddenly, Josephine popped into view, and instead of growling or hissing, or mewling in sadness, she stretched, sat on her haunches, and began licking her paw to clean herself.

Chapter Twenty-Nine
Mud and Gore

The world around Josephine was still, her senses telling her it was everything, and nothing. She walked forward a few steps, feeling the grass beneath her paws, and smelling the fresh soil and open air. It brought a sense of peace to her. A voice that came from everywhere, and nowhere. The disembodied was deep and controlled.

"Watch and learn."

She crouched, her hair standing on end and her tail thickening to try to ward off any potential threats. It didn't matter, as the world around her spun and twisted. The vision in front of her became one of familiarity. She was back at her home when she was a small kitten, and her mother was teaching her how to fight. They were jumping and spinning through the different obstacles that were arranged, increasing her overall athleticism. She remembered this and purred fondly.

Bastet nuzzled her small kitten and purred softly, "I love you my sweet Josie."

The vision had changed into a moment that Josephine recognized as one of her most painful memories. It was when her mother had to go off to fight in Ra's war. To this day, Josephine didn't understand why the Sun God, who was the general of the Eternal, would need to have a war that was seemingly everlasting, and without reason.

She watched as her mother explained to her that she had to leave, with her crying and begging her mother not to leave her. It was how it had to be. The spectral Josephine stared in sadness as her mother left, and a single tear fell down her face, in acceptance. She let out a soft mewl, signaling a longing that could never be sated.

The way the vision shifted this time was different than the previous two, which brought things to a more alert attention to Josephine. She blinked away her tears as everything had checked like a chess board then uprooted and spiraled as if in a tornado. The colors all twisting and morphing into a final indistinguishable funnel of blur. When it finally settled, Josephine saw a battlefield of mud and gore.

There were trillions of combatants scattered across a blood red pitted hilly terrain. There were large, blackened scorch marks on the ground, and huge heaping piles of corpses. Josephine could see spear and pike tips sporadically across the battlefield, making the entirety of the moving mass seem like a porcupine.

Individual combatants would be cut down, then finished off by two or three more defenders, just to have a mass of other defenders to charge forward and fill the small opening that was created in the bloody mud. She stared in horror as the legs of combatants would be entangled in the intestines of their fallen opponents and comrades alike, which most of the time resulted in the addition of another corpse on this field of death.

As Josephine watched the horrors that a true war entailed, a true battle of the ages, she seemed to be able to see all of it, and none of it. There was too much information at hand for her to be able to take it all in. Suddenly, it was as if the rest of the battlefield got hazy and lost cohesion. Her vision narrowed until she saw a valley of corpses piled high on either side of a lone combatant. It was a powerful feline warrior. Her mother, Bastet, was slicing down opponent after opponent, adding their screams and blood to the turmoil of the dying and dead that grew the walls of her trench.

The mighty Bastet pushed forward into the everlasting battle, leaping from opponent to opponent, ripping out throats and disemboweling them with every movement. Her large cougar sized body moved like a grandmaster fighter, everything she did had a purpose, every movement was exact, not too little, and not too great. She would strike as fast as she would retreat, in order to strike again to finish her opponent.

Time seemed to slow down for Josephine, as she watched her mother battle and fight for the honor of a lesser god. She remembered her mothers' teachings, that The Eternal was the one true God, and that all the other gods were just kind of like his gentry. Sure, they were important in their own right, but only as important as a lightning bug is to a summer evening. They look pretty, and they feed the frogs and other insects and small critters, but they do not really accomplish much of anything. The world is capable of living without them, because where the lightning bug is the lesser gods, The Eternal is the atmosphere that the critters and insects and all other life forms breathe. The Eternal is the dirt and the ground they live and thrive in, the trees and the plants, and the water that is needed. The Eternal is the additive and the culmination, as well as the entirety of all. No lesser god can even compare.

Time snapped back into full speed and her focus heightened to her peak as she watched her mother leap back after killing a particularly large enemy combatant. The small feline warrior came back and landed on a flail's spiked ball, stabbing through one of her paws, and hindering her capabilities of dodging. She tried to retreat back towards her self-made trench of death when the area around her began to close in with enemy combatants.

Her first mistake, it seemed, was pushing too far into the enemy controlled portions of the battlefield, which resulted in her not having access to any support or reinforcements. She was cut off. Growing in size, Bastet became more human sized and shaped, with hands and feet, and beautiful purple fur lined leather armor. It was her trump card, her most defensive form that she could take, which would possibly enable her to survive. Fortunately, the damaged paw she had received was to her front left paw, which turned into a bleeding left hand, with a hole in the center of the palm.

Josephine watched in wonder, having never seen her mother, or any other sphynx take this form. She knew that sphynx had the capability to change, but she had never known how, and that was a lesson her mother had yet to ever teach her. She stared as her mother grabbed the very flail that forced this situation upon her, and then wrenched a small flat shield out of the death grasp of another fallen warrior. All of this took place over a matter of seconds, which ended with Bastet standing ready, staring daggers of challenge at her enemies.

"Come."

They came rapidly, stabbing her and slashing towards her legs, almost hitting them. Bastet swung her flail, taking out the legs of one enemy, then slammed her shield into the face of another. The combatants began to lessen around Bastet as she killed them one at a time. She did not make it without injury though, as a fallen man had stabbed his dagger into the back of her thigh. Another warrior had managed to strike her left shoulder, getting around her flail in a counterattack.

Josephine cried, knowing that her mother was running out of time. There was nowhere for her to escape, the end was coming soon. A female elfish warrior stepped forward, with Bastet gasping and breathing hard. Josephine saw that this bloody warrior had spikes all over her head and back, with blood splatters on her clothing and skin. The elf had rivers of blood flowing off of her skull, likely having taken damage from others during the battle. She wore little, as combatants of her species gained power and strength from the absorption of blood. Her vision was beginning to fade, with blood loss and exhaustion. Bastet went for an overhand strike at the spikey blood covered warrior, who just stepped back, allowing the flail to hit the ground. In response, the warrior stabbed forward with a long straight sword, piercing the sphynx warrior through her stomach. With a smirk, the elf twisted the blade, then retracted it, stepping back to watch the enemy who had killed so many of her allies, die.

Bastet fell to her knees, dropping the flail and the shield. She looked up towards the burning sun in the sky. She breathed ragged rasping breaths, taking a deep breath before shouting loudly in a growling voice, "LORD! Care for my baby girl! Protect and save her from herself!"

"It shall be done my champion. You have done well, rest."

The voice was not the voice of Ra who had answered her, but of the ethereal commanding voice of The Eternal. She had never heard Their voice, knowing that it was only capable of being heard by a soul that was crossing into the lands of the dead, heading for her judgement. For a living mortal to hear or see The Eternal, would result in their immediate death. The living flesh cannot survive such power.

Knowing she was answered, and that her demand would be oversaw appropriately, Bastet let out a final breath, willing her last remaining vestiges of power to leave her body, to seek out her only living child. An inheritance only a sphynx of the Celestial Order can pass on. A silvery light shot out of Bastet, into the atmosphere, only to circle around the skyline before disappearing over the far horizon, out into space.

Josephine wept as she watched her mother pass into the land of judgement. She wept in sadness to see her mother would never return, because a small part of her wondered if her mother were actually alive and was fighting to get back to her. That chapter of her life was closed now forever. Another part of her wept with pride, pride for the strength her mother had, and how she had fought bravely and without reserve until her last breath. Even to the point of demanding something from a God.

The world twisted and spun once more, bringing her back into the glade of grass. She was such a small animal, but in this moment, she felt mighty and proud. She puffed her chest out and stared in challenge at the demanding presence that pushed down upon her from everywhere.

"What did you learn?"

"I learned that my mother did indeed perish on the battlefields. I learned that she loved me eternally, and that is enough."

Josephine rarely spoke out loud, because the words felt funny coming out of her snout, around her teeth and over her tongue. She spoke out loud this time because she felt like this moment demanded something more than her telepathic response. She needed the words to be heard by the world, by the atmosphere, and the air. Her voice was strong, and young, but it held the same defiance her mother's spirit had.

Adding onto what she said, before the presence responded, she said, "I am proud, that Bastet is my mother."

"Acceptable."

With a flash, and a wavery view, she blinked, then saw that she was surrounded by Sesh, Pip, and a yellow haired human. Without saying anything to anyone, she began to clean herself, licking her paw and wiped her….

Out of nowhere, a flash of light slammed into her from the outer layer of the atmosphere. With that, she felt the power and love from her mother. She aged rapidly, no longer a small kitten, but a full-sized Sphynx. The remaining tufts of fur on her tail were no longer visible, and her tail had regrown and fixed itself after being partially severed by the Dreadweaver. Josephine had grown in size, easily adding another forty to fifty pounds. She was now the size of a small cougar, mighty and ferocious. Josephine Quickly fell unconscious, her mind and body completely exhausted from the rapid growth. The last thing she saw, in her fading vision, was Sesh as he rushed over, concern obvious on his face.

Chapter Thirty
Lillith

Morana scowled. She knew this type of soul wrenching time magic. The world was at a standstill, to the point where she couldn't even burn the grass surrounding her. She was completely powerless in this god forsaken place of life.

Stretching out a finger, she flicked her stagnant floating body, to the detriment of nothing. Her incorporeal finger passed through her body like it was passing through water, with just a small amount of resistance. Even the flames on her body, that her soul was separated from, had ceased their ever-flickering movements. Her flesh was no longer peeling and rotting away, it merely held its form, and stayed as scabbed half-living flesh. She had learned of this type of thing from her mother, Lillith.

A power came over her, one she had rarely felt its equal to. It was oppressive, and sinister. She felt a kindred connection to it, one that spoke to her on an innate level. Looking around in every direction, Morana saw nothing. When she looked to the sky, she heard the voice boom into her mind, and spirit.

"Daughter of Lillith and Moloch, you should not have come here."

"Who are you to tell me what I should and should not do?" She spoke with pride and fury, as one would if they were royalty, being spoken to by a lesser station.

"I am Judah, the betrayer. Commander and ruler over this small glade."

"I know of your name Judah. You betrayed the Eternals gift. Sacrificed him for a mere pittance." Morana scoffed, "'twas a move of a servant, not a ruler."

"Surely, an error, one where I lacked foresight. Why are you here in my glade Morana?"

"I hunt."

Lightning lit up the sky, with thunder following. Clouds rolled and billowed, blocking out what little light came from the sky. As if in response, Judah spoke again, "As it is, you must watch and learn."

The world around Morana burst into flames, bright orange and black. They flickered and burned, leaving no smoke. Her vision itself seemed to melt away, and as the flames died down, the vision came again. She stood there, staring at a beautiful powerful angel, her father. He was watching a small planet in a universe full of rocks come to form. He watched as the Eternal, whom Morana could not see, created the perfect habitat for Their favorite creation, humanity.

As the first humans came to the planet, the Eternal gave them a perfect garden, as they were perfect souls. They did not know the depth of their capability for choice but followed blindly. Placed in the garden, was a single tree of knowledge, or a seed of temptation.

"Why give them the seed of temptation, Eternal? Since they are going to be blind followers, why not remove that tree of knowledge, so they cannot betray Your trust?"

A ringing sound screamed through her ears and her vision warbled a little, as Morana tried to hear what was said in response to her father's question. She heard nothing but saw her father's reaction. He looked appalled.

"Why would You create Your favorite creature and give it such a large capacity for choice?"

More ringing.

"Understood Eternal. Thank you for the lesson and guidance."

Morana watched as Moloch struggled with supplication, but still complied. She could see in his face and demeanor that he did not agree but still followed what was commanded. At least for now.

The world burned and melted away again, revealing a new scene. Her father had chosen to try to teach the Eternal a lesson, by tempting his favorite creation even more. Morana could tell that he was jealous of the attention they were getting, because he was used to being the favorite one. He began to create a plan, to enter the garden and tempt the human into violating the Eternal's trust. If he were going to be sneaky, he would be the sneakiest of creatures, the slithering serpent.

While sneaking around the Garden of Eden, Moloch continued to see the beautiful woman, who was the male human's wife. He watched her laugh and play with the animals and creatures around her. Moloch spent months just watching her move, and live. After many months, Moloch came to the woman, changing into his original form, and whispered her name. She was alone in the small pristine pond, cleaning herself.

"Lillith."

Morana was shaken to her core. Her mother was a human. Her mother had been the wife of the first man. She watched as her father sweetly talked to the beautiful human, making her laugh and smile. He continued to press his advance, until she giggled, looked around, then gave in, beckoning him into the water with her. Morana watched with avid fascination and disgust as her parents consummated, unknowingly at the time, creating Morana.

In the same melting burning fashion, the world around Morana changed again. Her mother was very visibly pregnant. The look on her face was distant, as she tried to entertain her husband, Adam. It was on this particular day, Lillith looked to Adam, and told her she had lain with another, and that the child was not his, but belonged to the man she truly loved Moloch. Adam, feeling betrayed, prayed to the Eternal, asking for a new wife, as his current one was unfit to be his wife. He prayed that she would be cast out, and persecuted.

Morana smiled in pure joy as the pain on Adam's face was profound. He was a broken man, because of the woman he loved. Love was all he had ever known, and all he knew how to do. This was the first time the human man felt something closer to hatred, and anger. It made him wallow in self-despair and pity. It was a feeling he had never known or felt before.

The world burned and melted once more. When she could see the world around her again, she was in the celestial city, and she could feel the palpable feeling of anger. The Eternal was furious at her father. Morana smiled, enjoying the feeling. She watched as her father was thrown from the celestial city, forced to the pits of the burning depths of the planet earth. Like an enormous falling star, Moloch crashed to the earth. On impact he obliterated everything in his path, except the garden, as it was protected by the Eternal God. The large creatures of old, ancient serpents of power beyond reckoning were all killed in the waste that became the planet. Plants burned and caught fire, rivers and lakes dried up, and the planet fell into a crumbling nothingness, its first true apocalypse. The only life was a beautiful green garden, which remained untouched by the ravages of the fallen angel.

Adam turned to Lillith and cast her out of the Garden of Eden. He did not shout, but merely did as he was instructed. She was thrown into the burning and decrepit landscape that was outside the Garden. All that remained of living life on planet Earth, outside the garden, was now Lillith.

Anger filled Morana. She watched as her mother, belly swollen and large with her late-stage pregnancy, walked away from the Garden, trying to find somewhere safe. It was mere moments to Lillith, but what felt like centuries for Morana, when Moloch appeared before Lillith.

"Come my love. You will become my queen, first of the demons, and I, Lord of the Flies, King of the Darkness, and Dictator of Evil, will be your husband."

"My love." Lillith looked at her husband, no longer beautiful, but burnt, and charred. His gorgeous, angled face, and muscular body was no longer such, as he looked like he had been burned from head to toe. His skin flaked and decayed in front of her eyes. In the joints of his body, were large cracks, which flickered with bright red and green flames, and his eyes were pure cerulean. Lillith knew it was

Moloch, the man she fell in love with. So, she reached out her dirty hand towards the burned man.

When he took her hand, a visible change could be seen on Lillith's face. She knew the inner workings of the world now; she had been given the gift of knowledge by her beloved king. Her face changed, lightening, and becoming more purple and violet than the beautiful golden brown and tan of her middle eastern skin-tone. She grew a tail, with a spearhead on the end of it, that she felt could be used as a weapon if need be. Her fingers became long, and her nails grew and sharpened. Her body became lithe and slender, the only bulge being her pregnancy. All of her hair fell out of her head, and she grew a couple of rams horns out of the side, next to her ears. They also sprouted across the roundness of her head, creating a hair-like structure of horn, where her hair used to be. To Morana, her mother, became the beautiful being she was always meant to be, the first demoness. In a flash, her mother and father disappeared into the pits of hell, to create their empire.

A haze began to fill Morana's vision, until all she could see was the gray of smoke, and occasional flicker of orange flame. Suddenly, a wind blew through the area, removing the smoke, and revealing the open green glade around her once again. She felt the powerful voice of Judah, once more.

"What did you learn daughter of Lillith and Moloch?"

"That my mother was once the wife of the first human, and she chose my father over him."

"Acceptable."

Smirking, she asked with derision, "Wasn't I supposed to learn some notable lesson that would change my path?"

"You must only learn."

"I am only proud of my beginnings, there is nothing else to learn here."

Without another word, the oppressive feeling was removed from her shoulders, and she once again felt the flames from her body and felt the continuous rot and decay of her flesh. She was herself again, and she immediately felt her prey, merely feet away from her. Turning towards the direction her senses directed her, she saw the backs of three individuals, sitting on the grass, surrounding a large unconscious cat.

Unable to help herself, she hissed, "At last… You… Die!"

Chapter Thirty-One
An Age Old Battle

Sesh had just run over and slid down next to where Josephine had fallen. He gently ran his fingers over her fur, stroking, and scratching lovingly. Katie had edged over as well, giving the large cat a curious look, without touching her.

"It's okay, she's friendly. This is Josephine, the sphynx that I was telling you about earlier. I don't know why she grew like this, but she is definitely still the same cat."

"Yea, Sesh is right, she is the same, she's just not a little kitten anymore. She's going to be insufferable with calling me a fairy again, bah!"

"She calls you a fairy?" Katie giggled.

As they sat there discussing the sleeping feline, a sonic boom sounded through the atmosphere, and a large wooden sign slammed into the ground in front of them. Katie leapt back in fright, Pip took to the air, ready for anything, and Sesh just looked up, seemingly unconcerned.

"What was that!?" Katie yelped, not noticing the sign, just reacting to the noise.

"It's just one of those signs we were telling you about, remember?"

"Yes, I just didn't expect to see one actually appear. All the ones I've seen, were just there already."

The weathered wooden sign read:

The Doomed Maze Central Square
You have successfully faced your darkest day.
Congratulations.
You still have one issue to resolve, I wish you luck.

"One issue to resolve?" Sesh questioned Pip.

"Yes, apparently, we are not done with this maze, though you never did find your heavenly weapon, so that must be it. Since it appeared to all of us, it must mean that Katie also has one issue to resolve. I do not have an inkling of an idea of where we should go. There does not seem to be any time requirement continuation, as I feel that the sign would have told us. So, let's wait until our dear grown kitten here awakens, then we will continue on with pride and gusto!"

"So, did all the signs' you guys had appear like that? With all the booming and dramatic dropping into the ground?"

"Oh no, they were just there for us. This is the first for us too. I got a feeling of a sense of dread, let's wait near Josephine, and then get the heck out of here." Sesh said.

Sesh looked at Pip again, then back to Katie, and they both nodded, agreeing. They went back over to where Josephine lay on the ground, and sat down, surrounding her. After sitting for a few moments in silence, they all felt a palpable rise in temperature. A horrid acrid stench of burned hair and rotten meat overtook them. Sesh looked towards Katie, and then they heard it.

"At last…You… Die!"

Sesh rose to his feet, turning quickly and seeing the disgusting demoness Morana, for the first time. Katie also saw the demon and gasped in fear. She remembered this would be torturer and what she did when she escaped from that forgotten dark castle. Katie remembered the way the green flaming demon chased her into that dense forest. She barely had time to think, 'You followed me?' before the demon was upon her.

Morana flickered forward, slashing a flaming claw-like hand towards Katie's midsection. The demoness was fast, far faster than any of them, except maybe Josephine. Sesh had time to slam into Katie's shoulder, shoving her out of the way. When Katie went flailing to the ground, feet away from where she had been standing before, she looked back and screamed.

Morana had impaled Sesh through the stomach with her flaming hand. The tips of Morana's long sharpened nails could be seen sticking out of his back on either side of his spine. A wicked toothy grin could be seen on Morana's face, as she looked towards a screaming Katie, mere feet away. Before Morana had time to rip Sesh's spine out of his stomach, a powerful angel's presence came into the area. Sir Trillion Pippenstein the Third grew to his full size, sporting his dark gray armor and powerful sword. His presence gave off a powerful aura that seemed to have a physical attribute to it. It pushed and tore at the flames coming off the demoness.

Just before Morana could finish off Sesh, Pip flashed and lunged towards Morana with his mighty two-handed broadsword, forcing her to retreat or be impaled. Sesh fell to the ground next to an unconscious Josephine.

Katie showed her true grit, rising and running to Sesh. She ripped his torn shirt off, and folded it the way her grandfather taught her, shoving it into the lightly bleeding wound. She noticed the wound wasn't bleeding nearly as much as it should have been, because the heat from Morana's hands had partially cauterized the entire thing. She threw her body over Sesh, as a powerful angel came tumbling over her, missing her by mere inches.

In the life and death battle, an age old one of angel versus demon, Pip charged at Morana, swinging his sword in the way he had trained for centuries. He was trained to fight demons, but most of the demons were lesser creatures, which lacked the power needed to stand toe to toe with a true angel. Morana was not one of them. She blocked his mighty swing with a forearm, sending chunks and wedges of flesh flying from her, but not even leaving a scratch on her heat tempered bones. Morana countered with a flicker, appearing behind Pip, to swipe at his head. Pip used the momentum of his blocked strike to spin his body and slam his sword into her swiping hand, severing two fingers.

Morana screamed, flickering again, and appeared directly behind Pip, slamming a powerful fist into his chest. Pip went flying backwards, head over heels, he tumbled, keeping himself artificially elevated so as not to injure the two humans and sphynx lying on the ground. Now the three innocents were between Morana and Pip. Pip flashed, heightening his speed to dash around the humans, drawing Morana away from them. She had to focus on the angel, because if she ignored him, he would become a true danger to her. Demons could only be slain by a heavenly weapon, such as Pip's, likewise demons were one of the only ways that Angels could be slain as well.

"I… will… destroy… you." Morana threatened Pip, as he circled, trying to draw her further away from Sesh, Katie, and Josephine.

"Then come try, demoness. I shall cut you down, as if you were a stalk of wheat, and my sword was a scythe." Pip's mighty voice matched his mighty size.

Morana flickered towards Pip in mind dazzling speed, burning the grass on the glade to a crisp. She swung at Pip again and again with her emerald flamed claws, hissing and growling with each sinister strike. Pip manages to block and deflect every powerful blow. The sound alone was enough to stir up the wind and cause the burning grass to spread. The earth beneath the mighty battle was cracked and dented from the battle between good and evil. Morana was meant to consume and destroy, which was her innermost desire and motive, whereas Pip was taught and ingrained to purify and protect. It was the innate code of the Angels.

With each strike, flames erupted around Pip, and he lost a little bit of his power. He countered a particularly good deflection, and managed to chop into Morana's shoulder, severing one of her arms at the joint. Molten green lava oozed out of the socket, slowly cooling, and hardening into another arm. It would take her some time to regrow that arm, so Pip pressed his advantage.

Katie was shaking Sesh, trying to get him to keep his eyes open. He was going into shock. She did everything she remembered to do to prevent that, from covering him with what little she could to warm him, including pulling the unconscious sphynx closer to him for warmth. She raised his legs with her bundled up satchel and jacket. Holding pressure on his wound, she continued to treat him with what minimal things she had available.

She had remembered a small skin-stitching needle and thread she had kept in a small hidden survival kit in her boot. Her grandfather had taught her to survive. She also kept a spare handcuff key in there, and a cutting wire, a small knife, and some flint. She pulled the bandage out of Sesh's wound and began to stitch closed the massive hole. She had no idea if it would even be enough, with how much internal damage he must have taken, but she had to try. Meanwhile, the battle of good and evil around her waged on.

Sensing her disadvantage, Morana transformed into her true form, it was a little less speedy, but far more powerful. Morana began to rapidly flicker in place, growing huge bat-like wings and a sharp spear-like tail to aide in her movement. Large flames burst forth from her hands, as She attacked, disappearing from one spot, and reappearing in another. She would strike at the flagging Angel with each appearance, landing blow after blow. She only had one arm, but it did not matter. When it came to raw and uncontrolled power, Morana had that in spades, far more than the punished angel. She did not know this, but Pip was unable to retain his reserves for his full power, due to being stuck as a small fairy sized guardian. He was running out of steam, and fast.

Sensing victory at hand, Morana kicked the angel in the legs, sending him tumbling to the ground. She lashed him across the face with her sharpened tail, buffeting the air with her wings. On his way to the ground, she lashed out with another kick, and struck his mighty broadsword, sending it skittering away into the burning grasslands. Pip lay on his back, staring up at the grinning Morana. She rose above him on her mighty wings, as he shrank back to his small, diminutive size.

***

Carmen watched in horror as the love of her life, her soul companion, lost. She wept because she could do nothing to save him.

He fought bravely, but his punishment proved to be too much, and he was unable to maintain his strength. The demoness proved to be far too powerful, she had concerns that even she wouldn't be able to face her little half-sister and defeat her.

***

Morana stared down at the fairy sized Pip and laughed. Her laugh was evil and grating, full of sinister thoughts and intentions. She stared at the small angel and glided closer to him.

"I thought you would be more. Who knew that Angels were this weak. How disappointing."

Just then, a mighty roar sounded behind Morana. Josephine had awakened, and she was furious to see her little friend fighting the demoness alone, and that he was losing. Her muscles rippled and bulged as she leapt towards Morana, slashing the demoness with huge claws. Josephine thought about her mother as she battled the demon, slashing and cutting with every swing. Josephine was faster than the disappearing Morana, and it showed.

Morana would disappear, flickering backwards, and Josephine would be there waiting for her. Her feline reflexes seemed to alert her to exactly where the demoness would appear. When Morana would appear, Josephine would swipe at her, slicing away more, and more of her flesh.

Morana was old, and experienced with her body, whereas Josephine was only her current size and power threshold for moments. Morana could tell that the sphynx was still young, and unaccustomed to fighting such a mighty foe. She stayed on the defensive, mitigating the damage from the sphynx. She knew eventually, the cat would make a mistake, and then she would capitalize. Minutes passed of Morana being on the defensive, slowly losing more and more of her substance. She began to wonder if Josephine would actually make a mistake and was just about to try something else before it happened. Josephine jumped into the air, swinging a mighty blow aimed at Morana's head. Morana knew that she couldn't adjust in midair, so she flickered to the left side of Josephine lashed out with her still regrowing arm and took a huge chunk out of the cat's hind quarters. Josephine hissed in pain, biting down on a burning arm, and pulling. The bone snapped at the

193

forearm. Morana had recovered enough from her missing arm to use it in limited capacity for the attack, but now lost it again.

Hissing in frustration, she flickered back several times, then began to toss large globules of green molten matter. Josephine easily dodged all of the makeshift fireballs. Josephine dashed forward, her claws glowing brightly with a celestial light. She was dozens of feet away from the demoness when she started swiping with huge luminating strikes. Each swipe would send four large bright arcs of light towards Morana. Each arc was hundreds of times the size of Josephines claws. Josephine began to increase the quantity of swipes, Morana's only respite being when Josephine had to dodge.

Morana took a golden arc of light to the chest, sending showers of flames and flesh everywhere in a five-yard radius. She howled, anger raising the temperature of her flames by factors. Suddenly, Pip was in the fight again. He zipped around the demon, slamming into her as a small bright light. Together, Pip and Josephine attacked, alternating hits on the hissing and screaming Morana. Josephine went high, aiming for Morana's neck, when Pip came in from behind, and slammed into Morana's lower back. With a sickening crunch, Morana's head went flying into the sky. The light in her eyes winked out, the burning, decayed rot of her flesh ceased its constant transformation, as her body crumbled to the ground. A smoldering green ember under a pile of skin and bones was all that remained of Lillith's first daughter. Morana had been defeated.

Chapter Thirty-Two
Success and Treasure

esh awoke several hours later. He opened his eyes and saw the closest of friends he had ever had, and a beautiful blonde girl, named Katie. He had no doubt that she would become one of the closest people he ever had too, they just hadn't known each other long enough. Coming to consciousness, Sesh was still groggy and unable to properly focus on how he physically felt. After a few seconds, the pain hit him. It felt to him like it hit harder than his truck and Katie's SUV colliding.

Groaning loudly, Sesh put a hand on his stomach, "ugggggghhhhhhhh. What happened?"

"Well, you took a demon's flaming fist through your gullet. She was seconds away from ripping your spine out of your belly button," Pip explained.

"How am I alive?"

Looking down at his stitched-up stomach, Sesh listened attentively to Pip's retelling of the story quietly.

"So, you see, after she knocked me down and I was drained of energy, Josephine came heroically to battle, saving all of us. Together, she and I vanquished the foe. Meanwhile, Katie here, took care of you, though I'm still uncertain as to how she managed to cross stitch your wound." Looking towards Katie, Pip asked, "How did you cross stitch his wound?"

Nervously looking around, Katie responded, "I always keep an emergency kit, stashed away in my boot. My grandfather taught me that I would never know when I would need it." Lifting her boot, she showed them a small pull away compartment that fit seamlessly into the slightly taller than average heel. She continued, "I happened to be lucky enough that I had a flesh needle and stitching, as well as several other things needed for survival, like a small knife, and capability to start a fire."

"What marvelous foresight, Katie!" Pip beamed broadly at Katie.

Indeed, you did well. I would like to add that demon tasted like hammered hamster dung.

Josephine had spoken to all of them telepathically. Everyone just looked at her, then burst into laughter all at once. It was a joyous occasion to be alive. Sesh's eyes twinkled with happiness, as he stared at the big beautiful violet sphynx.

"How did you get so big Josie?"

Pip nodded, "Yes, I'd like to know that as well, how did you get so big?"

Josephine glanced at Katie, nodded, accepting her as a part of their group, then responded telepathically to all of them again.

In my vision, I saw my mother. I saw her battle thousands upon thousands of enemies, in a battle that stretched as far as my eyes could see. I watched her fight valiantly, until she made a mistake, and pushed too far into the enemies-controlled land. It was not the only mistake she made, as she also landed wrongly in one of her attacks, which caused her to have a damaged limb. As the enemies surrounded her, and she took her last breath, she willed her last remaining power to me. It is only something that a sphynx from the Celestial Order can pass on. The Celestial Order is just an order of combatants that the gentry of gods have. They are trained up and sent to fight on the front lines of evil.

As if that was enough, Josephine stopped speaking, deciding to keep many of the finer aspects of her vision to herself. As they all sat there, enjoying each other's company, a peaceful quiet came over them. They could hear a distant birdsong, from the non-existent trees and forests. They could smell the flowers, and taste the honeysuckle on a breeze, that they could not feel. They each gained a true feeling of tranquility.

THWACK!

A large wooden sign appeared in front of them, slamming down into the ground and standing. This weathered sign was a little more extravagant than all of the other signs that had appeared before them. It was weathered wood, with a gold border. The lettering was stunning calligraphy, written in shining gold. It read:

Congratulations on completing the Doomed Maze.
Congratulations on completing your tasks!
Sesh, you have found your heavenly weapon.
Katie, you have saved the stranger from the fingertips of Death.
The five of you will be greeted by Gabriel in a few short minutes.
Gather yourselves together, well done.

"Five of us?" Sesh asked, before anyone else could speak.

"Yes... I do not know what that implies." Pip responded, looking around at his companions. "Who could the fifth person be? My only guess would be Katie's guardian angel. We do not know who he or she may be, as they have not had the need to reveal themselves. If that is the case, then I would like to be the first, to formally thank you for being a comforting supporter of our adventures."

"That makes sense, I did feel like I was often not alone, especially when I slept on that super comfortable couch. Gosh, I wish I could catch a small nap on that couch again. I'm exhausted," Katie added.

"Wait, you slept on the resting couch?" Sesh asked.

"Is that what that white couch where that food table was?"

"Yes, that's exactly what that was," Sesh glanced at Pip before adding, "then that practically confirms it, that Katie's guardian angel is our fifth. That was who woke her up from the resting couch." He looked back at Katie then continued, "you see, the resting couch is something that if you go to sleep on it, you will have the most restful sleep of your entire life. You can get a full night's rest in a truly short time. The downside is you have to have someone wake you up…. Or you will sleep forever."

Katie looked at him then gasped, "So you think that my guardian angel woke me up? There was no one around me when I got up, I just kept travelling through the maze."

"Yes, I think that's exactly what happened. That being said, I also want to formally thank the mysterious guardian angel, because without Katie being here, I would have most assuredly perished."

They all felt the presence of Gabriel, the archangel come over them. His presence was just too powerful, far more powerful than Judah, who ruled this glade as punishment.

"Congratulations on passing the maze." Gabriel eyed them all, then said, "Please, come join me, as I take you back to the entrance of the maze, where you will have to travel back up the valley, through the rose garden, and back into Gateway Township."

They all gathered close to Gabriel, as they felt the wind pick back up. It swirled and gusted before their visions all blinked out for a split second, before coming back into focus, being at the mouth of the hole that served as the entrance to the Doomed Maze.

Sesh looked at Gabriel, then asked him, "Sir, I'm confused. The sign said I found my heavenly weapon, and I don't know what that consists of. What weapon did I find?"

Looking at him for a moment, Gabriel nodded as if deciding internally that telling him would harm nothing. "You have found a true companionship, with your friends. Please understand that all true companionships are signed off from the Heavens. Your paths have been so intertwined that upon finding each other, you were all automatically going the same direction. It is truly a gift from The Eternal. Your heavenly weapon, is your friendship."

"I see." Sesh nodded, smiling. He really did have great friends, even Katie.

"Now, I must be leaving you four to continue your return to the Gateway Township. I have duties that I must do, elsewhere. Saint Peter will join you in the Rose Garden. Before you go, be advised that this is merely the beginning of your journey through the seven levels of purgatory. I will not say that all the levels will be as difficult, or diverse of adventure, but I will say they will all have their own challenges, that if managed poorly, could result in the death of one, or all of you. With that, I must go. Please be on your way." With that, Gabriel winked out of existence with a small flash of light.

***

Judah watched closely as the five individuals left with the mighty Archangel. The second they were gone, he turned his attention instantly towards a small green flame, flickering on a molten ember. He could feel her presence still, it was faint, but still there. He appeared directly in front of the ember, standing in the blackened and burned plains. Bending down, he scooped up the flame, which turned out to be a piece of the bone from Morana's skull. The rest of it had crumbled, when she had lost her battle with the sphynx and guardian.

Whispering to the flame, Judah said, "Shh…. shh… It's okay my sweet, sweet, darling. I will feed you, until you return to your former glory."

Judah cupped the ember closely to his chest, and blinked out of the glade, returning to his place of existence, once again. This time, carrying his treasured prize. He would stop at nothing, until he brought the mighty Morana, back to former state, and then he would pursue her, and make her his wife.

Chapter Thirty-Three
Entrance to the Levels

Gabriel was gone. The four companions stood around the valley floor, just grinning stupidly at each other. While they could not see Carmen, she grinned right along with them, happy about their survival. As if coming to an unspoken agreement, they all turned, and started walking towards the switchbacks, that made up the pathway to the crest of the valley.

"You know, I really am sorry Katie."

"For what?"

"For hitting you with my truck and bringing you here."

"Oh, piffle Sesh, think nothing of it. It happened and we have no control over any of it to change it. I forgive you. I really do." Katie smiled at Sesh, a big, beautiful smile, with perfect straight white teeth. She looked at him directly in his kind eyes. She really did always like a man with kind eyes.

He smiled back, as they climbed the switchbacks up towards the back entrance of the beautiful Rose Garden. Thinking about it, he realized that Katie had never seen any of this. It was confirmed by her occasionally glancing at the wisps of spirits that occupied some of the darker recesses of the valley.

"They are spirits." He told her, without prompting.

"Huh?"

"Those wisps, they are spirits that never took the step to enter the maze. They were too afraid, so they stayed in the valley. After a while, they just lost their cohesion to being a true soul, and ended up as that, a spirit wisp that merely occupies."

"How do you know this?"

"Peter told me."

"Who is Peter?"

"Saint Peter, he's the keykeeper of the gates of Heaven. You'll like him, he's like a super happy, kind old man, not to mention he has a huge, huge, hellhound as a pet slash mount."

They walked in silence for a little longer, continuing their climb. To Sesh, it felt like the climb up was far longer than it had been when he was heading into the maze. Maybe it was just nervous apprehension when he was entering, he didn't know. He looked at Pip, the angel was in quiet contemplation himself, as he rode on the back of a sauntering Josephine. She seemed way more aware of everything around her, in her fully grown state.

As they reached the crest of the valley, Sesh got a little déjà vu. He remembered reaching the crest of a vastly different valley in the maze when they were leaving the desert temple. That seemed like so long ago. They have gone through so much, just to get to this point. It was amazing that they had even survived. Thinking about some of the horrors they faced, Sesh wasn't paying attention, so he almost walked into the fence surrounding the Rose Garden.

"Hey, you okay?" Katie looked at Sesh and asked quietly in concern.

"Yeah, just thinking about… well everything that we went through to get here. It was a lot."

"It was, but we made it. Let's go see what that old man right there with the big dog wants. He looks super happy to see you."

Looking up at Saint Peter, Sesh put a huge grin on his face that matched Peters and said, "That's Peter! Come on!"

They all seemed to put a little extra pep in their step as they entered the garden through the beautiful arching gateway. Sitting on a bench, which was now conveniently facing them, instead of facing the other direction like before Sesh entered the maze, was Saint Peter. Off to the side, in his favorite patch of thorns and bushes, lying on his back and rolling back and forth, was Theodore the hellhound.

"I see you made it, and you made some friends along the way."

"I did, Peter, this is Katie, Sir Trillion Pippenstein, and Josephine. Guys, this is Saint Peter."

"I thought I recognized little Pip there. How are you, old friend?"

"I am well. It is good to see you again Pete."

"Great. It's also a pleasure to meet you as well, Ms. Katie and Ms. Josephine. One does not often see a fully grown sphynx walking about. It is nice to see. That's Theodore over there, he's a big friendly luff, so don't worry about his size or appearance."

"Did you really wait for me the entire time I was in there?"

"Well, it was only eight hours, right?"

Sesh laughed, "it sure did not feel like eight hours."

"Well, in actuality, it was far longer. Please, come sit with me, all of you."

Strangely, the small bench was now much longer, and accommodated them all equally. After they had all sat down, and gotten comfortable, Saint Peter continued, "Okay, so I'll start at a time that was around three thousand years ago. You see, I told you before you entered the Doomed Maze, that only one other person had completed the maze, and passed their task. Since you entered the Doomed Maze, that number has now gone up to four total. You two and your brother are the three newest additions to that noticeably short list. Can you guess who the fourth person is?"

Looking at each other, both Sesh and Katie shook their heads no. After seeing this, Peter continued, "It was The Eternals' gift to humanity. His name was Yeshua. I'm sure you've both heard the story. Though you likely had heard his name called Jesus. There are many different translations of Yeshua's name. That is irrelevant to the story at this time. Yeshua was killed on the cross, ultimately being sacrificed for the sinners of the planet. At least, he was in such a deep coma, to anyone who felt for his liveliness would have felt nothing. He was as close to dead as one can possibly get. There was no technology back then, so it was out of the question to even get an accurate measurement of his heartbeat or oxygen intake.”

“Besides that, the point remained the same. He was sacrificed. In his coma, which was not unlike yours in a lot of ways, if he had failed, he would have been weighed by the scales. After taking on all the sins of humanity, his scales could not have possibly been balanced, and as such, he would have been sent to hell to be tortured by the demons therein. Yeshua had to make it through the Doomed Maze and find something I will not discuss, in order to return to your world. The Eternal knew what was going to happen, there is nothing hidden from them, in either past, present, or future. That being said, They are an avid believer in freedom of choice. So, They let things play out the way they did.”

“Yeshua completed the Doomed Maze, in three days. In reality, he was inside the Doomed Maze to him, for merely hours.”

“Wait, you’re saying that to him it was merely hours, and it was three days... to us, that felt like... days... many days. Does that mean we were in the Doomed Maze for weeks?”

“Yes. Three weeks, two days, and fourteen hours, and an odd number of minutes.”

“Wow. How does this affect our living bodies?”

“It doesn’t. If you pass the seven levels of purgatory, your soul will be returned to your body, and you will live.”

“Remarkable. Jesus was something special, wasn’t he?” Katie said.

Saint Peter looked at her and nodded, before adding, “He was really incredible, not saying that you four aren’t, it’s just saying that he was beyond what anyone could dream of. After he completed the Doomed Maze, which took thousands of years for anyone to complete, it was then said that no one will complete the Doomed Maze again until one day, when the world was at its brink of complete collapse. When that day comes, it will be completed. It’s said that the one who completes it, will hold the power capable of righting the world, and balancing the scales of the planet. I would assume here, that this means the life-stone you have on your living body, or near it. One thing that I don’t understand is why your brother, who has been weighed, found balanced, and was allowed to continue on into the celestial city, was able to complete it, as he has no effect on the living world any longer. I can only gather, that because of your choices in the Doomed Maze, you were able to assist your brother through the ultimate power. That's the power of love."

"That does make sense. I was told how I could use it to fix the world."

"Wait, you can fix our world?" Katie looked at Sesh excitedly.

"Yes, I just have to make it through the seven levels of Purgatory."

"That's…. incredible. How is this possible?"

"Well, I found a little green swirling stone, and I'm supposed to put it into a natural spring, to allow the water to flow once again. All springs on our planet are connected, so… yeah. I just got to do that, and then everything will start to get better."

"Well, let's get through the seven levels of purgatory then and save the world!"

Smiling grandly, Peter looked at the four companions and nodded sagely. "Yes, that is what must happen. First though, I will take you into the Gateway Township and get you outfitted for the first level of Purgatory. I cannot give you much information about it, as I only know the basics. I know that it is going to be much different than the Doomed Maze, but it is entirely full of hazards. We can go speak to Gabriel once more and see if he can give us some advice on each of the levels. So, come with me, let's go to the outfitters."

As they walked through the garden, Katie really got to look around and see it in its full magnificence.

She said, "This garden really is stunning."

"Yes, it used to be a part of the Garden of Eden."

Sesh told her the little story he had heard, which amazed her and awed her. Upon entering Gateway Township, she was amazed even further, after seeing the western style buildings and dirty dusty roads. Sesh pointed out the cloud building down the way.

Josephine and Pip were ultimately quiet this entire trip, Sesh assumed they were just communicating telepathically to each other, and being at peace. The entire situation was incredibly surreal. They went and visited Gabriel once more, only for him to turn them away, telling them that they had been given enough information. He wished them luck, then turned back into a stone angel door knocker.

The small western town was not bustling with as much activity this time through. Sesh noticed that the people were more friendly too, they would smile and wave at their group. The little dusty faces, sticking out of dusty buildings, smiling, and waving. The occasional wagon would clomp by drawn by horses, with a driver tipping his hat in salutation. Things were much more pleasant this time through for Sesh.

"Okay, this is the outfitters." Saint Peter had said. He really did seem like a gentle old man, without the huge hellhound at his side. Theodore had decided to stay in the garden and get a good nap in the midday sun.

Saint Peter had allowed them all to take quick well-needed naps on the resting couch, to help recover some of their energy from their trying journey so far. While they slept, he gathered them adventure packs, filled to the brim with important items that one would need for surviving the wilderness, or many potential hazards that the levels of purgatory would throw at them.

Things like rope, fire starting materials, cutting materials, wire, and even weapons. Katie was given a small crossbow, with extra eight-inch bolts. Sesh was given a good-sized cutting blade, which could be used in a pinch, for survival, or as a weapon if need be. Pip and Josephine were given nothing, except a small satchel that Josephine could carry, that contained some food and water purification tablets.

After getting outfitted for the long adventure ahead of them, Saint Peter escorted them back out of the town, and away from the dusty people that the small town housed. They walked towards the Rose Garden once again, but instead of entering it, they walked along the edge of it. The lack of conversation between the travelers really heightened the anxiety that they all felt. All of them, except for maybe Peter.

Occasionally one of them would try to start a conversation, only for it to fall flat. It wasn't long before they came upon a towering oak tree, next to and surrounded by the gorgeous roses of every color imaginable. After they passed the huge oak, the roses around them began to blur, and move away from them. It seemed as if they were all being sucked into a single direction. The blurring continued and got stronger, until everything began to spin and twist together. Ahead of them, they could see a huge wormhole forming. It was a spinning conglomerate of all the colors of roses mixed with the astronomical view of a solar system, spinning incredibly fast.

Stopping a good bit away from the portal, Peter turned and faced them. He said, "I don't know what you're going to face beyond that portal, but I do believe you can handle it. Your friendship and love for one another is strong enough to be considered a weapon from heaven. Use it, rely on each other, and embrace your unity. Together you are strong."

They all smiled, and then leaned in and hugged the friendly older man. Nodding to each other, Sesh turned, looked back over his shoulder, and yelled, "Bye Pete!" then took off running towards the portal, followed closely by Katie, Pip, and Josephine.

As they got closer to the portal their bodies began to unravel, twisting and blending in with the blurring roses. It blended and spun faster as they joined the mixture of colors in the wormhole. They would enter the first level together, and together, they would conquer whatever was presented to them. Sesh, Katie, Pip, and Josephine disappeared into the portal, entering the first floor of purgatory.

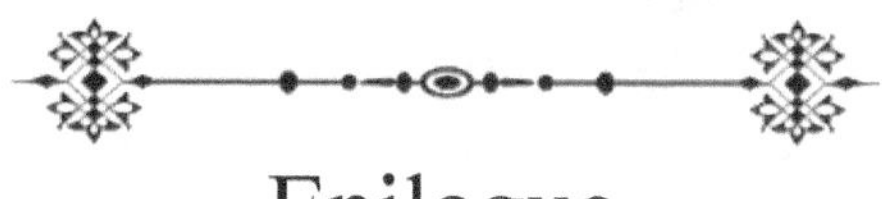

Epilogue

A heartbeat monitor was going off, slowly and rhythmically. Dust had settled on most of the windowsills and spare equipment that didn't get much use. There wasn't a cleaning crew at the hospital anymore, to make sure the rooms were clean of detritus and dust. An old man sat in a thread-bare chair, looking at his straw haired granddaughter. He scowled occasionally because she was forced to share a room with the young man who put her in the coma.

Occasionally, he would look over to the young man, weary, and sullen. He watched, wondering if he was going to die before his granddaughter. The singular nurse on staff would occasionally come in, and he would voice his concerns about why she had to share a room with him. It didn't make sense to him; the hospital was not occupied by very many people. It didn't matter that the nurse was the only one that worked on this floor. In fact, she lived here, in one of the rooms close to the nurse's station, alone, as just another widowed old lady, who happened to be a nurse.

There was a lone doctor who worked and oversaw the entire hospital. With a weary look on his face, he had explained to the parents of the young man, and the old man, that the two comatose patients were in fact, very much still alive. They have incredibly active brainwaves, and he didn't understand why they didn't wake up. Physically, the bruises on their brains and the small superficial damages to their bodies, would heal. Their minds just needed to take a step out of the darkness, and into the light. For that to happen, they needed time.

The reason they were both put into this room, was because it was one of the few remaining rooms where the lights functioned properly, only flickering occasionally, instead of being burnt out altogether. The hospital was run down, like the rest of the world. The old man tried to clean a little, to make things a little bit more sanitary, but there was only so much he could do. Nothing he did seemed to help the stench, the old man considered the smell and decided it only smelled like one thing, and that was death.

The old man stayed here, with his granddaughter every day. He never left her side. She was all he had left. It was strange to him, that the boy on the other side of the divider, would get a visit from a man and a woman from time to time. They initially started visiting, right after the accident, every single day. As the days went by, it went from both of them every single day, to one of them every other day, to both of them individually once a week. Now, as it's been nearly three weeks, they stopped coming completely.

He noticed their faces too, looking more and more gaunt, sporting the deep dark circles under their eyes. He knew what was next if they didn't eat or get a bit more sleep. That's likely why they weren't coming in as much, they were focusing on trying to find food, and grow their gardens. It's a shame what the world had come to.

As the weeks passed, the elderly man's appearance became more malnourished. The nurse was only feeding the boy and the girl once per day, through their feeding tube, so they wouldn't starve. She fed them baby formula, because that seemed to be the most common form of foodstuffs the government had access too. This was likely because the children weren't being born, so they had stockpiles. Occasionally, she would bring the old man some food too, just a bowl here and there, to make sure he didn't die on her watch. When she didn't bring him food, she brought him a small mixture of formula in a cup. Any form of sustenance was welcome.

The nurse got a small supply of food occasionally from the government, which helped keep her last two remaining patients alive. She would check on the small garden she was growing on the roof of the hospital, and sometimes get a vegetable or two, to keep herself in vittles too. Lately, for the last few weeks, the garden has exploded in growth. The usual paltry plant growth was now growing rapidly, and she guessed they would begin producing much more, within the next few days. Afterwards it wouldn't take as much to stretch the little bit of food and include the old man in their sparce meals.

If one were watching, they would notice how the two elderly folks' gaze would linger on the other from time to time, but never at the same time. He found her enchanting, the way she selflessly cared for others, who could not care for themselves. She found his dedication to his granddaughter an exotic quality that few men left in the world, possessed. Perhaps, in another life, in another time, they would have found each other, and pursued more. Alas, it wasn't another time, nor another place, and he was just a frail old man, and she a frail old woman, taking care of a couple of young people, who couldn't care for themselves.

The occasional flicker of green light coming from the young man's cubby, where his clothing and limited belongings were kept, would have been witnessed, if anyone cared enough to pay attention. The fact that no one noticed the light, or cared enough to look into what the pulse was, could simply be attributed to the gnawing hunger that they all felt, as a constant companion.

***

"How do you think they will do Gabriel?" Saint Peter asked Gabriel, as they stood alone on the porch of the cloud house.

"I do not know. There is still much growth that needs to take place, for them to be able to surpass all of the levels."

"Do you know what the first level is?"

"I know what it can be, but it varies from time to time, and person to person. With the five of them entering together, counting Carmen, it's possible they will face a completely different string of events for the first level. There will be a welcoming archangel to each level starting at the first one, to tell them some of the finer guidelines and goals they must follow and complete. I believe it's Michael, for the floors. He may even be over all of them, I cannot recall."

Saint Peter just nodded and stayed silent. He hoped those young folks would be successful in their endeavors. The Levels were tricky, and dangerous. Planet Earth needed to be saved, and those two humans were the ones to do it.

***

Tamara went through the cupboards one more time, trying to find anything she could turn into a little bit of food. She found nothing, once again. It was time to go out and try to find something to eat, in the small town. Chances were small that she would be able to. Frank

209

already left to try to get some meat from the old man that Sesh works for from time to time.

Tears fell down her emaciated face. Her baby boy was the last of her children. They were all dead now. There was no way he was going to wake up from the coma, so she counted him amongst the dead. She had nothing to live for anymore, just her need for food. She used to love Frank, but when she was honest with herself, she stopped loving him, the day Eloise died. If he had been there, he could have stopped them. She knew deep down that nothing could have stopped them, but she felt the need to blame someone, so it would be him. She opened the drawer that held all of their cutlery, tarnished, and blemished from age and lack of use. Her fingers closed around one of the longer blades.

"If you don't come back with some food, you will be the food."

***

Frank knocked on Mr. Fallows door. After waiting for several minutes, it finally creaked open, and a couple of old gray eyes looked out at him. A foot under the eyes, were the large round barrels of a double-barreled shotgun.

"What do you want?"

"Sesh is in the hospital, he's in a coma. We haven't been able to eat because we have been going to check on him. Do you have a small bit of food, you can spare for us? It's just me and his mom."

The tip of the barrels dropped a couple of inches but stayed pointing at Frank.

"He is a good boy. A diligent worker at that. I suppose I can advance you a little on his work. When he wakes up, he will have to come earn this back. Do you hear me?"

"Oh, thank you sir, absolutely. He will definitely come and work a little. I can even do some work for you too if you need me to. Anything, to keep my family alive."

"Wait here."

The door slammed shut, and deadbolts, chain bolts, and locks could all be heard latching and turning. Frank did not know how long it was going to take, but he hoped it would not be long. He knew that Tam did not have much longer before she surrendered to

210

being one of the waking dead. He had to get her some food, even if it meant cutting his own arm off, and feeding it to her.

Ten minutes later, Frank began to wonder if the old man was coming back at all. He had beaten another man to death with his bare hands once, but that was the only time he had ever hurt another person. He was just contemplating the ways in which he would go in and take care of the old man, so he could feed his wife and himself, when he heard the latches on the door begin to open once again.

End of Book 1

About the Author

In August of 1986, Sam was born in Northern California but spent his prominent years in the back woods of Arkansas. After graduation, he joined the Air Force to go see the world. Ultimately, settling back down in Arkansas after his service, he went to work and helped rear his budding family. Sam is the father of four beautiful and intelligent children, and he is happily married to the best supporting spouse a man could ask for. It should be known that he is a master at laughing when someone falls down, but only after they reveal they haven't been injured. He sometimes hyper-fixates on some of the most mundane of things, only to conclude, it's just not for him. On road-trips he likes saying things like: "I bet dere's fish in dere" in the most southern of accents he can muster. His daughter does the same, and it's quite funny. While driving in some of the southern states, it changes to, "I bet dere's a gator in dere!"